MW01166964

Reluctant Captive

by Joyce Jackson

∞∞∞

Indigo Love Stories
Sensuous
are publshed by

Genesis Press, Inc.
315 Third Avenue North
Columbus, MS 39701

This book may not be reproduced in whole or in part, by mimeograph or any other means, without permission. Published in the United States of America by The Genesis Press, Inc. For information write The Genesis Press, Inc. 315 3rd Avenue North, Columbus, MS 39701.

Copyright© 2000 by Joyce Jackson

The Reluctant Captive

All rights reserved
ISBN: 1-58571-040-7
Manufactured in the United States of America

First Edition

This book is dedicated to my sister-in-law, Nelda Stredic-Jackson who was with me every step of the way. She pushed, prodded, nagged, encouraged, was my number one critic and cheerleader and never let me give up my dream.

To Francis Ray, more than a prolific author, whose many words of encouragement gave me the added drive to be presistent in my goals.

Dr. Elvin "Dee" Holt for supplying me with information. To Thomas, my good friend from Kenya whose stories fueled my ideas.

and
to the entire Jackson clan.

"Good grief, stop staring at me like that," she retorted, irritated that he made her nervous. She backed away when he took a step in her direction, her breathing accelerating. She would fight him this time. His caresses and his unexpected gentleness would not lull her into easy acceptance of his unwanted attentions. Not this time. She moistened her lips, drawing his eyes to the motion of her pink tongue while she fought off the memory of his devastating kisses.

She was at the wall with no place else to go. "I thought you didn't want me," she mocked, throwing his words back at him in a rush when Jackson lifted his arm over her head. Her chin was up, her eyes flashing fire as she waited for his next move.

Chapter One

Have you spotted them?" The deep-throated voice hissed from behind the waiter who was surreptitiously peering through a diamond-shaped pane of glass embedded in the swinging double doors of the kitchen.

The waiter nodded his head.

"Are you sure it is who we seek?"

Again, he nodded his head in silent affirmation.

"Mzuri [good]," she replied loftily, increasing her comrade's annoyance. She smiled triumphantly. "We take the woman when the opportunity arises. Tonight." Eyeing the food in front of her, she wrinkled her nose with distaste. The smell was delectable but she knew beforehand the waste of it would be scandalous. Food would be thrown away here tonight that could feed a medium-sized village. She made a move to heft the canapé laden serving tray up past her shoulder but the waiter's troubled voice halted her actions.

"A message must be taken to Jackson for his okay on this crazy plan of yours," he insisted in their language. "You know as well as I there will be hell to pay if we move without his say-so." The man's face sagged with dread. The knowledge of what Jackson Shugaa would do to them if they carried out this crazy plan without his sanction caused him to swallow noisily.

The kitchen hummed with activity around the pair. Nziguniziju eyed her comrade rather contemptuously. "David, we must take advantage of the opportunity given to us. There is no time to get a message to Jackson. You know he's not in Kenya. I will assume full responsibility. After all, I am in command when Jackson and Kimya are not here, am I not?" Her tone defied him to dispute her.

"Eeei [yes], but-," he began, only to be stopped short with a sharp reprimand from the headwaiter.

"I thought you said you and your sister needed this job in a most terrible way. If you do not get this food and drink out to the president's guests, I will replace you on the spot. There are hundreds of hungry mouths who would be grateful for the shillings this job pays."

He slammed a serving tray on the stone table and began setting empty wine glasses on it. "Fill these," he barked and thrust a chilled bottle of Perrier Jouet in David's hand without waiting for his response. "Then serve them without delay." Turning, he grabbed the arm of a passing waitress and shoved her towards a platter of hot hors d'oeuvres. "Serve these now!" he ordered. For good measure, he scowled at Nziguniziju who was placing the raw vegetables and fruits on her tray then spun sharply on his heels and exited the kitchen.

Before David could return to his argument with N Zee, Nziguniziju's pet name used by those who knew her, she spoke, keeping a watchful eye on the swinging doors. "Look at all this food," she grumbled gesturing with her arms at the mounds of appetizers that were to be served before the main course. "This wine and champagne alone cost thousands of American dollars." In the large ovens behind them duck and lamb were roasting. Wildebeest, gazelle, giraffe and crocodile meats were being prepared on traditional Masai swords for roasting over an open flame. Smoked salmon and white tuna were marinating in spicy vinaigrettes while exotic soups simmered on top of the massive stoves. Cooks labored over salads and side vegetables while others prepared the accompanying sauces and dressings.

"It is assured most of our people will go hungry tonight or be forced to eat porridge! Nothing but grain and water for our children. If they are lucky, maybe they will have a bowl of marerima [wild vegetables] or come across a gituyu [a large forest rat]. These people come to our country on the pretense of helping our citizens and are treated like royalty!" She threw the last baby carrot on the tray and hefted it to her shoulder. "They must be made to understand the gravity of our country's situation, David."

The look of apprehension remained fixed on David's face even as he nodded his agreement with her statement. It didn't matter if N Zee's plan proved successful; they could still pay dearly for doing this.

N Zee was brave, fearless—a woman whom many of the male rebels admired for her wits and her womanly charms. Still, Jackson Shugaa was not a man to cross and those who knew him avoided doing so.

David squared his shoulders, inhaled a breath and followed his comrade out the double doors. With a cool impersonal smile curving her lips, she walked directly towards their intended target, carrying a laden tray. Ghanima [good fortune] would surely be with them because what they were about to do was for Kenya and her people.

∞∞ ∞∞ ∞∞

"Are you mad?" David questioned in disbelief to N Zee when they were back in the kitchen preparing to serve the fourth course to Matoi's dinner guests. "Has a swarm of locusts eaten your brains?"

N Zee calmly placed a plate of foie gras garnished with crisp lettuce and rosemary on a sterling silver tray before turning to David.

"Of course I'm not mad," she replied serenely. "Who would suspect it could happen here? This way we catch everyone by surprise and at the same time show that we are brave enough to infiltrate their so-called impenetrable circle. Besides," she added, "the diplomats and visiting guests are surrounded by guards going to and from their official residences. We would not get within five hundred feet of their cars. Our truck would stand out like a giraffe trying to fit inside this kitchen." N Zee referred to the ancient flatbed they had left parked near a grove of trees well out of the eyesight of the guests with their sleek expensive vehicles.

What she said was true. David could not dispute the logic. But to toss their original plan and kidnap such an important dinner guest, the daughter of the American, Julius Wellington! It just could not be done!

David read the gleam in N Zee's eyes. He knew she would not be deterred. Voicing his question with less skepticism than he'd initially felt, he swallowed back the sick feeling building in his stomach. "How is this thing to be done without us ending up dead?"

"As the Americans are wont to say, I'm so glad you asked." N Zee smiled. With a forefinger and a sultry sway of her shapely hips, she beckoned David to follow her.

∞∞∞∞∞∞

Katherine was proud to be attending the dinner party honoring her uncle's appointment as one of the twenty-four directors of the World Bank. Julius Wellington was the first and only African American in the Bank's hierarchy. The appointment was history-making and Julius had wanted Katherine to be here with him. He'd called her in Washington from his temporary home in Germany to ask that she come to Kenya.

Immensely proud of her uncle's achievements, Katherine's grin had spread from ear to ear listening to him talk about all the things he intended to do to make sure the poorest Third World countries got some of the millions in loans to help their leaders beat back poverty, improve technology and ensure every child an education. She'd hesitated mere seconds before accepting his offer of a first class, round trip ticket and taking a leave of absence from her job as a consultant to small and mid-size financial institutions.

On the flight over, Katherine was excited at the thought of seeing her uncle, who'd been out of the States for more than two years. His wife Abra, on the other hand, had come back to the States frequently for brief periods during the last year and a half. Each time the two women had come in contact with each other, Katherine was painfully aware that Abra's resentment of her had not abated. So it was no surprise to her that her uncle and cousin Edward were the only family to greet her at the airport.

Upon arriving at the Grand Regency Hotel, she'd received a less than enthusiastic greeting from her aunt Abra. A simple "Hello, Kathy dear, you're looking...nice." And from JaLisa, a dry "what's up cuz" and a swift buss on the cheek.

Earlier, as Katherine was dressing for the party that evening, Abra had come into her room, taken one look at the backless peach number that ended above the knees and sneered. "The women in this country don't expose their flesh like that, dear Kathy. They have more respect for themselves." In a voice heavy with censure and sarcasm she'd continued, "Take a cue from your cousin and dress appropriately. Don't insult these people and expose our family to ridicule."

Her thoughts returning to the present, Katherine could not, no matter what she did, shake the feeling that she was being observed, intently. Several of the men standing in their circle were watching her with interest, including the much-married American Ambassador to Kenya. She was acutely conscious of the unwanted attention as the men weren't trying to hide their blatant admiration. But that didn't totally explain the feeling.

Once or twice she thought she caught one of the waitresses eyeing her. She immediately shook off the notion. Why would she be of interest to a waitress, in Kenya, no less?

Or maybe it was the feeling of guilt she'd experienced ten minutes after walking through the door of the president's residence. She was defiantly wearing the controversial dress and she felt out of place with all of the attention she was garnering. She was loathe to think she would have been better off listening to Abra.

As Katherine's whisky-colored eyes roamed the room while being served roasted giraffe and new potatoes, she observed something that intensified her curiosity. The waitress who had been staring at her earlier was speaking in low tones to her coworker while serving the guests from the platter of grilled meats she held. Katherine couldn't hear what she was saying to him but whatever it was, he was frowning.

"By his very silence, the president is allowing the police to torture and kill Kenyan citizens, David. Men, women and children are starving in the street as he and his guests sit down to a six course meal which you serve them. The Americans sanction giving aid to a tyrant who doles out funds only to those most loyal to him and to those who continue to do his bidding by maiming and inflicting torture! Those loyal to president Matoi are allowing the unlawful removal of land from the rightful owners by looking the other way and becoming rich themselves." N Zee pressed her point home with her next statement. "Are you going to just stand by and watch this happen to your own people without a fight? Are you going to be a part of the problem or a part of the solution, David? Tonight, we make a serious statement, a non-verbal statement that will get the world's attention."

Suddenly the waitress was glaring at Katherine from across the table. Katherine quickly averted her eyes from the waitress. Shaking off her feeling of unease, she looked at the portraits and photographs of Kenya's president amidst the rich furnishing's in the room. There were pictures of him greeting dignitaries from around the world, of him in his office working. His visage seemed to be everywhere. On the ride from Kenyatta airport, she'd seen President Matoi's image in the shop windows and on the state buildings of Nairobi. She'd never seen anything like it.

A man's voice near her shoulder pulled her from her reverie.

"Aren't you and your brother proud of your father's accomplishment?" The question came from a second-generation English settler who owned hundreds of acres of prime land in the highlands. Katherine turned to the man, ready to correct his mistake.

"I'm not..."

"Katherine is not ours," Abra vocalized from across the table, drawing attention their way. "She is my husband's niece. We took her in after her father and mother were killed in a traffic accident when she was thirteen. She's been with us one way or another since that time. We've done the best we could in raising her." The steel edge was absent from her voice when she added, "Our daughter, JaLisa, is back at the hotel suite. She became quite ill from a piece of fish she ate. She truly hated to miss this dinner given in her father's honor but the doctor insisted she stay in bed for the next eight hours. We are very disappointed that she could not be here with the family tonight."

Ignoring the looks of sympathy and open speculation cast her way, Katherine prepared to leave the table to escape Abra's not-so-subtle verbal putdown. Before she was up out of her seat, Robert Biwott, the police commissioner, extracted a folded piece of paper from the inside pocket of his military jacket. He laid it on the table beside his plate, painstakingly unfolding the squared ends. Carefully protected inside the butcher-type paper was a photograph. Biwott stared down at it, an expression of intense dislike covering his features. He glanced around the people seated at the table, his hatred for the person in the photo clearly visible.

"Has anyone in this room seen this man recently?" A hush descended on the table as the paper was passed from hand to hand. Even Abra's conceited smile was gone and the wait staff moved among the guests more unobtrusively than before.

As the guests scrutinized the photo, the police commissioner's eagle eyes catalogued the expression of every man and woman seated at the table. With each negative shake of the head his features turned more sour.

President Matoi's eyes were alive with disapproval at the commissioner's actions. He glared his annoyance at him as the paper continued to be passed around.

The commissioner withdrew the photo from the hands of a parliament member's wife who was studying the photo overly long, and passed it on. He glowered at the woman before speaking to the others. "At any other time I would not be so presumptuous as to bring up so unpleasant a subject, especially on so auspicious an occasion. However, times are quickly changing and terrorist acts are escalating as we speak. It is time our friends and neighbors were made aware of the dangerous times we live in. They must be made to know that internal enemies of our country would destroy all of the progress our president has made and continues to make in this country."

The heavy scowl remained on the president's face but the anger dulled in his eyes. "I want each of you to look closely at the man in that photo, which is about two years old. He is very elusive, and we have been unable to obtain a more recent picture of him. We strongly believe this is how he looks today. He is so arrogant in his belief and his deeds he does not attempt to alter his features or use a disguise. He is without a doubt the most dangerous man in Kenya today." The commissioner paused, allowing his words to sink in.

As he did so, Katherine noticed the expressions of fear, curiosity and revulsion on the faces of some of the guests. She also noticed veiled admiration in the eyes of more than one female guest. The commissioner spoke once more in accented English. "This man is bold beyond belief. Despite his terrorist activities, he has been known to walk the streets of Kenya during the day as free as you and I. Please, if you should hear anything, any lead however small it may seem, let me or one of my men know."

A Central Bank member sitting beside Katherine, who had attempted to engage her interest in him shortly after her arrival, pressed the slick paper into her palm, grazing her knuckles. Ignoring the obtrusive gesture, Katherine's eyes dropped to the black and white photo.

It was a head-to-waist shot. The man was clean-shaven, his features vividly defined, nearly gaunt, his cheekbones prominent. He was broad-shouldered though lean across the chest. His folded arms, one on top of the other, ended in large hands with long, tapered fingers. The heavy lids had impossibly thick lashes and the eyes of undeterminable color were focused and sharp. His face was unsmiling, grim. His eyes were cold, hard, and stared out of the photograph into Katherine's soul. Not an iota of emotion was reflected on the man's visage. She did not doubt the validity of the commissioner's claim. This man was clearly dangerous. She didn't have to be in his physical presence to know it.

Unable to tear her eyes away from the photo even as she pushed it into the next palm, Katherine shuddered slightly. It wasn't a face she would soon forget.

Without waiting to hear the man's name, Katherine stood, this time determined to escape the tension-filled room. She was cognizant of the daggers Abra threw her way as she made her way out of the dining hall.

Katherine found her way through the long hallway's twists and turns to the lavatory. With immense relief, she pushed open the door leading into the ladies' lounge and came face to face with the waitress who'd unwaveringly stared her down. Nonplused that the wait staff was using the same bathroom as the guests and despite the faint animosity emanating from the woman, Katherine couldn't help admiring her up close.

Her smooth skin was a dark sandy brown. A black and white cap on her head covered the many fine braids that were secured at the nape of her neck in a tight ball. She was less than two inches taller than Katherine and generously proportioned. She was attractive, but with cold and unfriendly eyes. Attempting to break the ice, Katherine smiled into the stony eyes. She didn't realize she was holding her breath until the woman brushed past her, expressionless, and out the door.

After answering nature's call, Katherine studied the face staring back at her in the gilded, lit mirror as she washed her hands. Except for the small black mole above her upper lip, her honey gold skin was unblemished. At twenty-nine years of age, she would describe herself as attractive, maybe even sexy to some. Katherine sighed. She applied mauve lipstick to her pouting lower lip, then her top one and smacked them together. Satisfied with the reflection, she turned from the mirror and left the powder room.

Turning a corner retracing her steps back to the dining hall, she came upon the same waitress who'd left the bathroom just minutes ago. She made a move to go around the woman and found her path blocked.

"Excuse me." Katherine made a move to go around on her other side. The woman continued to block her path. A frisson of apprehension began to crawl up Katherine's spine as she stared into the dark eyes. "You're blocking my way, please move…"

That was all Katherine got out before the woman's hand slapped over her nose and mouth with a damp cloth. Katherine opened her mouth to scream. The sound that came forth was a faint squeak before she slumped forward into the woman's arms.

N Zee held on tightly to the unconscious woman, glanced quickly both ways down the hall-way, then hurriedly began to drag Katherine's inert body towards the back entrance. In doing so, one of Katherine's slingback pumps slipped off her foot. Her limp body was carelessly dropped to the floor.

Running back, N Zee scooped up the cham-pagne-colored pump. She'd bet the shoes cost enough money to feed all six of her brothers and sisters for at least a week. The only reason she'd gone back for the pump was she did not want any-one to discover the woman was missing, at least not yet.

Before picking Katherine up, she snatched the other matching shoe off her slender foot. Then, none too gently, she hefted Katherine's limp body under both arms and pulled it swiftly down the long hall.

"What is this?" David demanded nervously when she rounded the corner. The noises and accompanying commands coming from the kitchen were much too close for comfort. Someone would step out the door and spot them standing with a limp body between them.

N Zee's voice was calm when she answered. "This is who we came for." Holding Katherine's unconscious body loosely, she passed David the shoes. On reflex he took them, glaring his disapproval at the risk she took.

"Here, you can carry her too." N Zee abruptly let Katherine's body go, allowing David mere seconds to catch her before her body slammed to the floor. He scooped the slender form up, shoes and all, and followed N Zee's long-legged stride out the back door.

David's heart pounded in his chest so hard it actually hurt. Perspiration ran down his face and body as if a cloud were perched over his head unleashing its downpour on him alone. His eyes flew wildly about from side to side. His body was tense, waiting for someone to spot them kidnapping the American woman.

If they were caught, they would not be going to jail to await a trial date. If they survived the abuse at police headquarters, they would be led to one of Kenya's surrounding forests, tortured, kept alive, depending on the attending doctor's skills, then tortured some more before being finally, and mercifully, killed. But before that happened N Zee would be raped, passed around from man to man. According to rumors, that had happened to some female members of Jackson's family and had, without a doubt, happened to countless other women imprisoned on trumped-up charges. All because they supported the rebels' cause and offered aid to the rebels in their fight against a corrupt government.

They stepped out into a clear warm night without incident. A half moon hung high amongst glowing stars.

David exhaled in relief when he saw no one was waiting for them on the other side of the door and just as quickly cursed, calling to N Zee in a harsh whisper not to move so fast. She turned to him, thrusting the damp cloth held moments ago under Katherine's nose into his hand. "Use this if she starts to wake up. Wait in this spot, I will return as quickly as possible." With those parting words she disappeared into the darkness, sprinting for the thicket of trees outlined a quarter of a mile away.

He stared down into the comely brown face and grimaced as if in pain. If the truth were told, they hadn't put much thought or planning into this outrageously dangerous scheme. Neither Jackson nor Kimya was aware of what the two of them were about. No matter the outcome of the kidnapping of this woman, Jackson Shugaa would be very angry. Angry enough to banish them from his presence and the camp. Too much was at stake to put the overall operation in jeopardy. And besotted fool that he was, he had gone along with N Zee without question until now.

His lust for her had led him to this. Was this what he would tell Jackson when he questioned

them both if they made it back to camp alive
he allowed N Zee to talk him into this crazy
because he could not resist her? Probably b
than anyone Jackson knew of N Zee's charms.
often David had spied her attempting to work h
wiles on their leader.

And what of Kimya? He was second in command and could also make it very uncomfortable for
him. Unlike David, Kimya did not let N Zee twist him
around her finger. He was loyal first and always to
Jackson Shugaa. No one came between those two
men—no one.

David so wanted to be a part of the cama-
raderie. He wanted Jackson to depend on him the
way he depended on Kimya and even N Zee. That
was one of the reasons he'd given little thought to N
Zee's plan but had plunged headlong into it. Here
was a chance, he thought, to elevate himself in
Jackson's eyes. However, he now realized that getting involved with N Zee might prove fatal.

Blast it! His mind was traveling around in useless circles. What good did the knowledge do him
at this juncture? Glancing over his shoulder at the
heavy wooden door, he willed it to remain closed.
Although he was standing in near darkness, anyone
coming outside could easily spot him and his burden.

He moved to the end of the corridor leading to

he grounds, keeping his back pressed close to the stone wall. Reaching the outer edge, his eyes searched the dimly lit area. No enemy was in sight but neither was N Zee or the car that was supposed to be here to help them.

"Mbaya. Mbaya sana [Bad. Very bad]," he uttered, peering down at his captive. His arms felt numb. He wanted to lay his burden down. Instead, he leaned his head against the stone wall of the double-story residence and closed his eyes.

"What are you doing? Sleeping standing up?" an amused voice queried. Nearly leaping out of his skin, David jerked forward, banging Katherine's head on the stone. She groaned, twitching in her drugged sleep. N Zee snatched the crumpled but still damp cloth from David's fingers and clamped it over Katherine's nostrils. Seconds later, she quieted.

Nervousness and relief caused David to speak louder than he intended. "I have been waiting for you forever. Where is our truck and where did you get a change of clothes?" David looked in amazement at the military fatigues and khaki shirt N Zee now sported.

"Come. Jessie has transportation nearby," she answered calmly. "I did not bring our truck because it would lead directly to us. And keep your voice down," she instructed tersely.

"Transportation to where?" David aske_
laden, yet attempting to keep pace with the
moving woman. He got a glimpse of the vast
icured lawn. Was she crazy? They were pract_
ly out in the open. Surely guards were post_
somewhere. "Have you lost your mind. Someon_
is bound to see us!"

"And if they don't see us they will surely hear
you," N Zee replied in a voice heavy with sarcasm.
"Shut up and follow me, David. I know what I am
doing." If possible, she moved even faster across
the thick grass.

"You cannot command me," David hurled at her
retreating back. He threw Katherine over his shoul-
der as if she were a sack of maize. He'd had just
about enough of N Zee's high-handed ways. She
took too much for granted. "You may be third in
rank but in this venture you and I are equal."

Receiving no response, David scowled at N
Zee's back like a pouting child. She was ignoring
him as though he was a dudu kuga [dead bug],
beneath her feet.

Without further comment, he mimicked her
steps to the grove of trees, wondering with each
step they took where the guards were. Why weren't
bullets stinging him between his shoulder blades or
worse yet, why weren't he and Nzigunzigu being
hauled off to jail? He was sure there were dozens

of pairs of eyes boring into him from all sides, but he refused to lift his head to look around.

Minutes later, they were standing on the edge of darkness before a dilapidated-looking flatbed truck with elevated wooden sides. From where he was standing, the back end of the truck seemed to be an extension of the trees on the side of the road. Someone was sitting behind the wheel, though David could not discern his or her features. The engine sounded as if it might shut down permanently at any moment. With all of the noise coming from under its hood, it was a wonder guards weren't circling them right now.

"Why are you standing there like your feet have suddenly grown roots?" N Zee snapped at David's side, startling him.

"Do my legs look like they have grown stilts?" David answered with equal heat. His gestures clearly indicated that the bed of the truck was much too high for him to climb onto with the woman in his arms.

"Pass her to me after I get in." Walking to the end of the truck N Zee artfully dodged the low hanging limbs. Grasping a lower flimsy wooden rail, she slung a long leg onto the truck's side, levered herself up and onto its bed. On her haunches, she scooted to the end of the truck and held out her arms for the woman.

Skeptically eyeing N Zee's outstretched arms, David hesitated. He judged the reach to be much too high.

"Give her to me," N Zee insisted. "We don't have all night. We must leave here at once." With a sound of impatience and throwing David a look of disgust, she stretched her arms out and grasped Katherine's limp legs. David held onto the upper part of her body.

"Careful," David cautioned.

"What for?" N Zee jerked Katherine's body from David's hands onto the truck. Her limp body fell with a soft thump. David was swinging himself onto the bed when the driver gunned the engine. The smell of too ripe fruit coming from wooden crates stacked against the cab assailed his nostrils, almost overwhelming him. As the truck slowly pulled away from the residence, David sat beside Katherine's body, which lay across a pile of rags.

"Do you realize Jackson and Kimya will surely be upset if the American is injured? Why add it to our already full plate?"

Something in David's tone forestalled N Zee's denial. She was confident she could handle Kimya, though it would take some doing because of his loyalty to Jackson. But he was also in love with her. She knew it and used it to her advantage when needed. Jackson Shugaa was another matter altogether. Nobody handled him. What better way to know than from experience? Her failure to bewitch Jackson and have him succumb to her will was like a running sore that never healed.

In the darkness she stared down into the face of the American captive. She couldn't see her features clearly but remembered them—very well. Truly, she would love to do some damage to the woman.

But there was truth in what David had said. Jackson would be exceedingly angry with them if they did harm to the woman. She must do nothing else to bring his wrath down on their heads. She began mentally preparing herself for his reaction when they met face to face. Because in the end this venture would benefit the rebels and their cause, she would willingly take the brunt of Jackson's anger.

Watching David crouch beside the American, she read his thoughts. He was terrified. The reality of what they had done was only now penetrating his consciousness. All without the permission of the 'oh-so-great' Jackson Shugaa.

That she had ruthlessly used the man sitting across from her did not faze her. His lust for her was hers to bend as she saw fit. And use it to her advantage she did. This venture tonight was for Kenya and the rebels. And for Jackson. Maybe, just maybe, he would see how much she was willing to sacrifice. How much she cared, how much...

"Cover her," N Zee ordered briskly. "Then ourselves."

Responding with a malevolent glare, which N Zee ignored as she placed her head near the end of two stacked crates filled with ripe mangoes, David drew a rough, moldy sheet over Katherine's head, making sure her nostrils were not covered.

Trying his best to ignore the smells assaulting him, David stretched out in the narrow space between stacked fruit and vegetable crates. While there was no way he could rest easy until they were well within the forest, across from him N Zee chuckled softly at what the dinner guests would discover when they decided the woman had been gone too long from the table. The smile on her face remained as she allowed the swinging motion of the truck to lull her to sleep.

Chapter Two

A low groan brought Katherine groggily out of her drug-induced slumber. Rolling to her side, she held her aching head in unsteady hands and squeezed her eyes tightly shut, mentally willing the pain screaming behind her temples to vanish. It didn't. All too soon she became conscious of the pain in the back of her legs, her shoulders and her butt. She struggled to raise a hand above her head and for long seconds could not. Her teeth and tongue hurt and she couldn't produce enough saliva to rid her mouth of the foul taste of some sort of rag that had been stuffed inside, no matter how much she hacked and tried to spit. The rocking motion was creating nausea in the pit of her stomach. Katherine opened her eyes but could not see a thing.

"Get it off me," she tried to scream, her voice muffled. "Get it off me this instant." She pushed against the rough fabric, becoming frantic when it refused to budge. A weight pressed down on her chest and she thrashed about in panic, her elbow striking the sharp end of the wooden crate at her side.

"Somebody get it off me, pleeease! Now, I want it off!" Her insistent muffled cries reached the ears of David and N Zee, who quickly sat up and peered over at the thrashing body under the covers. Pulling them back, N Zee promptly gave Katherine a hard slap across her face.

"What did you do that for?" David asked in wonder, staring from the now motionless, startled figure to his comrade. Pulling a lighter from his shirt pocket, he flicked it, producing a small flame. The satisfaction from her deed on N Zee's face didn't escape his notice.

"The American will know who is in charge," came the crisp reply. "We must—" The sharp crack of a palm against a cheek stopped the flow of words from N Zee's tongue. The force of the blow whipped her head around. The captive was sitting up, breathing rapidly, her face fierce.

If David had not been amazed, he would have laughed out loud at the look on N Zee's face after the American's unexpected response. Even in these mean, uncertain times, her expression was priceless.

He didn't have time to savor the moment because N Zee retaliated with another resounding whack to the American's other cheek, knocking her back down. Before she could follow through on a triple, David caught her arms. He spoke harshly in Swahili as the woman struggled to free her arm.

"Stop it, N Zee! What good will she do us abused?"

Intense rage obscured N Zee's vision as she continued trying to get free of David's hands. She did not hear him. She saw only the greedy, offending American who had dared to lay a hand on her.

That she could be needlessly cruel David no longer doubted. Because of his desire for her, he'd always looked the other way. Tonight would not be one of those times. If he allowed it, N Zee would truly harm this woman. He gave her a vigorous shake.

He could feel the captive, who had yet to recover from the second attack, eyeing them with wide eyes as she lay between them.

"Get control of yourself, woman!" His angry gaze swam over her. "I will hold you like this all the way to our destination unless you promise to keep your hands to yourself."

"I will if she will," N Zee spat, glaring down in the darkness at Katherine, who watched the pair warily, but defiantly.

"She is awaking from a drug administered by force. She is groggy, unaware of her surroundings and does not know us. Yet you attack her for no reason. How else is she supposed to respond?" he reasoned.

"If I had known you were going to be this woman's champion, I would have left you back in the forest and done the job myself," N Zee sputtered, bristling with rage.

"Will you leave off," David replied through clenched teeth. He didn't point out to N Zee that it was foolish to think she could have carried out this plan alone. She had needed him. No one else would have gone along with such an outrageous scenario.

Instead of answering, N Zee sat back on her haunches, her expression goading him into releasing her arms. As he did he grumbled, "It will be hard enough explaining why we carried out this crazy plan, much less explaining the bruises on the woman."

N Zee sucked her teeth and turned her head in disgust.

"Who are you? Where am I? What do you want with me?" The smoky voice was unsure, shaky, and seemed to float around them. Katherine faced David, somehow instinctively knowing she would get no answer from the woman. Her questions came again, stronger this time.

"Why am I here? What do you want? What do you intend to do with me?" Cautiously, slowly, she eased into a sitting position until the woman pressed a hand to her chest to halt her progress.

Without looking Katherine's way, she spoke to David in their tongue. "Don't you dare speak to her."

"Don't you tell me what to do. I am not a child nor am I an idiot." Clenching his jaw, David shifted away from N Zee. His command of the English language was limited, so was N Zee's. But he'd heard the panic in the captive's voice, knew that she was questioning her circumstances.

"Do you speak English? Where am I? Where are you taking me?" Wheels were spinning in Katherine's head, causing it to hurt more. "Is it money you're after? Tell me what you want, please." Her dark eyes pleaded with David in the moonlight. He appeared the least hostile of the two.

At the party tonight —it was still tonight, wasn't it? she wondered fuzzily—Police Commissioner Biwott had asked questions and warned everyone present about a rebel leader. A dangerous man...oh, what was his name? Katherine's head pounded but her haze began to dissipate as she realized that in her haste to escape her aunt's presence she hadn't stayed long enough to hear the commissioner mention the man's name.

Was this pair kidnapping her? Did they know that she was an American citizen? That her uncle was a member of the World Bank, an internationally powerful organization? Were they aware that the executive directors, based in Washington, D.C., were responsible for policy decisions affecting World Bank operations and for the approval of loans to countries in need of financial help as Kenya was? Were they aware that a word from her uncle in the right ear could help assure a country received much needed capital to continue its development? Katherine sat up so fast N Zee didn't have time to stop her.

"Where are you taking me?" She turned her head frantically from male to female. Silence was her only answer.

A headache raged behind her brow, and aches and pains were everywhere. Added to those dismal facts, she was in a foreign country, headed she knew not where. Did anyone know that she was missing? They had to by now. One could spend only so much time in a bathroom.

But where were they going? Katherine stared through the wooden railing into the darkness. She had no idea where they were or how long they'd been traveling. And she knew nothing, absolutely nothing about Kenya's geography. She could see plenty of trees but not much else. The road they were traveling was either unpaved or boasted many potholes because it was certainly bumpy.

All at once Alex Stewart's pleasant-looking face flashed in her mind. Good, dependable, agreeable Alex. Alex Sebastian Stewart was an only child. He was a partner, along with his father, uncle and cousin in the family's prestigious law firm. In addition, Alex had his own fortune, besides what he had inherited from his grandfather, who had been in the lumber business. For three years they had dated each other exclusively. Steady, upstanding, conservative, utterly boring Alex. The same boring man that women all over Washington would give their teeth to marry. The man who was now putting pressure on her to give in to his proposal for marriage and to set a wedding date.

Alex had never indicated anything but complete satisfaction with her. Once she was back home, she would let him know that she was ready to marry him. He cared for her and she for him. She might not see stars, hear bells, or spend hours mooning over the mere mention of her lover's name, but what she felt for Alex was genuine. He was easy on the eyes, and had enough clout and resources to allow them to indulge in all sorts of pleasures. Above all, he was patient with her. That's what made him so safe. Never had he seemed so desirable as right now.

The truck began a slow descent. At last it came to a stop. The driver cut the engine and for a brief period all was quiet. Katherine listened to the door of the cab open and close, and her body tensed, preparing for the worst. The driver walked to the side and said something to the woman. Both man and woman met him at the open back. The woman tugged on Katherine's arm, dragging her along with them.

It was on the tip of David's tongue to ask N Zee where she thought the American woman could possibly go, but he squashed his question. For whatever reason, N Zee was determined to handle the woman roughly.

Glad to be able to move off her backside, Katherine settled on her knees between the pair and listened to them speak in their language to the man standing next to the bed of the truck. The flashlight he held in his hands was pointed directly at the trio. The bright light drifted over each of them, then returned to Katherine, lingering until the woman snapped at the man. Grinning crudely, he aimed the beam at the ground.

The rise and fall of the voices became loud and

agitated and though Katherine didn't understand the words, she detected the anger, especially from the woman, whose fingers were biting into her wrist. Twisting her arm loose, Katherine was surprised when the woman didn't put up a fight.

The woman reached into the breast pocket of the military jacket, withdrew something and threw it at the man's feet. He shone the light on the ground until he spotted the small bundle. Unfolding it, he tucked the light under his arm, held his hands aloft and proceeded to count the money. Katherine could see they were paper bills but could not determine if they were American currency.

The smile left the man's face and he adamantly shook his head. Using a forefinger, he pointed at the wad of cash in his hand, shook his head again and spat on the ground. He looked up at the trio again and his expression was anything but friendly. This was not a good sign. The driver argued loudly with her two captors. The woman pulled out empty pockets on both the shirt and pants of the battle uniform she wore. This caused their driver to yell even louder and draw his pistol, aiming it straight at Katherine's head. Her male captor stepped in front of the gun and held both hands up, speaking in a calm voice. Whatever he said, the driver finally placed the gun back in the waistband of his pants. Totally amicable, his menacing demeanor vanquished, the driver stepped forward, lifted up his arms to help the woman down. The woman's partner hurriedly climbed down and indicated by gestures that Katherine was to climb down into his arms, for which Katherine was grateful. The man stood her gingerly on her feet.

Her relief was short-lived when the woman focused her attention on Katherine, pointing to her shoes, speaking harshly in their tongue. Katherine understood at once what she was asking for, though she said it in Swahilli. She shook her head vehemently.

"No, no, no!" she plunged on, ignoring the possible consequences of her defiance.

"Lift her up, David," N Zee instructed impatiently. Before Katherine knew what they were about, the man swept her up in his arms. Though Katherine struggled, the woman easily slid the shoes off her slender feet. With some effort she snapped off the heels, and threw the damaged pumps onto the ground next to Katherine's feet.
The woman's partner said something to the driver, who looked his way and chuckled. At last he sauntered over to the driver's side of the truck and climbed inside. The woman took hold of Katherine's arms and pulled her towards the edge of the dark uneven road. From the looks of it, their ride was over and they were now on foot. It seemed

as if they didn't have enough cash to pay the man and so consequently were forced to relinquish their vehicle as payment, or get shot.

"Wait, my shoes!" Katherine screeched. If the woman understood what Katherine said, she gave no indication of it. Instead, she tugged on Katherine's arms, moving rapidly away from the direction the truck was going.

It was too dark for Katherine to see where she was stepping. Her sheer hose provided little protection from the small pebbles and debris that created havoc on the bottom of her tender soles. Grunting in pain after a sharp stone pierced her instep, Katherine did her best to maintain her balance as the woman dragged her along. Her legs were nearly as long as the woman's but she had to run to keep up. The strength in the woman's arms was unbelievable. No matter how Katherine struggled, she managed to pull her along behind her.

The man was speaking sharply to the woman but she paid him no heed, her long legs carrying her swiftly over the dirt road. He called out in a loud voice, finally reaching out to spin the woman around, in the process knocking Katherine's arm from her grasp.

"Enough," David shouted. "Give her these shoes." He thrust the altered shoes he'd retrieved moments earlier at Katherine, who clutched them gratefully with damp fingers.

It was too dark for the man to read the gratitude in her eyes. "Thank you," she said, bending down to quickly slip the awkward-looking shoes on her feet. Katherine didn't care how they looked. She was only too happy to have something to shield her soles from the rocky, dirt road.

So much time had lapsed that Katherine could hardly tell day from night. They trudged the torturous trail of scraping vines and thorny trees for hours. They stopped once to allow Katherine to relieve herself while the woman stood guard, shining the light into her face instead of on the ground. She promised herself afterwards that she would not stop again until they reached their destination, wherever that was. It was too humiliating.

Katherine wanted water in the worst way and her feet were two size seven blisters. Her stamina amazed her. She wasn't the most athletic person and had a low tolerance for pain. But somehow she endured.

Suddenly the woman paused in the dimly lit trail ahead of them and issued a series of whistles. Not just ordinary whistles. They were some kind of code, each burst vocal and piercing. The answering response was as loud and as piercing. The woman repeated a series of whistles similar to the first, though of shorter duration. The answering response was shorter.

Without warning, two bodies dropped soundlessly from somewhere over their heads and landed in front of them. Katherine was too tired to be startled. Squinting above her head, she tried to determine where the men had come from. She could discern nothing in which the men could have hidden since branches didn't begin to extend from the tall trees in front of them until near the top of the canopy.

She focused her attention back on the ground to find the woman shining the light at an enormous trunk ahead of them. From out of a massive opening in its side stepped a third man. Katherine gasped. She'd never seen anything quite like it. The opening the man emerged from could comfortably hold at least four men.

The men surrounded them and spoke in a tongue Katherine was becoming familiar with. The woman spoke in animated tones, gesturing at Katherine. One man had a small flashlight that he shone directly on Katherine. Speechless, all three stared for so long Katherine became uneasy. Especially when they each took a step her way. She stared back into each impassive face, then fell to the ground in a dead faint.

"Is Jackson aware of what you've done?" one of the sentries asked N Zee.

"No, Magayu," she answered in a steady voice.

Magayu whipped his attention around to David, who squirmed under his glare. He made a clicking sound with his teeth. "Adam, you carry the prisoner," he said. At his curt command the sentries moved single file through the forest with N Zee and David following. Adam led the procession, carrying Katherine in his arms.

N Zee didn't care what any of them thought. She didn't answer to them. She was third in command behind Kimya. As a matter of fact, she was in command here! She forged ahead of the men. She would make them all see. Kimya, the only man with any influence over Jackson, would be the first to convince. Once Kimya understood her reasons, so would Jackson.

As always, despite the advance guards leading the way into camp, the rebels entered with caution. It was a hard and fast rule Jackson demanded they live by—caution in all things. Though the campsite was empty, unseen eyes were watching them from everywhere, on the ground hidden in the thicket and from wooden flat platforms hanging high up in the trees like the one Adam and his cohort kept watch on.

As the group entered the clearing, Katherine spied a wooden platform built from saplings standing in front of a small, sturdy-looking wooden structure ahead of them. As if on cue, a tall, broad-shouldered man opened the crude door and stepped outside. In the silence of the approaching dawn, Kimya looked across the compound at the individuals.

"What is this?" His hands were at his side while his eyes were on the female slowly regaining consciousness in Adam's arms.

Head held high, a defiant glint in her eye, N Zee spoke. "She is an important American hostage. Her presence will help us gain the attention needed to make world leaders listen to us. Having her as our hostage will help us win this war."

The man's voice whipped out deep and gravelly, stiffening each spine. "How is this? Who is this woman?"

N Zee supplied the answer. The man commanded Adam to bring Katherine closer. He stared down into her face, opened his mouth to speak and snapped it shut. Frowning, he looked from David to N Zee. "Who gave you permission to do this thing?"

"No one. I acted alone." N Zee met the man's

angry stare without blinking. David moved to her side. He reached for her hand but N Zee thrust it behind her back.

"I too am responsible for bringing the American here. I was with N Zee all the way."

A fully conscious Katherine listened to the foreign exchange of words between her captors and another strange man who looked visibly upset. She looked at each face, trying to gauge their emotions. All were tense. The woman appeared to smirk. It dawned on Katherine that she could see each face clearly. Daylight, finally arrived, was filtering through the leaves high above their heads.

The rectangular structure in front of her commanded her attention. It was a small, crudely built house. It stood in a beam of sunlight which had pierced a mid-sized gap in the canopy of trees. On the outer edge of the clearing stood four or five tents and a few huts fashioned from leaves, mud and sticks.

Fascinated, Katherine listened to the alien sounds around her. The forest was coming to life. In the spot where they stood, it was relatively cool, and condensation from leaves on tall bushes and skinny trees fell onto her hair and face.

Katherine boldly tapped the chest of the man holding her in a death grip. Gaining his attention, she pointed to the ground, indicating she wanted to get down.

"Hey," she persisted when he failed to comply, "you can put me down."

The man peered down into her face and his lips split into a wide, leering grin, revealing slightly protruding teeth.

"Put me down," Katherine asserted forcefully. She wiggled, straining to be released. The man grinned wider. Katherine realized he liked her moving about in his arms. His rough hand was spread wide across her bare back and the other tightened meaningfully around her thighs. He inclined his head at the man standing in front of them, speaking.

Katherine searched around for her protector but found him also listening to the man dressed in the beige khaki trousers and matching shirt. Obviously the man had authority since the woman was listening to him without interruption. When he finished, the woman spoke.

"Where is Jackson?" N Zee asked sullenly.

"Sleeping," came the terse reply.

"At this hour?" Adam asked.

The insubordinate question brought a flare of displeasure to the brown eyes. His answer was given in a tight voice. "Our leader came into camp only hours ago from a very dangerous mission. Because of him we now have weapons enough to continue our struggle. He has traveled on foot for almost a week without much sleep or nourishment. Each of you has heard about what he suffered in prison two years ago, though he will not speak of it. The rumors do not do the truth justice. Jackson has sacrificed much. His body cannot endure continued punishment. For as long as he wishes, he will rest."

Adam dropped his eyes from Kimya's censuring expression, his lips tightening in anger. He did not like being chastised, especially in front of others. He was a rebel, a fierce fighter and as good a man as Jackson Shugaa. Had not he proven himself in battle? Everyone spoke the praises of Jackson Shugaa, but they would learn that he was a mere mortal like everyone else.

N Zee took several steps toward the small struc- ture before Kimya realized her intent and held up his hand, forestalling her progress. "Jackson will rest." His tone brooked no argument.

Behind him, the door constructed of thin hard strips of wood suddenly pushed outward and a man filled its opening. Quiet reigned. Katherine watched as they stiffened to attention. The man who wouldn't let the woman proceed further stepped aside, his eyes on the man emerging from the hut.

Stooping low to exit the small abode, the new stranger stared across the way at them. He was dressed in beige khaki pants but wore a sea green cotton undershirt. Deep in the shoulders with a lean build, he looked to be at least 6' 3". His pants were loosely belted and rode low over narrow hips. The legs that went on forever were slightly bowed at the calf. His bare feet were long and narrow. A gun was strapped around his lean waist. He spoke quietly and Kimya moved closer to listen. He bobbed his head up and down as the newcomer talked for his ears alone. Finally, with a negligent wave of his hand, the newcomer bade the man to move aside so that he could approach the others.

Unable to help herself, Katherine gaped at the man whose picture had been passed around at the dinner. In the flesh he looked even more menacing, yet in some ways, desirable.

Chapter Three

The man turned his attention to the rebel still holding Katherine and then to Katherine. A chill skittered through her body when their eyes met. His golden eyes, stark against his skin coloring, were as dry and remote as the Sahara. The absence of emotion or warmth gave him a sinister aura. Enveloping him was an air of indifference that made Katherine perceive him to be looking through her.

Her attention dropped to the lethal-looking handgun at his side, and then quickly she raised her eyes back to his face. Katherine's heart raced.

The heavy lids, fringed by impossibly thick black lashes, narrowed a fraction. Katherine, caught up in his hypnotic eyes, did her best not to squirm but found herself shrinking down into the man's arms. The same warning that had crept into her head when she stared at the man's picture at the banquet, flashed through her now. This man was dangerous!

Silently, the man watched Katherine watching him. Despite the fear threading through her, she could not pull her eyes away from his stunning face. His cold eyes ran the length of her slim form held snugly in the rebel's arms. They started at her battered shoes, rose past legs without hose, then up over the tattered peach dress to her auburn-streaked hair hanging in tangled disarray over the man's arm. His voice when he spoke to the rebel was a biting lash. "Why are you holding her? Is she a cripple?"

Shaking his head in protest, Adam opened his mouth to speak. "Let her go," Jackson commanded.

With apparent reluctance, Katherine was eased to the ground. She stumbled backwards when her sore, tired feet touched the hard-packed earth. The man who had carried her caught her and held her at his side. When he was spoken to in a terse manner, he quickly moved away from Katherine. He saluted Jackson sharply, spun on his booted heels and left, taking the two guards with him.

"Inside, N Zee, David." Expecting total obedience Jackson dismissed the pair and spoke to his friend Kimya. "Bring her. We must sort through this mess at once."

Bending low, Jackson followed the others inside the thatched structure. After the slightly lopsided door was shut, it took only moments for Katherine's eyes to adjust to the gloomy, tight interior of the small room. It was dimly lit by the early morning sunlight that filtered through tiny slits along the walls of the hut. A petite woman dressed in traditional military fatigues lit a kerosene lamp. She wore black thongs on her feet. Her sandy brown braids were tightly bound on top of her head. She ignored Katherine and quietly went about her task of ladling water from a bucket hanging from a string in the corner of the room into tin cups.

Katharine's eyes scanned the gloomy space. A folding table approximately the size of a card table dominated the room. Two chairs faced each other on either side. In one corner of the room was a rickety-looking stool holding a plastic bucket. Next to it was a twin-sized mattress lying on a bed of leaves on the dirt floor. It was covered with a thin cotton sheet. In that same corner pegs protruded from the walls. On these hung various articles of men's clothing. There were no windows in the room. Only a very small hole, chest high, was cut in the wall next to the door. Pinned above it was a piece of cloth used to cover it at night.

Finished ladling water, the silent woman placed the cups on the table, positioning the kerosene lamp in the center. She lit candles and placed them in two corners of the room. A door much like the front one led to another room to their immediate right. Katherine saw standing in another corner, a canvas bag. At least half a dozen rifle butts extended from its opening.

Swallowing with some difficulty, Katherine warded off panic. What on earth was going on here? Gratefully she accepted the cup of flat, warm water offered her. She tilted the cup up and drank thirstily. When she handed the empty cup back to the woman, she found all eyes on her.

"Haven't you all ever seen a thirsty woman before?" she asked no one in particular. The others had yet to pick up their water. Katherine's already taunt nerves frayed. What was she supposed to do? Wait until she got permission? The woman had given her the cup, for heavens sake!

The room was closing in on her and she was having trouble breathing. She'd never suffered from claustrophobia before but was overwhelmed by it at this moment. Too many people in too small a space. She couldn't bear it!

The man with the gold eyes was at her side. He said something to her kidnappers, who eased themselves down on the mattress. His hand wrapped around Katherine's upper arm. He spoke to the man at his side but his eyes never left her face. Katherine flinched and stared down at the long, lean fingers enclosing her flesh. His calloused palms were cool on her skin.

Katherine looked up at the man and wished she hadn't. Her heart skidded, then caught in her throat. A slight tremor started in her limbs and she tried to extricate herself from his hold.

Jackson's lips thinned. "Take her in there and lay her down in my room. She looks as if she is about to drop on her feet," he said in Swahili. Kimya moved to comply.

Katherine realized that whatever the man said did not please the woman who had drugged and kidnapped her. She cut her eyes at Katherine and the dislike was palpable. Her breathing became as labored as Katherine's was moments ago. Katherine would dearly love to know what was said. The woman was controlling her emotions with a visible effort. Obviously this man was their leader and she was much too afraid to defy him.

"Why your bed?" N Zee asked with repressed anger and jealously. "The woman is filthy."

"So are you," Jackson returned calmly. N Zee flushed with embarrassment. David's gaze dropped to his soiled clothing. He looked at N Zee from under his lashes, hoping to convey to her his affinity for her distress.

"So was I after so arduous a journey," Jackson added, easing the hurt from N Zee's expression. He was extremely upset with her. Still, he had no wish to wound her needlessly. "After traveling on foot for a length of time without benefit of soap and water, what else is there?"

"She needs a bath. We all do," David offered tentatively. Reaching into the inside pocket of the waiter's jacket, he extracted Katherine's purse. Unable to stop himself, he held it to his nose and sniffed. It smelled just like the American. He passed the beaded bag to Jackson.

"She will get one," Jackson stated, briefly eyeing David.

"Since when are we in the habit of treating our captives so well?" N Zee asked irritably, still not reconciled to the idea of Katherine sleeping in Jackson's bed.

"Since you got into the habit of kidnapping innocent individuals and bringing them into the camp." The quiet, impassive tone had N Zee lifting her eyes to Jackson's. The look in his warned her not to push her luck for fear of alienating Kimya. She would need Kimya on her side. She could only hope that his passion for her would make him an ally.

∞∞ ∞∞ ∞∞

The door led into another dimly lit room smaller than the first. The man lit a candle and Katherine saw that this room was dominated by a sleeping platform built from forest wood and bound into a wooden frame. A coverlet lay on top of a smaller-than-average size mattress. A large metal tub, the kind which Katherine had seen in antique shops or magazines depicting country living, rested in a corner behind the door. A tree trunk, its top smoothed over, sat upright next to the bed. At the foot of the mattress was an army knapsack, its ends secured tight.

A bright ray of sunlight shone though another hole cut in the wall. This one was close enough to the ceiling to require something to stand on to see outside. This room was just as gloomy as the first, though not stuffy. Kimya led Katherine by the arm to the mattress, indicating by hand gestures that she was to lie down.

"Oh no, mister!" She backed up to the door, shaking her head vigorously, her streaked locks flying about her shoulders.

"Lie down," Kimya instructed in Swahili. He pointed again at the bed. Why must this one be stubborn? He saw the weariness in her face and the slump of her shoulders.

"Uh-uh. You'll have to catch me first, then kill me. I didn't survive the trip here with that evil one out there to be raped by you or anyone else." Katherine bolted for the door. She was nearly through it before Kimya yanked her back inside.

She shrieked in fear and anger and fought Kimya with renewed energy and desperation. Perspiration made Katherine's limbs slick, and Kimya struggled to hold onto her. The sounds of her tearing dress barely registered with Katherine. All she was cognizant of was not giving in to these brutes without a fight. She raised her knee and it found its target as the door opened behind them. Kimya doubled over in pain and muttered a streak of curses but somehow managed to keep his hold on Katherine.

"What is going on in here?" an icy voice demanded.

"I...do not know...what's...what is wrong with her," Kimya replied in a strained voice. He was huffing and puffing, barely dodging Katherine's flailing arms. "She became a wildcat when I pointed to the bed for her to lie down. Talking nonsense about r...ump." The rest of Kimya's words were lost when the arm he'd captured was jerked away and slammed into the center of his hard stomach.

Understanding dawned on Jackson. Exhaling a breath, he stepped into the fray, grasping

Katherine's twisting, bending body as her brown eyes darkened with terror. Pulling her against him, he held both her hands behind her back without much effort as she continued to pant and strain away. "Stop it!"

Too intent on escaping these new clutches, the language Jackson used failed to register in Katherine's mind. She was dimly conscious of her arm stinging from the blow she'd landed in Kimya's stomach. Two against one was ringing in her ear. There was no way she could fight such well built men. There wasn't an ounce of extra flesh on either one of them. "Oh God," she prayed. "Just let me die right here, right now. Please!" She squeezed her eyes shut and the tears she'd held back since this nightmare began rolled down her cheeks.

"You will not die. You will live until we decide what to do with you. No one, including Kimya, will harm you in any way, I assure you. Do you under-stand?" Jackson stared at her intently, silently not-ing the stark terror glittering in her eyes. He shook her slender frame for good measure, then raised his eyes to Kimya. An expression of acknowledgment entered Kimya's eyes. He left the room, closing the door behind him, forcing N Zee, who was on her knees eavesdropping at the door, back onto the mattress.

Katherine stared at the retreating back of the

man Jackson had called Kimya, then turned to look at Jackson in amazement, her fear momentarily forgotten, the stunned look in her eyes replaced by relief. She'd understood what he said. Every word he uttered. "Oh my, you speak English." And what a speaking voice it was. She was cognizant of its cadence in the midst of a maelstrom of emotions.

"Thank you, Father." She rolled her eyes heavenward. "Someone can finally tell me what this craziness is all about." Her eyes warmed and she found herself smiling.

Seemingly spellbound, Jackson got caught up in the emotions flickering across the American's face. Here she was, weighing less than half his body weight, and she'd fought like someone possessed. The punch she'd delivered to his friend carried some weight. She was strong and by the look of determination in the depths of her eyes, brave.

Her thick, auburn-streaked hair fell in her face, obscuring one eye. The one watching him was large, deep brown and red-rimmed, probably due to lack of sleep.

"Who are you? Where am I and why am I here? What do you want from me?" Katherine watched Jackson expectantly, seeking answers.

"You lie down on the bed and remain there until I speak with the others." Jackson's tone was matter-of-fact and did not offer more.

This wasn't the response Katherine wished to hear. Her brows knit. "I don't want to lie down. I want some answers."

The gold eyes iced over and Katherine's fear returned. "If you please," she sputtered.

It was at that moment that she became vividly aware of how close their bodies were. The tips of her breasts just lightly brushed his chest; her nipples were erect and pushing through the thin fabric of her torn dress. His heart was pumping steadily against her bosom, while hers pumped so furiously it was like the thumping of a drum in her ears.

"Let me go," she demanded brusquely.

The heavy eyes became hooded as he continued to watch Katherine with a disconcerting directness, yet didn't release her. She could only wonder why these men were always holding her and refusing to let her go. She strained against Jackson's wide chest.

The man's grip was like iron. Fighting him was ludicrous. When he released her, it would be his choice, his eyes seemed to say. He kept her close to him as Katherine stared back at him sullenly. After what seemed forever, he dropped his arms and stepped away.

"Lie down here." He pointed to the mattress. There was a steely, unyielding quality to Jackson's accent-tinted voice. Katherine knew it wouldn't be wise to disobey him. Still, she was never one to give in easily, especially when someone was ordering her around.

With a defiant tilt of her chin, she backed away and sat carefully on the edge of the platform bed. Her expression told Jackson that she would lie down when she wanted to and not before.

The gold eyes turned flat in a face totally devoid of emotion. As casually as she could, Katherine draped an arm over her knee, doing her best to still the tremors coursing through her. What she really wanted to do was scamper to an empty, shadowed corner to escape the soulless eyes.

"When we are finished, you will clean yourself up." Jackson left the room, closing the door behind him.

Scowling after him at the shut door, Katherine stuck her tongue out. "Clean myself up indeed." Despite her haughty retort to the empty room, she cringed. The man made her feel dirty. She looked down at the grime-smeared legs stretched before her and up the length of her dress. "And indeed I am," she sighed.

Up came her chin. She would not feel self-conscious around these people! They were criminals, for heavens sake, and she was a hostage. What did she care if she smelled and looked like hell?

Still, the logic couldn't quite quell the urge to sniff herself. Then, leaning over, she pressed her nose close to the bed covering and smelled it.

Maybe she would stretch her dirty body out on the rumpled but clean-smelling coverlet for a little while. But not right now, she decided, standing upright. She scrutinized the austere room, paying close attention to the items missed in her initial observance. Pegs extended from these walls also. Khaki shirts and pants hung from one. A knapsack hung from another. Curiosity had Katherine peering inside. Sticking a hand in, she pulled out socks, undershirts and men's briefs.

Hastily dropping them back into the sack, she stepped away from the wall. The log standing next to the mattress grabbed her attention, as well as the cut-out hole over the bed. Investigating this discovery was worth the effort, she decided.

She rolled the heavy log and positioned it under an opening the size of a twelve-inch photo frame. There was no way she could fit through it, but Katherine was anxious to see what was going on outside. Standing flat-footed on the low log, she peered through the opening. Sunlight was filtering through the gaps in the trees but Katherine could not see the sky. She couldn't see much of anything else outside either.

Katherine stretched out on the platform that was

inches off the dirt floor. It was like the log she'd recently stood on, surprisingly sturdy. She supposed it would have to be to hold its occupant. While not bulky in size, the man whom everyone deferred to was tall and solidly built. Once Katherine became aware of being held in his arms, she'd been conscious of nothing but muscle. A sudden wave of physical and mental fatigue flushed through her body, and then she drifted off to sleep.

Chapter Four

*J*ackson and Kimya were at the table with barely enough room for their long legs. The petite woman called Rose was no longer in the room. Both men faced N Zee and David, who remained sitting on the mattress. N Zee hated being in that position. Their legs jutted out in front of them and she could barely move her feet without bumping into the table legs. Mostly it felt sub-servient to the two men sitting above her.

"Why is the American woman here?" Jackson queried. His eyes shifted between David and N Zee.

"To gain us leverage in our fight," was N Zee's cryptic answer.

"Leverage with whom?" Kimya asked

"With Kenya's government," David answered.

Cutting David an irritated glare, N Zee sat forward on the mattress. Her expression forbade him to speak any more. "The woman will be used as a bargaining tool with the World Bank members. Through us, those members will make certain demands on Matoi."

Watching the pair impassively, Jackson raised a brow but said nothing.

"And?" Kimya prompted when N Zee fell silent, her eyes on Jackson, full of anticipation.

"The American's father is an important member of the World Bank, an executive officer of color, who was recently appointed. We are all aware of how dependent our country has become on funds loaned out by its members. Our once thriving country can barely feed many of its citizens.

"I fail to see how any of this will help us," Kimya replied shortly.

N Zee's lips parted in a smug smile as she held the glance of the man she knew to be secretly in love with her. "The captive's father will help us once he learns that we have his daughter."

"How?"

"By using his seat on the board to force Matoi to step down. He will do that by influencing the other members to refuse to loan Kenya more money. Without the money, our country will not survive its present status much longer. Poverty and displacement are increasing at a rapid pace. Pressure will be brought to bear on Matoi and his corrupt cabinet to step down.

Once the American knows we have his daughter, he will do as we dictate. He will not get her back until Matoi steps down." N Zee's features softened. She was sure Kimya would see the logic in her plan.

"You say this woman is the daughter of one of the executives?"

"Yes," David answered swiftly, before N Zee had the chance to stop him. "He is the only board member of color in the history of the World Bank organization." Intent on listening to David, no one saw the frown mar Jackson's forehead.

"You two think it will be as simple as that? A newly-appointed member making such a demand? Someone who has no history with the World Bank? You expect one lone African American male to have influence over more than twenty powerful individuals?" Jackson bellowed.

A mask of uncertainty crossed David's features. N Zee lifted her chin in haughty confidence. "The World Bank is finally giving in to international pressure and appointing an African American member. They would not want to be seen by other countries as insensitive by refusing to help this man. After all, they constantly claim they have Third World countries' best interests at heart."

The expression on Jackson's face did not reveal his thought. N Zee couldn't tell if her words were getting through to him. She raised beseeching eyes to Kimya.

"How do you plan on getting your message to the American, to the World Bank?" Kimya asked.

"I will take the message myself to..."

"No!" The curtly issued word exploded in the small room. All eyes fell on Jackson. "We've lost too many because of misplaced bravery. And," Jackson added, his expression hard, his tone relentless, "it was by the Almighty's grace that you two were not caught, tortured, forced to talk, then slaughtered. An innocent woman could have been harmed also. It was foolish what you two did. Foolish and thoughtless. You did not have permission from me or Kimya to carry out this crazy plan. In your stupidity did either of you stop to think that you could have led Ntimama or his men to us?"

Jackson allowed his words to sink in before he spoke again, his cold eyes shifting to N Zee. "You are prone to acting instead of thinking, N Zee." Though it was usually cool on the forest floor it was fast becoming tight and hot in the small room. Neither Jackson or Kimya had broken a sweat but David and N Zee were clearly uncomfortable. Perspiration rolled down David's face and neck. N

Zee's forehead beaded with moisture.

A knock sounded on the door. The deafening roar of the howler monkey coincided with its opening as the newcomer was given permission to enter. Rose moved silently around the room, holding a metal coffee pot that had seen better days in her hand. At the inclination of Kimya's head, she poured boiled coffee into the empty cups. Her task complete, her eyes strayed from Kimya to Jackson and lingered. N Zee stared pointedly up at Rose.

"Thank you, Rose," Jackson offered, dismissing the woman, who exited as silently out the door as she had entered.

N Zee turned dry burning eyes first to Jackson, then to Kimya. She would not cry at this humiliation heaped on her by Jackson's biting tongue. She jerked her hand away from David's attempt to grasp it and console her. She needed pity from no man. That this man took the gift she'd brought him and threw it back in her face was too much to bear.

Compassion was written on Kimya's broad face but N Zee bitterly realized that he would not come to her defense, no matter how he felt about her. He would not defy Jackson. So be it! She did not need him or anyone. Forced to fend for herself before she was out of her teens, she knew how to take care of herself. "You and Kimya were away. I am in command in your absence. The opportunity was

presented to me and I took it. Time was of the
essence." She sat up, legs stiffly stretched out, her
upper body rigid.

"You should have waited until I returned from
my mission," Kimya reprimanded mildly. "We could
have talked this thing out and you would have realized your plan would never work. This was thrown
together hastily without thought of the consequences."

Risking a glance at Jackson's dark, immobile
face, N Zee retorted cooly, "Let's not argue. We
have the American. Our goal should be to use her
to our benefit. We must act quickly so everyone will
know we mean business."

David's face lit with animation. "There are
many ways to get our message across to the
woman's father." His eyes landed on Jackson and
he swallowed, his Adam's apple bobbing up and
down. Jackson drank from his tin cup and set it
down. Encouraged at his silence, David continued
speaking. "The woman is a valuable tool. No one
would dare touch us as long as we have her." He
nodded his head at this additional contribution, his
thin lips pulling up in a confident smile.

"The woman goes back to her father tomorrow."
All eyes flew to Jackson. N Zee made a sound of
protest in her throat. David stared, not sure of what
to say or do. Kimya watched his friend, patiently

waiting to hear what he would say next.

"What do you mean, she goes back? How can you say that after all we've been through?" N Zee's expression was thunderous, her tone belligerent.

"Having this woman here will complicate matters. If she is as important as you say, we will soon be hunted like game. This has the potential to become an international incident, involving the CIA and American soldiers."

Blanching, N Zee swallowed the hot words on her tongue as Jackson's words hit home. Still, she did not back down. "If so many people get involved in trying to get the woman back, don't you see how we could use the situation to force Matoi to step aside. If we threaten to end her life…"

"Quiet! Don't speak another word." Heat entered Jackson's eyes. N Zee winced at the forbidding expression on his face. "We will not threaten innocent lives. The American goes back to her father, unharmed. You will do nothing so rash again as long as you are with me, or you will cease to be with me. Is that understood?" Jackson stood up, signaling the meeting was at an end.

"The weapons I brought back are to be distributed for the attack day after tomorrow. Do it now, then get some rest."

"Please listen, Jackson."

"Now, N Zee," Jackson grated out.

When David would follow a disgruntled N Zee out the door, Jackson stopped him. David turned to Jackson, his expression cautious and questioning.

"Did N Zee tell us everything?"

David's lips puckered. He hurriedly wiped the expression from his face but not before Jackson saw it. His tone was stiff. "N Zee is honest. She would not lie to you."

There was a long pause before Kimya spoke. "Your loyalty is commendable but misplaced." His tone turned grim at the look on David's face. "Don't let N Zee use you again."

"N Zee wouldn't...she wouldn't...," David protested lamely.

"Leave us." Jackson dismissed the man, giving him his back.

Kimya surveyed his friend's sharp profile, gauging his mood. He was closer to Jackson than anyone alive and not even he could determine his thoughts at all times. "Maybe the American woman can be of use to us." He kept his eyes on his friend as he moved the table from the middle of the room. Jackson swung around to him, his thick black brows slanted in a frown.

"Having this woman here will cause more trouble than it's worth." Jackson inhaled a deep breath and his tall frame tensed. "She is trouble, Kimya. I feel it in my bones." His unblinking gold eyes held his friend's brown ones.

"What will we do?"

"Try and get her back to her family as quickly as possible. If not tomorrow, the next day, and pray it all ends there."

"Will that end your concerns once we've taken her back?"

Sighing wearily, Jackson's eyes lifted to stare out the open door. "No," he quietly replied.

Jackson moved soundlessly around the room. Katherine didn't stir. He lit a candle to dispel the rapidly falling shadows, and set it on the log beside the bed. With light in the room, his attention fell on the woman lying on her side so still in his bed. Her dress was dirty and ripped. Her hair was tousled over her shoulder and the pillow in every direction. Her taut back tapered down to a small waist and perfectly round, firm-looking buttocks. Her shapely brown legs were scratched and speckled with dried blood in places. He frowned when his eyes fell on her feet. They were bare and bruised to the ankles. The light soles were black in some places.

Jackson picked up a slender foot in his hand. He rolled his thumb across the tender instep. Katherine flinched but she didn't wake. His fingers continued to caress the soft skin as he lifted one of her battered shoes from the side of the bed. The heels were missing, the leather split and cracked. They were good for nothing except feeding a fire.

Moaning in her sleep, Katherine rolled onto her back, bringing Jackson's attention back to the dress which barely came down to mid-thigh. The scooped neckline was pulled taunt and allowed Jackson a capacious view of her smooth, brown bosom. He stilled for a moment, watching the rise and fall of her breasts.

Releasing her foot, he reached out with one hand and brought the tattered hemline of the dress as far down her thighs as possible. Her arms crossed over her middle in a protective gesture but she did not awake.

She was indeed beautiful, Jackson admitted dispassionately. Being disheveled and soiled did little to obscure her attributes. He also had a notion that she could be a handful, if his brief encounter with her was any indication. Regardless of the outcome, she had fought like a lioness when she thought she was being attacked. The kind of trouble this lone female could bring they did not need.

He and Kimya had determined that Kimya would leave tonight for Nairobi to find out what he could about the uproar the American's disappearance had caused. Once that was established, he,

Jackson Shugaa, would get her back to town, hopefully without incident.

Once the woman—the woman. They couldn't keep calling her the woman or the American. He would find out her given name and use it.

She sighed softly, almost mournfully, in her sleep and raised an arm above her head, murmuring in a husky voice words Jackson couldn't understand. He stared closely at her face.
Maybe it was best they learn nothing of her before her return. Maybe it was best she be known simply as the American.

Pivoting abruptly from the bed, Jackson strode into the vacant front room. There was much to be done. Now that they had the weapons, tonight they must prepare for the hit-and-run attacks to be carried out in seventy-two hours. The female rebels must be primed and ready to carry out the grenade attacks in the predawn hours preceding a full scale raid. No more delays like today. New fighters were standing by in Nanuki ready to take the oath and fight for citizens' rights. But the oath would not be forced on an individual using the threat of death, as was done by the opposition. With that type of forced loyalty, it was too easy to plant informants and encounter disloyalty. The oaths for Jackson's rebels would be given freely, without force. However, there would be no turning back once the oath was given.

Chapter Five

Katherine awoke disoriented and with a weariness of body as though she had not slept. She opened her eyes as wide as possible, and lay still until they focused in the dark room. With one arm folded across her trim middle and the other stretched across her forehead, she lay listening.

A low-pitched whoop touched her ears, inducing shivers along her spine. Seconds later, the loud gobble, gobble, gobble of a turkey followed. Hardly able to believe her ears, Katherine cocked an ear. It was hard to imagine the presence of turkeys in this forest. Having no idea she was hearing the Mangohey monkeys for the first time, she attempted to distinguish one foreign sound from another.

The feline roar that followed on the heels of the monkeys' distinctive sound raised the hair on Katherine's arms and neck. She sat up, wondering what species of cat she heard. Was it cheetah? Lion? She remained silent, straining toward the sounds of voices and strange noises she now heard from beyond the closed door.

What did it matter? she asked herself, losing interest immediately and slumping back down in the bed. They spoke what sounded like Swahili, and she couldn't understand it any more than she could understand most of the forest noises.

Unable to locate what was left of her beat-up shoes, Katherine stood on sore feet on the cool dirt floor, smoothing the rumpled dress down her thighs. Then she realized the voices sounded farther away. Limping slightly from stiff limbs and tender feet, she reached the door and opened it. Katherine scanned the corners of the room, looking for the canvas bag with weapons—it was gone. Deep male voices and female laughter drew her from her disappointing survey to the door leading to the outside, which was open.

Dozens of pairs of eyes held Katherine captive in the doorway and all conversation was suspended. Her eyes rounded at the sight of so many people. Groups of men and women were gathered around fires in the large clearing facing the small shelter. Standing or sitting on the hard ground, logs or overturned cans, they all appeared to be dressed in full military regalia, or a tee shirt and khaki pants or shorts. More tents had been set up in the clearing further back.

The sedate, petite woman who had waited on them after Katherine's arrival was bending over a butane stove stirring something in a large black, cast iron pot with a long-handled spoon. She used a metal cup to dip a powdery white substance from a fifty pound bag standing nearby and poured it into rapidly boiling water, stirring the mixture constantly and confidently as it thickened. Smothering the fire down, she moved to a pot of the same size cooking over an open fire enclosed by large rocks, stirring what was inside also.

Katherine was hungry enough to consume whatever was cooking in those pots. As long as she didn't see it before it became food.

Many eyes were on the cook, observing her every move, expressions of anticipation on their faces. To them, appeasement of hunger seemed more important than Katherine.

Her female kidnapper was sitting on an overturned bucket less than a yard away from where Katherine was standing, near a full-figured woman with a neat, short Afro. Both raised their eyes in Katherine's direction, glaring at her.

Another pair of eyes watched Katherine from near a tent positioned to the left of the shelter. The man's legs were crossed at the ankles and despite there being nothing to support his back, he appeared relaxed.

Refusing to acknowledge him, Katherine's eyes wandered around the campsite. Pockets of animosity were aimed her way. She tugged on her dress, suddenly self conscious of her disheveled state. Gulping painfully, she took a step back but did not disappear from sight.

Rose began ladling out portions of food to the impatiently waiting rebels, and conversation among them resumed. Out of the corner of her eye Katherine saw the golden-eyed man step up with his bowl to be filled. She inched back into the room, intending to escape his scrutiny. Finally all the way inside, she closed the door. The man made her extremely nervous.

Resting on the only seat in the room, a cloth folding chair, Katherine wrapped her arms around her middle and asked herself not for the first time about her circumstances. Barring a superficial cut to her side, from the female captor, no one had done her serious harm. Yet. But where was she? Why was she here? How would she get away? No solutions came to mind and Katherine hung her head in despair. Never had she felt so hopeless in her entire life.

The opening of the door had Katherine jumping up from the low chair and positioning herself flush against the wall. A shadow filled the doorway and the woman who had cooked the food came inside. She was holding a steaming bowl the size of a cup.

Breathing a sigh of relief, Katherine eased forward, smiling at the pretty, sandy brown face before accepting the proffered bowl. Whatever was inside smelled delicious. Katherine's stomach growled in anticipation. She recognized onions and potatoes. Could she hope against hope that the meat she spied floating in the juices was some sort of beef? At this point Katherine decided she didn't much care. She took the bowl from the woman, sat down in the chair and began to eat. The food was hot and more spicy than she usually liked, but Katherine didn't mind. The meat was tender and was similar enough in substance and taste to beef that she didn't question its source. When she raised her head the bowl was empty, the woman gone from the room, and her hunger only partially appeased. An uncontrollable burp escaped her. What she wouldn't give for a tall glass of cold, sweet water.

As if she heard her silent wish, the woman appeared with a tin cup filled with water. She drank down long swallows of water, realizing just how thirsty she was. When she set the cup down on the table, she found that the woman had disappeared again.

"Oh well," she spoke derisively. "Fed and watered and ready for the slaughter."

The words had no sooner had left her tongue than the door opened and in stepped two strange men carrying pails of water. They walked past her into the room where Katherine had napped earlier. They soon left and minutes later returned with more pails of water, steam escaping their tops. These they also took into the room and left with empty buckets.

Wide-eyed and speechless, Katherine watched them carry out their tasks. Her eyes narrowed to near slits when her female captor entered the room with a towel thrown over one arm and a misshapen piece of brown soap in the other. She stood over Katherine, pantomiming the bathing motion, her lips drawn up in a thin, mocking smile.

Nodding her head that she understood, Katherine offered a tentative smile to show that she was grateful for the chance to get clean. She reached out a hand for the items, intending to take to the water as soon as the woman left. The woman snatched the items back, pointing a finger to the room where the tub of water waited.

"Oh, I understand. I am to bathe," Katherine answered agreeably. "I can do it myself. Have

since I was about three or four. Do you understand?" Katherine asked dryly, looking to the
woman for acquiescence. Obviously not compre-
hending, the woman pointed again to the room
behind her.

At an impasse, Katherine allowed herself to be
led into the darkened room where the woman started to light candles. Finished, she beckoned
Katherine to the full tub of water, once again snatching the soap and towel out of her reach. A gleam of
wickedness lit her eyes. With rapid hand signals
she indicated that Katherine was to strip off her
clothes.

"When it's a cold day in hell," Katherine muttered through clinched teeth. "I can bathe myself,
woman." Before the woman could pull further back,
Katherine grabbed the items from her hand.

The woman reached out, snaring a fistful of
Katherine's dress and ripping it away. Breathing
fire, Katherine stared down at the only thing she
was wearing, pale pink lace panties. "Give that
back," she screeched. When she reached for her
useless dress, the woman shoved her backwards.

Off balance, her legs banged into the side of the
tub. Unable to gain her footing, Katherine stumbled
backward into the water, then struggled frantically to
lever herself out. Finally, she managed to get a
handful of the woman's pant leg, pulling herself

upright and tumbling N Zee headfirst into the tub in the process.

Before Katherine could savor the satisfaction of N Zee's position, she came up sputtering and screaming, braids dripping water, and gave Katherine a stinging slap across the face. Angry enough to see multi-colors, Katherine retaliated in kind, deftly dodging additional blows seconds before pushing N Zee back into the tub, bottom first.

"What is this? Stop it at once!" Jackson stood over the two fighting women, scowling. His full lips were compressed in anger, his noble nostrils flared. The look in his eyes was like dry desert sand. Harsh and biting. Katherine could not control her flinch.

Jackson pulled N Zee from the tub. Not quite contrite, she stood in front of him, water dripping from all points onto the floor, creating a muddy puddle. "Explain yourself, now!" The calm of his icy voice belied his surging emotions.

Crouching down beside the tub and crossing her hands over her breasts, Katherine did her best to hide her body from view. She need not have bothered for all the attention Jackson paid her.

"How is it you bring this woman items with which to bathe and a fight starts?"

"She started it," N Zee replied in a shrill voice, pointing an accusing finger in Katherine's direction.

"I don't know what she's saying but she started this mess, not me!" Katherine shot out heatedly, pointing a finger in the woman's direction. "I told her I could bathe myself and she refused to let me. Instead, she tore what's left of my dress off me. I was defending myself and I'll do it again if I have to."

Swinging himself around in Katherine's direction, Jackson stared at her coldly. His eyes raked over her pantiy-clad, wet body. Heat rushed to her face. Cringing, she clutched her hands tighter in front of her, raised her chin and held his stare. He turned back to N Zee.

Katherine saw the nasty glint in her eyes. N Zee had not missed the exchange between Jackson and Katherine. She smirked at Katherine.

"Get her something to put on since you have destroyed her clothes," Jackson demanded curtly.

"Do you believe it was the American who started this?" N Zee countered. Water ran unheeded down her face and body.

Weary, his patience nearing an end where N Zee was concerned, Jackson answered truthfully. "I do not."

N Zee continued, "What does it matter what she wears or if she wears anything at all. She is a hostage." Throwing Katherine a scornful glance, N Zee belatedly realized that statement wasn't quite true. She wanted no woman parading in front of

Jackson naked so that he might admire her body, especially when he refused to see or admire hers.

"Go. Now!" Jackson commanded.

N Zee exited the room without further protest, leaving Jackson and Katherine to eye one another warily. "What is your name?" Jackson asked, throwing her a towel.

Unable to gather her wits, Katherine clutched the towel about her and glared up at Jackson. The sensual sound of his voice sent ripples of awareness through her. Finding her tongue, she responded as steadily as possible.

"Katherine. What's yours?" For a long while she thought he might not answer. His silence, as well as his forthright stare, was beginning to make her uneasy.

"Jackson," came the short answer.

There it was again. That tingle of awareness. Katherine used her most formal, distant tone. "First name or last?"

The stoic expression cracked a tiny bit. Katherine wasn't sure with what. Humor, anger, surprise. "First. Stand up."

Startled by the brisk command, Katherine's eyes fell from Jackson's to the damp shirt plastered to his muscled chest. He stood away from the tub, his long fingers outstretched.

"I'm not coming anywhere near you dressed…or

shall I say, undressed like this," Katherine replied in an un-lady like snarl.

Jackson's eyes darkened dangerously, and without warning, Katherine was lifted from beside the tub to stand before him. She let out a moan of pain when his rough hands scraped across the forgotten wound in her side

"What's this?"

Katherine made a futile move to cover her breasts as Jackson stared at the wound in her side. A trickle of blood ran down her side. "How did this happen?" Jackson's expression was dark, his fingers gentle as he probed the cut. "Who did this to you?"

Chapter Six

Totally unprepared for her reaction to his fingers probing her flesh, Katherine could only stare at his bowed head. She gritted her teeth to keep from crying out in pain. Her skin burned yet it tingled, leaving her confused over the conflicting sensations. She couldn't determine from his tone if Jackson was angry. His voice was impassive, without inflection.

So much for modesty, she thought, as the fingers continued to probe. Katherine slapped at his hand, hoping to deter him while continuing to hold the towel to her breasts. Jackson stared into her face for a tense moment, his expression unreadable, then resumed his examination. One hand held her steady while the other touched and stroked, scraping across her soft skin, not unpleasantly.

Staring straight ahead into the candle's flame, Katherine refused to give in to panic. She also found it difficult to be indifferent to this stranger. After all, he was poking about her body.

"Give me the towel." Jackson held out his hand, his attention on the cut.

"No!"

"I've seen a woman's naked body before, Katherine. You have a beautiful body, as I'm sure you are aware, but I do not desire it. To me, it's like any other," Jackson bit out.

Tongue-tied, Katherine swung her eyes up to meet Jackson's remote ones. His candor stung, and it bothered her that it did. Numbly, she unwrapped herself and put the towel into his outstretched hand. Her hair, which had gotten drenched during her fight with N Zee, dripped water onto her shoulders and down her breasts. Jackson brushed the wet hair off her shoulders, seemingly captivated by the thick, snarled strands. Satisfied with his actions, he splayed one hand over her flat stomach, bent his dark head over her wound and gently wiped away the blood.

Though he was gentle, the wound was open and tender, causing Katherine to wince. She didn't voice a complaint or resist him anymore, but kept her head averted.

"You did not answer my question. Who did this to you?" Jackson's unblinking eyes searched Katherine's face. She drew herself up, proud and defiant in her near nakedness, and pinned him with a reproachful glare.

"I am not used to standing around virtually naked in front of a strange man engaged in casual chitchat with him while he pokes at my body," she asserted frostily.

"I don't chitchat, whatever that is," Jackson countered bluntly. "And you have yet to answer my question."

N Zee stomped back into the room and found the two of them locked in visual combat. Her eyes bugged at the sight of Jackson's hands on the hostage's nearly nude body. She wanted to scream at the injustice of it all. She threw the bundle of clothes she carried in Katherine's general direction. Jackson deftly caught them with one hand before they landed in the water.

In Swahili she demanded, "Why are you standing there with your hands all over her?" She shot daggers at Katherine and stepped menacingly close.

Ignoring N Zee's question, Jackson angled his head at the cut in Katherine's side. "Who did this to her?" He passed a teal-colored shirt and multi-colored wraparound skirt to Katherine. Both were old and worn, in some places through and through, but both were clean and would cover her nakedness. She inched away from the pair to cover herself.

Something akin to panic crossed N Zee's attractive features. "How should I know?" she answered, her eyes flying between Jackson and Katherine. The look in Jackson's eyes resembled granite.

"Did she have the wound before or after you and David took her?" His hard eyes bored into N Zee's. He knew the answer before N Zee spoke.

"After," she replied weakly.

"This woman is not to be touched again in any way by anyone in this camp. Is that understood?" The curt voice lashed out at N Zee. Jackson had never spoken to her in such a way before. And all because of some spoiled American.

"Yes," she spat out, pivoting on her heels for the door.

"Bring her back a pair of thongs," Jackson commanded to the retreating back, "some that fit, and do not throw them, N Zee," he warned.

"You may bathe now." Jackson turned to Katherine after N Zee stormed out of the room. "After you finish I have some salve for the wound.

Katherine opened her mouth to speak but Jackson forestalled her next words. "I have no desire to watch you bathe either." When he made a move to leave, Katherine's question had him halting in his tracks.

"What's her name?"

"Nzigunzigu. It translates into butterfly," he added, an ironic twist to his lips. "She is called N Zee by those who know her well."

Frowning at the impossible pronunciation and the meaning as it related to the woman, Katherine asked the name of N Zee's kidnaping partner.

After Jackson supplied David's name, she asked, "Why am I here? What do you intend to do with me?"

The extraordinary eyes stared into her own. "You will go to your family and to your father tomorrow night."

Immense relief overwhelmed Katherine even as she questioned her hearing. Surely Jackson meant her uncle. However, some of the guests at the party last night, or was it the night before, had been under the assumption that she and Julius were father and daughter. But she really didn't care who he thought she was. She was too happy to know she was going back.

"Why was I taken?" she couldn't help asking.

Jackson's expression turned to stone. "Those are all the questions I will answer." A few strides took him out of the room, the door closing behind him.

The noises outside the closed door had Katherine bending an ear before shedding her clothes. She wanted to be sure no one was coming in before she completed her bath. She knelt down in the tub in the tepid water as best she could and scrubbed herself vigorously. Her tender flesh stung as she scrubbed over scratches and bruises with the face towel.

Frustration welled up inside her, spreading up to her tender brown eyes. Here she was, not of her own free will, in little more than a shack with no electricity, no running water, most likely in unsanitary conditions. She had been wounded, superficially maybe, but wounded nevertheless. She had stood close to naked before a man she didn't know, a cold, solitary individual who had examined the wound deliberately given her by one of his people. She didn't think he was capable of showing compassion, yet he'd stopped N Zee's attack on her. He'd also said something to the woman about the cut on her side, which made the woman very unhappy. Or, Katherine surmised cynically, maybe he'd admonished the woman for attacking her too soon.

She realized how ludicrous the last thought

was. Jackson had said he was taking her back to her uncle. Why would he want her harmed? Still, she was unable to shake her unease. She wouldn't have peace of mind until she was out of this place. She focused on Jackson's words. By tomorrow she would be leaving here. Hallelujah! And she didn't care how. She had a mind not to remain in Kenya for the duration of her vacation, but instead head straight back to the States.

Katherine spattered water over the rim of the tub as she stood. Looking around the room, then staring at the ground, she realized she didn't have anything to stand on nor anything to dry off with. Talk about primitive. How was she supposed to dry off?

Her nerves were beginning to fray as she tunneled her fingers through her wet, chemically straightened hair. It was a thick, snarled mess. She combed through the damp strands as best she could, getting it straight enough to plait into a long, damp braid.

Earlier, when Jackson had lifted the dripping hair off of her shoulders, his touch was surprisingly gentle. Just as it had been when he examined her wound. What a contradiction he was. So dispassionate, yet displaying oddly gentle behavior.

Banishing thoughts of Jackson from her mind, she stood in the tub until most of her body was dry.

Satisfied, she threw a long leg over the tub. Jackson chose that moment to enter, carrying a piece of light-colored material, a pair of leather thongs, and a towel.

Gasping in exasperation, Katherine let go of several expletives, pulled her leg back inside and squatted back down into the cool water. She glowered up at Jackson, furious. She couldn't have been more shocked when something close to humor crossed his sharp features and his dark brow shot up.

"I don't care if you see women's naked bodies eight hours out of every day. I don't want mine exposed to you without my consent," she snapped, shielding her bare bosom with her hands as best she could. The candles burning low provided enough glow to reveal her shapely form quite well.

Those unblinking eyes sharpened on Katherine's face. Jackson took note of the fact that she'd braided her hair, bringing her alluring features clearly into focus. Her clear, dark eyes were much larger. Jackson also noted the wariness in their depths. Wisps of damp hair trailed down her slender neck past her collarbone.

"I brought you these," he said calmly, not in the least affected by her outburst. He held the multicolored fabric out to Katherine. "Dry off and step into them.

Katherine took the towel from Jackson.

"You may not like my body but you're certainly enjoying this, buster!"

Jackson leaned her way, his gold eyes contemplative. "I didn't say I did not like your body. I said I have seen naked bodies before." The quietly issued, accented statement sucked the words from Katherine's mouth.

Blinking repeatedly, she drew the towel around her body. "You don't desire it, you said so," she reminded him desperately. Surely he wouldn't attack her when she was most vulnerable? "Please leave," she demanded stiffly.

For long seconds Jackson studied Katherine. His tall form was reflected in her wide, frightened eyes. The soft glow of the candle's light bathed her creamy, honey brown skin in shimmering waves. Without comment, his lithe body moved through the door.

Breath escaped from Katherine's lungs. She listened carefully for any movement on the opposite side of the door. Satisfied that he was gone, she finished drying off and slid on the too big thongs. The man certainly made her uptight. The fact that he was holding her against her will played the major part in that emotion but there was another something she could not identify.

The shirt she slipped into was a man's and way

too large on her slim frame. The skirt, made from an African print, wrapped around her waist two complete times. The material was so thin in some areas that without the double wrap it was transparent.

Opening her purse, she was mildly surprised to see the few meager contents, sans the money, inside. She squeezed drops of the fragrant smelling lotion into her palm and rubbed it over her body. That small gesture returned some normalcy to her predicament and she felt immensely better physically.

She wandered around the room, what there was of it, reinvestigating the small room's contents. She wondered if anything had been added while she had slept.

The drone of voices drew her attention to the overhead opening. She drew the log under the window and climbed on it to look through the hole. In the glow of the lamps and candles, she could only see dense forest and heads covered with dark caps. If the voices were an indication, most of the heads under the caps were male. Occasionally a female voice or two interspersed the conversation, making Katherine wonder how many women actually were in the camp. When she realized she was listening for Jackson's distinctive male pitch, she climbed down off the log, her heart thumping irregularly. The mere thought of him filled her with a sense of foreboding. So much so she could hardly wait until tomorrow to return to her uncle.

A knock at the door interrupted her meanderings. Who was it? Jackson would probably just barge in. Maybe it was N Zee come to taunt and harass her some more. No, that she—wolf would not offer her the courtesy of knocking either.

The knock sounded again, more persistent. Katherine stopped speculating and opened the door to the solemn-faced woman who'd prepared the meal. Her eyes dropped to the bowl the woman had in her hand. The smells coming from it caused her stomach to rumble in pleasure.

Katherine stepped aside so the woman could enter. The woman set it on the log near the bed. She faced Katherine, their eyes meeting for the first time.

"Hello," Katherine said with a winning smile while the woman watched her with curiosity.

"Can you speak English?" she asked the silent woman.

"Hose." Her voice was so soft Katherine had trouble hearing her. "What did you say?"

Pointing, the woman pressed a finger to her chest. "Hose."

Enlightenment dawned on Katherine. "Rose?" Your name is Rose?"

Excited, the woman nodded. "Hroorse. Hose is name."

Smiling at the awkward pronunciation, Katherine pointed to herself. "My name is Katherine. Kath-er-ine." Katherine beamed at the woman who rolled her name around on her tongue and offered her a shy smile.

And, Katherine noted, Rose was an apt name. When the woman smiled, her soft brown eyes glowed. The solemn, brown face became animated, the round features very pretty.

Rose clamped a hand over her mouth, not quite hiding her smile, and pointed at Katherine. Puzzled at first, Katherine looked down and noticed that, despite all of her efforts, the wraparound skirt was coming undone. Chuckling along with Rose, she raised the shirt to reveal the bunched up waistband. The tied knot had come undone. With deft fingers Rose repositioned the skirt, making it look less bulky. She fashioned a simple but tight knot and stood back admiring her handiwork.

"I wish you could do something about this gigantic shirt." Katherine let the shirt fall past mid-thigh. "I'm beginning to think Nzig-un...N Zee gave it to me to spite me."

At the mention of N Zee's name, the smile vanished from Rose's face. Her expression was once again solemn as she exited the room as quietly as she'd come in, leaving Katherine to ponder what she'd said to cause the woman to shrink away from her.

One or two candles flickered weakly. Katherine knew it would be a brief time before they burned out. She wanted to be asleep when they did. Tomorrow would bring hope and light.

Chapter Seven

*J*ulius cradled the phone gingerly, ending his transatlantic call, his light brown face etched in grim lines. Two pairs of eyes were on him, waiting. Abra sat across from his place at the desk. His daughter, Ja Lisa, was lying down in the connecting suite. In her place, standing by the wet bar, was her ne'er-do-well husband, Hollis McMaster. He was staring at his father-in- law, his tongue practically lolling in anticipation of information concerning his cousin-in-law. The anticipation was more morbid curiosity than concern. Pointedly ignoring him, Julius spoke to his wife.

"That was Katherine's fiancé. Alex is quite concerned because Katherine didn't call him yesterday as she promised. If we don't hear something before the night ends, I'll have to call him and tell him the truth."

"Which is?" Abra asked cooly, crossing one waxed and hosed leg over the other, delicately sipping her tea.

Sweeping his eyes over his expertly coiffured wife, Julius paused with his answer. The look on her face was not one of concern, distress or caring. It hinted at annoyance and impatience. Despite her blatant disregard for his niece's welfare, Julius's emotions were a mixture of anger, longing and lingering love for the woman sitting model perfect in the imitation Queen Ann chair. It was a love that, in spite of her flaws, and the list grew with the passage of time, he would never completely outgrow, no matter how much he hoped that he would.

"That she has been kidnapped," he stated flatly.

"And how do you know that?" Abra asked, the mildness of her tone masking her skepticism.

"What other explanation is there?" he asked in exasperation.

"That she left of her own violation." Abra met her husband's furious look calmly.

"Before yesterday Katherine had never set foot on this continent. How can you suggest such a thing? She doesn't know anyone here except us, her family. You know as well as I do that Katherine is a sensible, practical young woman. She would never go somewhere in a foreign country without letting me know."

"Stranger things have happened," Abra suggested blithely. "Maybe she met someone at the dinner party last night,"

Julius cast his wife a look of disgust and spoke through gritted teeth. "If Katherine met someone last night, she is too levelheaded to up and leave with him without informing one of us." Frustration and irritation at Abra were visible. "Katherine knows that we—that I—would worry. She would never do something so heedless and rash."

Unlike our daughter, Abra added in bitter silence. Tiny, unattractive lines appeared along the sides of her compressed lips. Was her husband alluding to JaLisa's elopement with Hollis or her decision to invest a third of her trust fund inheritance into her husband's latest business venture? Both without informing her parents. Julius was as unaccepting of his daughter's marriage today as he was two years ago. As always, he paid more attention to his niece than to his own daughter who was at this moment lying in her bed, unwell. As usual, he'd jumped to Katherine's defense.

"Why would anyone want to take Katherine and where would they take her?" Abra did not try to hide her skepticism.

Having no answer for his wife's acerbic yet legit-
imate questions, Julius shifted his eyes from hers to
let them wander absently around the spacious, opu-
lent suite. The Kenyan government had spared no
expense in making them feel welcome.

Abruptly switching his thoughts from what was
in front of him to the poverty-stricken areas and the
despair he'd witnessed since arriving in Kenya,
Julius's grim expression increased. Their assigned
driver had been careful to steer clear of those areas
that might cause concern or induce questions from
the high profile visitors. After noticing the men,
women and especially the children sleeping on the
streets of Nairobi, Julius's curiosity had been
piqued and he'd directed the driver to take him to
the outer areas. He wanted to check for himself the
merit of the rumors he'd heard and the scenes he'd
witnessed on television.

While he knew American television and news-
papers were notorious for focusing on the negative
and adverse situations, especially as they related to
people of color, he was a man who took nothing for
granted.

Because he'd paid their chauffeur enough
money to disregard orders to keep the visitors and
tourists away from certain areas, the man had driv-
en him past the well-kept residential streets onto the
outlying borders of Nairobi, Nakuru, the Trans Nzoia

district, as well as the Bungona and Endebess districts. What he saw left him reeling with heavy-heartedness for hours afterwards.

People living in the makeshift refugee camps, which were little more than slums, were the victims of ethnic violence. Emaciated children, some in rags, some naked, sat in or stood in the middle of openings or lean-to cardboard shacks, barely able to raise heavy heads on their too thin necks to watch the crystal blue, stretch Mercedes as it rolled slowly by. A few of the more animated children played barefoot in the muddy ditches where debris and body waste stagnated in shallow water in front of and on the sides of the paper shelters.

In the rearview mirror Julius's eyes had met those of his driver who, lips curled tight, had looked neither left nor right, but stared straight ahead at the road. His relief was obvious when Julius ordered him back to the hotel.

Those images remained etched on Julius' brain. That day he kept his findings to himself but he intended to investigate further and get some answers to his many questions before more loans were approved for Kenya.

He didn't understand why his wife's careless question would prompt his thoughts to return to the scene at the camps. For a moment something disjointed and totally farfetched entered his consciousness.

"I don't know why," he answered truthfully. "Katherine is an extremely attractive young lady. Someone could have a number of sick reasons for kidnapping her."

Abra's lips thinned at her husband's description of Katherine. The girl had passable looks but she couldn't hold a candle to their daughter. "Well," she drawled, "what do you intend to do if she was forced to leave against her will?" Abra's emphasis and tone left little doubt of what she really thought.

Refusing to debate the topic any longer, Julius picked up his electronic Rolodex from the night-stand drawer. He pushed a key and waited a few seconds for the file to light up. He scrolled through names and phone numbers at the American Embassy until he came across the one he was searching for.

Julius turned to faced his now seated son-in-law who'd been quiet the entire time but had listened avidly to all that was said. "JaLisa would probably love to have you by her side," he said with a significant lift of his heavy brow. His level tone carried an undercurrent of censure.

Hollis's grey eyes slid from his father-in-law's barely veiled dislike to his mother-in-law. At the barely perceptible nod of her head, he pushed his tall, lanky frame from the wingback chair and took his time leaving.

The silence in the room was heavy. Abra tilted forward, her eyes intent on Julius. All pretense at nonchalance was gone. "Answer my question, Julius. How do you intend to find Kathy?"

"By any means necessary." Julius did not mask his determination. His visage left little doubt in anyone's mind that he was resolved to get his brother's child back safely.

∽∽∽ ∽∽∽ ∽∽∽

It was raining again. Jackson listened to the water strike dense foliage overhead. Drops slipped through openings in the trees and slid across his muscled arms to glide down his back, dampening his shirt. Jackson relished the rain. His grandfather had told him that water from the creator above was cleansing. In these uncertain times Jackson held onto that belief. There was much in his country that was unclean.

There was little movement at the site. Half of the men and women were at the outskirts of camp preparing for an early morning strike at the military base in Nakuru the day after tomorrow. This strike would make the president sweat. Jackson and Kimya were supposed to be with the others. However, other pressing matters were keeping them in camp.

Few candles and lamps burned, though darkness was heavy under the canopy. The rebels in camp who were awake moved about silently and undressed without the benefit of light. They were deep within the heart of the forest but were trained to do without, be on constant guard and take nothing for granted.

His topaz gaze scoped out the scene around him. Besides his accommodations, the men and women had constructed numerous fragile structures from flexible saplings pounded deep into the ground for covering and a sense of privacy. Limbs were bent forward to form peaked roofs. A space for ingress or egress was in the side or the front. The rebel's meager belongings were kept off the ground by small logs. Fresh leaves, twigs and other debris brought in twice a week were the only protection from the hard ground if one did not own a sleeping bag.

Some rebels, by hook or crook, had enough materials to set up fairly comfortable tents. One or two of the structures were fashioned from mangrove poles and palm leaves. Inside, a hammock of sorts was fashioned to accommodate a person lying down.

It was for one of these shelters Jackson struck out, surefooted in the darkness. He recognized voices calling out greetings to him as he moved along and he answered in kind. He hoped to avoid one individual on his way to his destination but was not surprised when N Zee eased from her sleeping hut and blocked his progress.

"Unakwendu wapi [where are you going]?" she asked in a sultry voice. She stood closer to Jackson than was necessary or proper. He saw her white irises in the darkness. He could smell her female scent, feel the heat emanating from her body. Her breasts brushed his hard chest.

"I am on my way to check on Victor," he replied mildly. He rocked back on his heels, allowing space between them.

"I will come too."

"Hapana [no]." The refusal halted N Zee in her tracks. She squinted at the firm jaw and set face. Shrugging, she spoke with studied nonchalance.

"I will wait here for you."

"Get your rest, N Zee." Tempering his order with an ironic smile, he added, "You have had a busy thirty-six hours."

N Zee hesitated then asked, "Where will you rest tonight?"

Jackson tilted his head at an angle. There was a hidden meaning behind N Zee's question. How he answered would determine how quickly he could get to his destination. "Where I always sleep when

I am in camp."

"And where will the American hostage sleep?" she responded sullenly.

"With me until she returns to her family."

N Zee's nostrils flared with fury. "In your bed?" In the cool, dark camp air, N Zee was conscious of a sudden chill. She couldn't read Jackson's expression but sensed his remoteness.

"Where the woman sleeps is no concern of yours. And she is not our hostage."

"Hapana [no]! She will sleep with me in my tent. Or with Rose." Brown eyes clawed at Jackson as N Zee's breathing accelerated.

"You will not dictate to me, N Zee. You overstep your bounds." Jackson's response was curt. He crossed his arms over his wide chest. "You have done enough damage for one day. Besides, there is hardly enough room inside your tent for you. One of you would have to sleep outside on the ground."

Moving her head from side to side, N Zee spoke barely above a whisper, "I will sleep with you." She covered the distance he'd put between them. Her braless breasts grazed Jackson's arm. She stroked over his crossed wrists, up the taunt skin to his biceps. Her fingers reached the width of his shoulders and Jackson heard her sharp intake of breath.

Frowning his disapproval, he stepped back and dropped his arms, forcing N Zee to drop her hands to her side. By blood he was Kikuyu and Masai, a half breed. By tradition and clan he was Kikuyu, with very strict moral codes which frowned upon public displays of affection towards the opposite sex. Though the camp was basically settled down for rest, Jackson was cognizant of eyes on them and ears wide open.

"You will return to your tent and rest," Jackson ordered firmly. "Stop this nonsense. You already have some of the men losing their concentration because of you and your antics."

Instead of the words angering N Zee, they emboldened her, bolstering her confidence in her attributes. Her lips turned up in an inviting smile. "It is only you I am interested in. I do not care about the others." Her voice was full of entreaty.

"Well, I do!" Jackson replied harshly. "Go, N Zee. Now! I grow weary with telling you the same thing over and over."

Gnawing on her lower lip, N Zee closed her eyes to hide her pain and disappointment. When she opened them, Jackson was gone. She held her hand out to the spot where he'd stood, touching only moist, warm air. Just like the man himself, she thought wistfully. Virtually impossible to catch and hold.

Chapter Eight

*J*ackson's mind was full of the day's events. He did not doubt that he'd hurt and embarrassed N Zee. He'd seen no other way to make her realize that they could be no more than what they were now, friends. He had not led her on. He'd offered her nothing but friendship. Many times he had tried to get her to see that there was no future for them. Each time she had turned a deaf ear to his assertions. For all of her good points, when she desired something, N Zee was oblivious to all else.

Jackson admired N Zee's intelligence and courage. While she was fearless, her tongue could be razor sharp and her temperament pugnacious. She was possessive and of late she'd exhibited a selfish nature. It would be a mistake to sleep with N Zee, although at times, the offer was tempting.

They'd met a decade ago at the University of Nairobi when she was twenty and he was twenty-three. The copper-skinned N Zee, of the Luhya clan, was both beautiful and strong-willed. Her aggressive nature and forwardness belied her culture and strict upbringing. She'd wasted no time in letting Jackson know that she was keenly interested in him and was more than willing to pursue a more intimate relationship.

After completing school, Jackson had left Kenya for England to pursue graduate studies and lost contact with N Zee. His father's disappearance had brought the two of them back in contact with one another.

His father, William Shugaa, had been a prominent lawyer and a key member of Kenya's African Democratic Union—the current ruling party's chief opposition at that time. William had been vocal in his allegations of graft and corruption within Matoi's government.

The Kenya African National Union—KANU—to which the ruling party belonged, pursued the philosophy of federalism called majimboism, which meant the expulsion of the Kikuyu, Luo, and Luhya who had been legally settled in the Rift Valley since before the 1920s. Formerly productive, law-abiding citizens were stripped of their lands and relegated to over-crowded refugee camps, some not fit for animals.

Immediately after Kenya gained independence in 1963, the president's ruling party, the Kikuyu, dominated politics. They had their faults as well. The first president had tolerated a degree of free expression, whereas Matoi was hard-nosed and intolerant. Any dissent was tantamount to treason.

Church officials were ruthlessly harassed because of their efforts to assist refugees and clash victims. Biwott's men were inactive and unresponsive to any violence against any clan accept the Kalenjins and their supporters.

William Shugaa had been of those citizens stripped of his property when threats and severe beatings could not silence him. Clients stayed away from his law practice for fear of harassment, beatings or worse.

William had disappeared from his office one day without warning or a trace. After Jackson and his friend Kimya had searched in vain for his father, N Zee had used her feminine wiles to learn that William had been taken by force and transported to parts unknown. It was presumed he was dead.

Jackson had discovered his father's remains buried on the edge of Nakuru's forest. It was futile to demand answers to his questions but Jackson did so anyway. He was thwarted at every turn and not so subtle warnings were issued for him to leave off. His mother, frantic with worry that something would happen to her only child, nearly fell apart. She had begged Jackson to go into exile.

While Jackson understood and sympathized with his mother's concerns, he could not abide by her wishes. His father, whom he had respected and loved deeply, was a symbol of what was good and decent. He would not rest until those responsible for his death were brought to justice.

It was during this time that Jackson Shugaa, law abiding citizen, professor and doctoral candidate became an enemy of the state. His rebel movement started with Kimya by his side, a handful of their closest friends and one female fighter—N Zee. The two had been at his side since the rebellion's inception.

He was fast becoming a worse thorn in Matoi's side than his father ever was. He and his fighters met government-backed violence with resistance and speedy action that was chipping away at the protective shield built around Matoi.

Their movement was steady and had captured the attention of Africa Watch. The rest of the world was sluggishly opening its eyes to the corruption running rampant within the current government. Citizens were becoming more outspoken and demanding change.

Jackson and his followers' goal was to keep the attention of the world focused on Kenya and thereby bring pressure to bear on the government to force either stepping down or changing their repressive rule. If enough financial pressure were brought to bear, Matoi's stranglehold was bound to bend, if not break. Thus, N Zee's misguided attempt to force Matoi's hand.

Closing his eyes for long seconds, Jackson cleared his head of the clamoring problems and set his sight on a tent in a small clearing. Three sides were open; the one fronting the dense forest was closed. The top was a tarpaulin supported by sturdy wood from the forest. He stepped into the tent's opening and saw the outline of an empty hammock near the back. In front of that, on a raised platform, lay a broken body.

Jackson's nostrils twitched at the pungent smells assaulting him. His boots crunched leaves underfoot as the odors drifted his way. They were sweet smelling leaves used to keep away insects as well as to purify the air and to neutralize bad smells caused by open wounds.

A small figure moved about in the darkness. The striking of a match on stone drew Jackson's attention to Rose sitting on her haunches beside the limp form. She smiled up at Jackson after lighting some candles.

"Habari [hello]," she said softly, watching Jackson mimic her position on the opposite side of the wounded man.

"How is he?" Jackson's voice was laced with concern. Victor was in his mid-twenties. He and a cousin of Jackson's were both wounded after they and a handful of followers walked into an ambush at Malo, an area of the Nakuru district. Their plan was a hit and run attack on the military base, but it never materialized. The explosives they would have used were left behind and the fire bombs in their possession were used against them instead.

Youth, recklessness and a severe case of hero worship had plunged both youths into the path of danger. Each had been anxious to show Jackson that they were worthy of his admiration and respect. They had wanted to make him proud and the two men had valiantly held off their attackers.

Jackson, learning of their danger, had gone to their aid. In the ensuing battle, Victor had flung himself in the path of a simis, a wicked, double-edged, spatula-shaped sword which had left a wound from Victor's shoulder to his knee.

Jackson and three rebels had stolen into the home of his father's former friend, Dr. Zuberi, who now supported Matoi. The good doctor had been dragged from his bed, thrown into an ancient truck covered with a cloth tarpaulin and parked some kilometers away, and had been forced to tend Victor's wound as best he could.

Zuberi had vehemently protested having to service the rebels. The fact that two rebels had been in his home holding his family hostage while he worked over Victor would mean little to Biwott if he found out.

For the brief second he boldly stared into Jackson's eyes, a different kind of fear had assailed him. Quickly averting his eyes, he had moved to the wounded rebel's side to staunch the flow of blood and give Victor something for the pain.

Jackson was cautiously optimistic that Victor would recuperate under the watchful eye of Rose. She had incorporated Dr. Zuberi's instructions with her own method in caring for the wound and used the antibiotics received from the doctor with traditional medicines she gathered in the surrounding forest.

Victor's smooth ebony chest rose and fell slowly in the glowing light. His wound looked puffy, bloated. Because Victor's wound had not been sutured, Rose had closed it by a method she'd read about when she was young, when learning about the struggles of those who had fought for Kenya's independence. She had carefully gathered soldier ants, held them over the cut so that their powerful jaws gripped the sides, drawing the flesh together. The tiny heads were twisted from their bodies but the jaws remained intact, successfully closing the cut. A latex-like substance was then smeared around the cut. An anesthetic from the stems and leaves of the isogosya and isoambumbu trees.

The list of casualties in this struggle was growing. Added to it were Louis, Victor, David and N Zee, each recklessly trying to prove something instead of thinking of the consequences of their actions.

Shrugging off the dark thoughts, Jackson touched his hand to Victor's forehead. He was cooler than three hours ago and for the first time he was breathing easier.

"You are doing a good job." His voice was as warm as his smile. A happy glow warmed Rose and she returned Jackson's smile with a shy one of her own.

"Asanti sana [thank you very much]," she replied, her brown eyes shining in the candle-light.

"I will sit with Victor for a while."

Shaking her head vigorously, Rose hovered protectively over the sleeping body. "You have been away a week traveling through much danger. You've not had a chance to rest after all that has happened today..." Rose trailed off lamely, aware it was wise to leave that subject alone. "You need your rest."

"As do you." Jackson observed Rose, taking note of the droop in her shoulders. "You have been going since early morning, taking care of our needs as well as Victor's. You will rest for at least an hour or two."

One did not argue with Jackson Shugaa. At least Rose did not. He spoke his mind, gave an order and expected it to be obeyed.

"I will return in one hour," Rose said.

"Two." Already Jackson was giving his attention to the unconscious Victor.

Watching the strong back, Rose could not stop herself from asking, "The American woman, she is very beautiful, isn't she?"

"Goodnight, Rose," Jackson answered calmly, bending over Victor. Rose smiled wistfully at the bowed head before darkness enveloped her.

∞ ∞ ∞

Jackson paused in undressing and held the kerosene lamp shoulder high to watch the female form twist and turn on the small bed. Tears glistened on her prominent cheekbones, a frown was between her brows and she was muttering incoherently in her sleep. She slept in the clothes brought to her earlier. The skirt was twisted between smooth brown thighs and long lean legs. Buttons were undone on the too big shirt which had fallen past her shoulders.

Holding the lamp aloft, Jackson wiped his hand across his brow. The evening was hot but it remained relatively cool on the forest floor. Still, Jackson wore as little as possible, which usually meant nothing. Tonight, for the sake of propriety, he would strip down to his briefs.

Continuing to thrash about, Katherine flipped over on her back. The loose shirt rose higher, exposing velvet-looking skin covering her rib cage and the underside of her breasts. Jackson frowned.

Tears were coursing down brown cheeks. Jackson called Katherine's name softly. When she did not respond, he dropped to one knee beside the bed. The lamp bathed the perfect skin in soft, flattering light. Jackson leisurely examined the small nose, the slightly parted lips. Thick, black lashes glistened with moisture. Tears did not detract from her loveliness.

Poised over her ear, Jackson spoke her name gently. "Katherine, wake up. You are dreaming."

"I did nothing wrong." The heartbroken whisper reached Jackson's ear.

"Katherine?"

Katherine's eyes fluttered and for a brief second Jackson assumed she was awake.

"Uncle Julius, tell her I did nothing wrong." She twisted right, then left.

Placing the lamp on the log beside the bed, Jackson raised Katherine to a sitting position. He placed his arms around her shoulders, holding her loosely. Her head dropped to the curve of his neck. Instantly his naked chest was wet with tears.

"Who made you so sad, little one?" He was conscious of her heart thundering in her chest. He began to speak quietly to her, switching back and forth between Swahili and Kikuyu. Hardly aware of his actions, he pressed his lips to her brow. Her satin skin was cool and smelled of flowers and the wind. Drawing back, Jackson stared down into the sleep-slackened face, at the lips so close to his. The hand soothing her back stilled.

The cessation of sound and caresses roused Katherine. She opened her eyes, staring directly into golden ones and was instantly mesmerized. Who was this intriguing man holding her? She was cognizant of heat. Oh my! He seemed very real in her dream, pressing to her side, creating tingles up her spine. He had replaced her nightmare, thank God. And what a replacement! That face! Those eyes—in that face! Blood pounded in her brain.

Her dream phantom did not return her smile and her good feelings began to evaporate as unease settled inside Katherine, who was fully awake now.

Why was he looking at her like that? As if he could see into her soul.

Not sure whether she was still dreaming, Katherine blinked furiously, swung her hand upward and encountered a solid chest. A flesh and blood man was bending over her. This wasn't a dream.

"What are you doing?" Her heart pounded in fear and anticipation. She was in Jackson's arms, her breasts smashed against his chest. His very wide and very naked chest. Her nipples were like granite. Her cheeks heated. Oh no, she admonished herself, horrified, you will not react in this manner to this man. "Let me go," she demanded.

She was surprised that Jackson complied. He stayed by her side, however, asking in that accent-tinged voice of his. "Do you usually cry when you have bad dreams?" He was watching her closely.

"What are you talking about? Bad dreams—crying?" Bewildered, Katherine brought her fingers to her lashes. They were damp. Sliding her fingers over her cheeks, she smeared across the dried salt tracks.

Had she been crying in her sleep? Is that why Jackson was holding her? Comforting her? Waking up in his arms, she had not immediately recalled the dream. Now remnants of it washed over her. She'd dreamed of how her uncle wanted her with him after her parents' death in a plane crash and of how his wife didn't. She'd dreamed of the verbal and emotional abuse suffered at Abra's hands. Of the many times she'd been accused of wrongdoing when she was innocent, and the many times her uncle had come to her defense.

She'd been so sure she'd put all of that misery behind her, but being here in this environment with these strangers, her captors, had brought it all back. Intuition warned her that she must be strong. Show no weakness to these people. Her eyes traveled around the dimly lit room. She was as far out of her element here as the earth was to the moon. The lean-to hut, the dirt-packed floor, the hard, unyielding platform passing for a bed and an ancient washtub for bathing. Was it any wonder she was having nightmares?

Her bedroom in her home was all lush chenille, silk and tapestry. Cool crisp sheets smelling of scented creams, lotions and fabric softeners and not distinctly of a male, this male. Goosedown comforter, half a dozen matching throw pillows and pillow shams on a king-sized bed, and plush carpet thick enough to muffle the harshest footfalls.

She arched her neck. Jackson was quietly observing every emotion flickering across her face while she was unable to read his. What kind of man was he? Katherine fought back her initial unease. She dug down deep for some of that control. Her tone was flip in response.

"The bogey woman is gone and not about to return, so you can leave me now." The shirt dipped low on one satin shoulder when, to prove her point, she sat up cross-legged on the narrow bed, waiting for Jackson to comply.

He stared at her in silence as if to determine whether she spoke the truth. Katherine was quite proud she didn't squirm under the intense scrutiny.

"You're taking this brooding, dark, mysterious stranger myth a bit far, aren't you?" she asked cynically. She deliberately left handsome out in her description. There was no reason to swell the man's head. After all, he was holding her against her will. She smiled at Jackson's frown, glad to finally get a rise out of him. Obviously he was one of those sour people who didn't appreciate her dry wit. The smile vanished when Jackson stepped to the middle of the room and commenced to shed his pants.

"What are you doing?" Katherine squeaked, coming to her knees. She froze in panic and disbelief while Jackson eased his pants down over his male hips.

"I asked, what are you doing?" Katherine repeated in a stronger voice as she searched the room frantically for something she knew she would not find, a weapon. While it was true she probably wouldn't receive any help from the others, she'd be damned if she'd make it easy for him.

"What does it look like I'm doing? I'm preparing for bed," Jackson replied crisply. He was down to his briefs. His snug fitting, very brief, briefs. Katherine gulped, her face aflame. She was unable to tear her eyes away, though she very much wanted to.

At least close your eyes! a voice of morality shouted at her. She did, but they popped right back open and skittered up Jackson's lean, muscled torso. There wasn't an ounce of extra skin on him anywhere. He was sleek and sculpted like dark, bronzed metal, from the top of his close-cut black hair to the bottom of his bootless, arched feet.

"I won't sleep with you," Katherine warned. "You'll have to hog-tie me first."

Jackson retrieved the burlap sack from the corner wall peg, neatly folded his pants and placed them inside and hung the sack back in its place. Katherine had a fairly good side view in the dim room of his tight buttocks, the taunt muscles rippling under the stretch fabric. Her eyes skidded past the narrow waist to the profile of chest and shoulders back down to the powerful thighs and long, long, muscled legs.

Anger stole over her. Who did he think he was? Was he trying to turn her on? Posing like some male model for men's underwear? Get real, Jackson, whoever you are.

"I don't know about this tying you to a hog," Jackson remarked, his expression quizzical upon fully facing Katherine. "But I do intend to sleep—alone." With that parting statement he extinguished the lamp and left the room.

On her knees in the bed in the dark, Katherine stared across the room at the flimsy shut door. Incredulity gave way to mirth. She collapsed on the bed in laughter. "I don't know about this tying you to a hog," she parroted. Wait until she told—Katherine sobered. Who would she tell? In her job as a financial consultant, she had numerous acquaintances, few friends, none of them very close. She doubted that Alex would find humor in the comment or appreciate the fact that she found anything her captors said or did laughable.

Katherine stretched out on her back. What she required was some perspective. One light moment did not detract from the seriousness of her predicament. And it was a predicament she could not laugh at, if ever, until she was safe at home. Closing her eyes, she called up a picture of Alex's pleasant features. There was nothing threatening or mysterious there. Her man was safe, sure, steady. And if she didn't see stars or rockets when she was intimate with him, well, that was okay too.

There was more to a relationship and life than fireworks. Like stability and comfort. With those calming thoughts, Katherine drifted off to sleep, praying a silent prayer that the bad dreams were at rest.

Chapter Nine

*D*awn in the jungle isn't touted by the rising of the sun, though its rays do manage to slip through the gaps amongst the treetops. In some, the light cast is surreal. The early morning is introduced by the sounds the howler monkeys and the cries of birds inhabiting the forest.

Jackson was up long before the first howler shouted. He didn't have to peer outside to know that the air was damp from the recent rain. He was fully clothed and sipping boiled coffee when a shout outside his door interrupted his thoughts.

He held back a scold, instantly recognizing the voice as he issued the traditional welcome, "Karibu."

N Zee strolled over the threshold with a covered

bowl in her hand. Easing past Jackson, she set the bowl next to the kerosene lamp on the makeshift table. "I made your breakfast this morning." She smiled up at Jackson, her eyes soft and appealing.

"Where is Rose?" Jackson inquired mildly.

"I told her to sleep awhile longer. She's had some tough days taking care of Victor and seeing to our needs." While speaking, N Zee's eyes scanned the area, searching for any sign that Jackson had spent the night in the tight room. There were none.

Her intention was to be present before Jackson arose so that the question that had plagued her all night about where he was sleeping would be answered. Disappointed, her intuitive eyes examined his face. He did not have the look of a man who had slept with a woman. She was reassured by the knowledge that the Kikuyu traditionally did not engage in amorous activities in the midst of battle. She was doubly assured by the knowledge that Jackson Shugaa would never force himself on a woman. There was no need. Too many women were willing to be with him by choice.

"Thank you for the breakfast, N Zee." Jackson's tone was pleasant enough but his delivery was a dismissal all the same.

"You still plan to take the hos...woman back today?"

Jackson simply stared at N Zee. She knew as

well as anyone in the camp that once he made a decision it was final. There was no going back.

Stubbornness vanquished the softness from N Zee's expression. "Her presence could help us. Why won't you admit that, Jackson?"

"Bringing the American to our camp was stupid and irresponsible. Why won't you admit that?" Jackson replied curtly.

"This is the reason you will not use her? Because I didn't wait for your permission first?" N Zee spat out. "I thought I was third in command. To make important decisions when you and Kimya are not around."

"This is not about who is in charge when the other is not around. Protocol has not changed. This is about decisions of life and death. This is about innocent people caught up in a power play between us and the government. Many of Matoi's supporters have proved ruthless time and again. There is no guarantee they will negotiate with us."

"Our entire fight is about taking chances. Nothing is guaranteed. Not even our next breath," N Zee argued. "You've said as much often enough. If we don't seize this opportunity now, when might the next one be presented to us?"

There was a distinct hardening of Jackson's expression. "The woman goes back after Kimya returns. Our discussion is ended." He scooped up the hot bowl but did not eat. N Zee's eyes lingered on his stern profile before she left without comment.

Movement from the other side of the door drew Jackson's attention. Listening to the sounds, his brooding expression remained in place at hearing a husky expletive followed by several more.

Katherine threw open the door and came face to face with him. She did a quick involuntary appraisal of his dark features. She wondered if Jackson could hear her heart thundering across the small space.

Irritatingly conscious of her wrinkled state, she inched away from the kerosene light. Instinctively, her fingers went to the thick mass on her head. Realizing what she was doing, she dropped her hand. This man wasn't some suitor come to court her. He was a wanted man.

"Well, what are you staring at?" she snapped. "How else am I supposed to look wearing the same clothes I slept in and not having a comb for my hair. I'm sure I look the part of a hostage."

Look at him standing there with that unnerving stare, not uttering a sound, like a bump on a log, she thought spitefully. "Don't you think you're taking this act a bit too far?" Katherine asked sarcastically, ready to sail past Jackson going she knew not where. She only knew she had to get away from him.

Jackson's firm grip on her arm halted her progress. Katherine tried to pull away. "What act are you speaking of?"

His low melodic voice and the warm, calloused palm circling her bare arm pushed her pulse into overdrive. "What in the world is wrong with me?" She held her hand to her cheek, clearly distressed with her reaction to Jackson's touch.

Edging closer, Jackson examined her face. "Are you ill?" A flicker of concern lit his fascinating eyes. His warm breath blew over Katherine's cheeks.

"What? Oh—I didn't realize I'd spoken out loud." Flustered, Katherine shied away from Jackson's probing eyes. He was so close, she smelled his male scent, was acutely conscious of the warmth emanating from his dark brown skin.

Jackson watched her, waiting for an answer to his question. "I feel fine," she replied in as steady a voice as she could muster. She swung her eyes back to his, unable to find the words to tell him to remove his hand from her arm.

"Are you sure?" He touched his lean fingers to her face, grazing the soft skin. With a thumb pressed on each cheekbone, he widened her eyes and peered into them.

"What are you doing?" There was an added huskiness to her usually smoky timbre. Her hand clutched his wrists, but she didn't push him away as was her intent.

"The eyes can speak of illness when a person is not aware of it or when they try and conceal the truth." The resonant voice lulled her so much Katherine found herself leaning towards the sound.

Twisting from his hold, Katherine sidestepped Jackson. "Well, go gaze into someone else's eyes. I don't want you staring into mine. I told you I feel fine and that is the truth." She put as much space between the two of them as possible.

All concern was wiped from Jackson's eyes. They were once more as dry and remote as the Sahara. "I will see if Rose can find you a change of clothing. There is your breakfast. He pointed to the bowl he had placed on the log. Turning his back, he exited the room.

With Jackson gone, Katherine was able to breathe easier. Curiosity drew her to the bowl. She turned her lips down. The thick brownish mush resembled oatmeal, a food she abhorred. Besides, she wasn't a breakfast person. At home there never was time. She touched her fingertips to the luke-warm bowl. If she didn't eat it, Jackson might return and stare at her, causing her to become all jumpy and nervous. Still, maybe she should dump it. If she dumped it, she could see what was happening outside.

When she stepped outside, Katherine nearly dropped the bowl at the sight of so many rebels. Many more than she'd seen yesterday. The large clearing was full to overflowing with people and movement.

She recognized N Zee's partner in crime, David. He had a rifle slung over one shoulder and a wooden bowl in one hand. He walked in front of Katherine, studiously ignoring her. There was another face she recognized. The man who'd held her on her arrival and would not release her until Jackson commanded him to. He paused in what he was doing with a gleaming, sharp-looking knife and grinned her way, revealing large, protruding, teeth. Katherine backed several steps into the doorway. A female rebel tapped the man none too gently on his arm with the butt of her rifle, diverting his attention from Katherine.

Katherine was chilled at the sight of so many rebels as they formed two arrow-straight lines and began marching past her. Some cast curious glances her way, while others stared straight ahead.

Curiosity overrode apprehension. Katherine intended to find out where the rebels were going. She waited until the last pair was some distance away before taking the same route. Suddenly, the woman who had given her the delicious soup last night was blocking her path.

Despite shaking her head firmly at Katherine, neither Rose's posture nor her expression was menacing. Indeed, she wore the most pleasant expression of anyone Katherine had encountered so far.

"Eat." Rose pointed to the forgotten bowl of congealed porridge. "Eat," she repeated more forcefully, pantomiming the act of spooning food into the mouth.

"Oh no, not even if I were starving, dear lady." Katherine shoved the bowl back at Rose, wiping the serene expression from Rose's face. She scowled and shook her head, causing her short braids to tremble over and around her face.

"What is going on here?" Both women's heads snapped toward the sound of the voice. Jackson emerged from a thicket that appeared impenetrable. He shoved the vines and branches aside as if they were a petty nuisance.

Before Jackson reached them, Rose was responding in their tongue, her eyes going to his dark, stony face. Katherine's chin jutted forth as his eyes narrowed on her.

He spoke to Rose in rapid, clipped tones, his expression never changing. Katherine detected ice in the voice, though the words were alien to her. Rose stared up at him mute, her lips compressed, her brown eyes losing their glow.

"We do not have food to waste," he stated flatly, his gaze on Katherine. "Reheat it and give it to Victor. He is awake." With a nimble bow of his head, he dismissed Rose. Head lowered, she did not glance in Katherine's direction as she left them standing at the side of the hut.

"What did you say to her?" Katherine asked in frigid tones, glaring her dislike at him.

Jackson stared back at her.

"Unless she held a gun to my head she couldn't make me eat that stuff. Don't take it out on her." A cocked black brow was Jackson's only response.

"You're a brute, you know it? A brute and a bully," Katherine added contemptuously. A part of her was aghast at the way she was deliberately provoking a man who was holding her hostage. After all, what did the woman mean to her? Except that it was in her nature to fight, especially for the underdog. Katherine became more incensed at Jackson's unresponsiveness. "What time am I leaving anyway?"

"Go back inside," he ordered, steering her toward the hut. Katherine's slender frame resisted the nudge as well as the warm contact of his open palm on her back. She knew she was courting trouble, yet she was unable to stop herself.

"Answer my question," she insisted stubbornly, shrugging off his hand.

Jackson gave her a quizzical look.   "I might decide to keep you."

Panic clutched Katherine.   Her eyes flew to Jackson's.   She searched his bland expression. "You promised," she replied hoarsely, uneasy at his statement.

"I am a brute and a bully. I can change my mind on a whim, can I not?" His hand found her shoulder, applying pressure.

Unsure if Jackson was mocking her, Katherine replied with heat, "I am not some trinket you can buy at one of your markets. You can't keep me, Jackson." She shied away from his hand, only to have him grasp her upper arms.

His clear eyes dueled with hers.   "Go inside, Katherine," he commanded. Before he could catch her arms in his hands, Katherine swung, striking his wide chest with curled fists.

"You are taking me back to my family like you promised, buddy, or you will live to regret it," Katherine threatened with false bravado.   She struck Jackson a blow with each word.

Shaking her briskly, Jackson jerked her close. Her head bobbed like that of a rag doll.   "Stop it, Katherine!" His voice was insistent, his expression bordering on annoyance. His lips were so close to her cheek his breath rushed over her ear, causing a tremor to spiral its way through her.

Katherine tilted her head back, reading the irritation on his face. "I will not stop it until you take me back to my family," she retorted, twisting this way and that to get loose. It was impossible. Jackson's grip was like iron. Still, she kept fighting him.

"I said stop it!" Jackson's smooth features were marred in frowning anger.

"Who are you to tell me what to do?" Katherine challenged, her face inches from Jackson's glowering one. She stared back defiantly. Alone in the clearing the two of them were joined from chest to thigh, oblivious to their surroundings. Katherine's labored breathing reached both their ears.

Jackson's eyes slipped down to her parted lips, lingering, to her breasts rising and falling in agitation. The too-large neckline of the shirt dipped low, revealing the swell of her bare breasts. Something flickered in Jackson's eyes, dimming the anger for just a moment.

Drawing her arms to her side, Jackson spoke in clipped, precise tones. "You will either sit or stand in front of the shelter where I can see you until Rose returns. If you make trouble, I will tie you and put you inside."

Katherine glared her dislike up at Jackson. He grabbed her arm and she did not resist him; she had no desire to be tied or cooped up inside against her will. She studied his sharp profile as she kept up with his long stride. She wasn't surprised by his autocratic actions but was rather taken aback by his visible hostility.

"And I will want an answer to my question regardless of where you stick me," Katherine ventured, not ready to give up her quest for the truth.

Jackson released Katherine in front of the shelter next to a log lying on its side. Her stubborn refusal to sit was wasted on Jackson, who ignored her and entered the hut. He came out within a short period with a black, battered notebook. Katherine gritted her teeth in frustration at the amount of space he put between them as he got comfortable on a low log.

"I will get you home when the time is right. I do not intend to keep you here."

Startled, Katherine's eyes flew to Jackson's. His held her immobile across the distance of the forest floor. Then he lowered his eyes and flipped open the notebook, bending his close-cropped head over it. Clearly, he was finished speaking.

Standing trance-like, Katherine stared at the bowed head. She'd been careful not to watch him too closely. Now she could have her fill. No matter what she thought of him personally, she could not help admiring the near mahogany-colored skin. It stretched taunt across bones and muscles and from what she was able to see, was blemish free. His long nose flaring at the tip was aristocratic. His lips with their perpetual grimace were full and strongly appealing. Thick, wide-spaced black brows lay smoothly above his eyes. And those eyes! What could she say about them except they could not be improved on.

His fatigue pants fit well over his solid thighs. A taupe-colored tee shirt fit snugly over his well-built shoulders. Even as she admonished herself not to admire him, Katherine had trouble looking away.

"Sit down, Katherine. There is a chair inside the hut if you do not want to sit on the log." Jackson did not raise his head as he spoke but continued to write.

Great day in the morning! What was she think-ing, ogling the man like that?

She took precise strides over to where Jackson was sitting. Peering over his shoulder she ques-tioned briskly, "What are you writing?"

Tipping his head back, Jackson regarded Katherine for curious seconds before answering. "A letter to my mother." He resumed his writing.

Katherine was so amazed at his answer that it was some seconds before she digested what he'd said. She tried to picture this brooding, distant man caring enough about someone, anyone, to write them and could not.

His hands moved swiftly across the buff-colored

paper. Katherine's attempts to read upside-down were for naught. "What's that language you're writing in?" Her forefinger smoothed over the printed page.

"Gikuyu," Jackson answering, continuing to write.

"Gi-ku-yu," Katherine parroted slowly, liking the sound of the name on her tongue.

Pausing in his writing, Jackson looked up. "The European way of spelling it is Kikuyu. Thus, it is how it is shown to the world. The true spelling is Gi-ku-yu.

"Is that what you all are speaking, Gikuyu?" Jackson laid his pen aside. An undercurrent of excitement rippled through Katherine as he gave her his full attention.

"More than one tribe or clan is represented here. Therefore more than one dialect is known. However, here we all speak Kiswahili."

"Oh," Katherine replied in a hushed voice. She blinked, swallowed and focused her gaze on Jackson's lips, which was a mistake. She raised it quickly to his nose, then his eyes. His waiting silence filled the air for an indeterminable period before he returned to his writing.

"So where is the mailbox?" Katherine asked flippantly, her large brown eyes scanning the area, taking in the folded tents, huts and tarpaulin-covered living quarters.

"Maybe I'll write a letter to my fiancé." She knew she'd said something wrong when she stared down into Jackson's face. The man had no sense of the absurd.

The gold in Jackson's eyes dissolved into chips of sandy rock as he stared back at Katherine. Katherine's palms were instantly sweaty. Outwardly she was calm. She'd learned long ago not to exhibit fear to the enemy.

"You are to be married?" The rich resonant voice was composed, the expression veiled. Katherine relaxed a bit.

"Oh that. Well, you see, I haven't...he doesn't know yet that I'm gonna marry him."

"You would force yourself on a man who doesn't want you?" His eyes searched her face, his lip slightly curled under.

Katherine's stiffened at the derision in his voice. Drawing herself up to her full 5' 8" height and managing to look regal in the too big blouse, the much washed and worn wrap- around, her eyes narrowed to slits as she stared over the top of her small nose at Jackson.

"I have never nor will I ever force myself on any man," she tossed back at him. Smiling frostily, she added, "Alex wants me. He has been asking me to marry him for over a year. He is one of the most eligible bachelors in Washington."

If Katherine hoped to impress Jackson with her speech about her soon-to-be fiancé's qualities, she was disappointed. He responded in a detached, bored manner. "If he is all you say, why has it taken you so long to say yes?"

"If he is all I say! If he is all I say!" Katherine sputtered, incensed that this stranger should question her about her personal life. "He is all that and more." She slapped her hands on her hips, daring him to dispute her claim.

The haughty action drew Jackson's attention to the tiny waist wrapped twice in the colorful skirt. His eyes traveled back to hers. "Well, why has it taken you so long?" he queried, again in that tone that set Katherine's teeth on edge.

"I made up my mind on the flight to Kenya. I uh...I haven't told him yes officially yet."

Arching a brow, Jackson did not respond. Katherine felt compelled to explain. "In the States most women and men don't rush into something as serious as marriage. I count myself in that group."

"What if your unofficial fiancé changes his mind about wanting to marry you?" Jackson inquired as though he were truly interested. He didn't fool Katherine. She knew there was ridicule somewhere in his question. She gave him a serene, confident smile.

"He won't."

Observing her, Jackson asked, "Do you love him?"

The question floored Katherine. This was too, too much. Whiskey-brown eyes flared into deep golden-brown ones. "You've got some nerve, Mr. 'Jackson Rebel Man' or whoever you are. I don't owe you an explanation about my private life. You just get me out of this jungle so I can get back to it."

"Answer my question, Katherine." There was a hard set to Jackson's sharp features and again Katherine was conscious of an undercurrent of tension.

"None of your business," she retorted sharply. Spinning on her heels, she reached the log and flopped down hard, sending splinters of pain up her tailbone. The folds of the skirt wrapped around and in between her long legs. She worked furiously at untangling it. She finally got it from between her thighs, wishing for something that fit, or better yet, her own clothes from her closet in her house in the States!

"Why would a simple question be so hard to answer or cause you such anger?" Jackson's deep voice carried across the way. He watched Katherine struggle with the skirt and his lip quirked.

"And why would my answer matter to you one way or the other?"

Well, that finally shut him up, Katherine remarked to herself in silent satisfaction when Jackson's head dropped over his paper without further comment. She tore her eyes away from the bowed head to her surroundings. Everything was in a neat semi-circle which extended well beyond her vision. The few huts were so small she doubted they could hold more than one person at a time. The shelters covered with tarpaulins probably gave little protection from the rain since all sides were open.

The smell of food lingered in the air, though some time had passed since breakfast. Katherine's stomach growled in protest at its emptiness. She couldn't help wondering when lunch was.

She looked up past funnel-shaped trees to the bits of blue sky and white clouds overhead. Leaves fluttered within her vision. Since she'd been here, she'd heard numerous sounds in the trees, but had not seen what was making them. Everyone here probably knew. It was the not knowing that made Katherine nervous.

The question she'd been avoiding took prominence over all others. Why couldn't she answer Jackson's question, impertinent or not? Yes, she loved Alex; no, she did not. No, she didn't. She knew it and so did Alex. She didn't try to fool him or herself. Saying out loud that you were marrying

someone you were not in love with sounded calcu-
lated and callous.

She was not naive enough to think love would
happen once the marriage took place. Both she
and Alex were of like mind and expected no mira-
cles. She cared deeply for him; otherwise, she
would not be able to marry him.

But love? Love was another matter altogether.
And, she concluded, with a tiny nod of her head,
people married for reasons other than love all the
time. She was perfectly happy with her decision.

If that was so, a voice nagged, why couldn't she
admit as much to Jackson. Shaking her head, she
threw off her melancholy and stiffened her spine
with firm purpose. She was not one for second-
guessing herself once a decision was made. Deep
in contemplation, she turned her rounded chin away
from Jackson, to the dense forest over her shoulder.

Finished with his letter, Jackson's attention was
drawn to Katherine's profile. Shafts of sunlight glint-
ed above her head and shoulder. Her burnished
auburn hair was tied back from her face with some
sort of string. Wisps of it escaped, trailing down her
graceful neck, down her back. A small breeze blew
some of the strands about her face, and she
brushed them impatiently aside.

In spite of her alien surroundings and the

absence of everyday comforts, her posture was at ease. His eyes traveled from the handmade thongs up the length of a smooth brown leg displayed through the slit in the wraparound skirt. He'd bet money Katherine wasn't aware that much flesh was showing. When he found his attention lingering and his mind questioning, he moved past the slim hands folded in her lap to the proud, squared shoulders.

His perusal halted at her face, noting the stubborn tilt of her chin. Her slender stature was deceptive. Jackson recognized the strength and determination in her. She had the heart and bearing of a proud warrior. His eyes narrowed further. A man marrying this one must be strong, yet allow her to be independent and not crush her spirit.

Rustling from the open path halted his musings. Without turning, he recognized the soft footfalls as belonging to Rose. The sounds were like the woman herself but they, like Katherine's slender frame, belied the strength within the woman.

She stopped in front of Jackson, holding the empty bowl in one hand. Jackson's focus shifted from the bowl to her face, questioning. "I am just returning from Victor's side. He ate most of the porridge. I ate the remaining spoonfuls left." Hope lit the soft eyes as Rose continued to speak. "His fever is not so high and some of the swelling around the wound has gone down."

Pushing himself into an upright position, Jackson took hold of Rose's shoulders. "You are doing a wonderful job with Victor. He has steadily improved under your care. I would have no one else by my side to help if something were to happen to me."

The smile left Rose's face. Her hands grasped Jackson's long, narrow fingers. "Nothing will happen to you. It mustn't."

"It is time to join the others in practice," Jackson replied, gently releasing Rose's hold. "Rhonda will see to the noon meal. "You will see to Katherine until we return. Kimya should be returning this day with some news of her family."

A beat of silence passed before she responded. "When Victor is better I will return to help you fight."

"It shall be," Jackson agreed, leaving Rose and passing by a staring Katherine without glancing her way. She listened to his footsteps recede into silence as he disappeared into the jungle.

Swinging around to Rose, she caught the expression on the woman's pretty face. She and Jackson had spoken Kiswahili and Katherine didn't understand a word, but she could decipher the expression on Rose's face. It was pretty darn close to the one N Zee wore whenever she was around Jackson.

Rose caught Katherine staring but wasn't fast or

adept enough in concealing her emotions as was her leader. Did that barracuda N Zee know what was in the wind or did she and Rose willingly share Jackson?

Oh well, it wasn't her business. Except for the barracuda, no one had mistreated her, but after today she hoped to never see any of these people again. Still, it was hard to shelve her natural curiosity.

"Come with me," Rose stated in halting English so thick with accent Katherine had trouble deciphering it. Rose repeated herself in a no nonsense voice accompanied by sharp hand signals and Katherine, figuring she had caused the woman enough grief, went with her without protest.

As they walked side by side, Rose's eyes were on her. When Katherine met the stare, expecting the woman to shy away, Rose surprised her by continuing her inquisitive probe. Quick to take note of the lack of animosity coming from the woman, Katherine offered her a tentative smile which was not returned.

Katherine wasn't offended but took it as a matter of course. Neither she nor the woman was here to make friends with each other. Intermittently, she was cognizant of those brown eyes on her until the path abruptly narrowed. Long-reaching limbs and vines closed them in on all sides and the pungent odor of rot permeated the still air.

Impatient to return to Victor and check on her cooking fires, Rose urged Katherine before her, guiding her steps with a firm hand centered in her back. A short distance later the trail veered into another open space. In their direct line of vision, side by side were a grass hut and a small tent. Katherine tried to see past the dark interior of the grass hut but could not. She fleetingly wondered if someone was inside.

As they walked closer, Katherine saw an empty hammock strung from two sturdy poles. A none-too-sturdy looking chair sat in front of it and beside the chair was a large, three-sided, tent-like structure positioned over a raised platform. Her eyes dropped to the still form of a man whose face was turned away.

Chapter Ten

Rose pointed to the lopsided chair, indicating Katherine was to sit, then hurried to the man. Deciding she'd rather stand than risk falling on her backside, Katherine eased beside one of the tent poles to watch Rose, who was kneeling over the man who let out a groan of pain.

Except for the square piece of cloth thrown over his lower abdomen, the man was naked. Katherine almost gagged at the sight of the scar which ran from the man's shoulder, down his side past his hip, to disappear under the cloth and reappear above his knee cap. The entire leg was swollen double the size of its smooth ebony twin.

The man turned his head toward Rose, who was speaking softly to him. Katherine saw his face clearly and was shocked at how young he looked. Barely out of his teens. The youthful face was hairless and smooth, the skin chalky. Without opening his eyes, the young man grimaced and moaned again, louder this time. Asleep or unconscious, Katherine had no doubt he was suffering.

Leaning over the body, Rose retrieved a bowl and placed it near her folded legs. She dipped her hand inside and gingerly smeared a green-looking paste around the long wound. Dipping a towel into a bowl of liquid on her right, she bathed the man's face and chest. All the while administering to him, Rose spoke in a soothing voice, eventually removing the frown from the man's face.

Katherine thought she detected a tiny smile on the man's lips and was startled when he opened his eyes and stared directly into hers. Fascinated, Katherine stared back. A huge grin split the man's face as he continued to stare at Katherine. He mouthed words she was unable to hear. Rose drew closer to him, then angled her head in Katherine's direction. The man said something again and Rose nodded and glanced over her shoulder at Katherine.

She gave her attention back to her patient and when he was resting to her satisfaction, she put the bowls and cloths aside and rose agilely from a position that would have immobilized many a person for some time.

"Pre-ti. Pre-ti. Victor pre-ti you."

It took a moment for Katherine to unscramble what Rose was saying. Her eyes strayed to Victor and back to Rose. She smiled. "Thank him for me when he wakes up. I don't feel pretty in this getup and I haven't had my customary morning shower."

The irony of her comments was lost on Rose, who was beginning the preparation for a meal. Here, as in the main camp, a hole was dug in the ground and filled with large stones which were smoldering with heat. Placing a large, hollowed-out stone on top of the smoldering piles, Rose filled it one quarter of the way with water from a gallon plastic jug. Droplets of moisture fell from the lip of the jug onto the rock, and hissed spewing steam.

Rising from her stooped position, Rose entered the shallow hut and emerged carrying a large bundle of leafy greens, wooden bowls and a knife. Setting them down and going back in, she returned with a long-handled, metal spoon, an iron pot, and two burlap pouches.

She opened the drawstring of the small burlap sack and scooped out salt with two fingers, adding it to the boiling water. After chopping the greens, she added them into the water.

When the greens finished cooking, she careful-ly removed the heavy stone using thin pieces of cloth on both sides. Katherine flinched at the heat she must be experiencing but continued to watch her in amazed silence.

The iron pot took the place of the stone. Rose allowed the water she poured into it to boil. From the larger bag she added white cornmeal, a spoonful at a time, until the mixture was a white, cake-like mass. It was soft when Rose removed it from the pot. She scooped this mixture out, put it into the wooden bowl and began the process all over again.

"Surely that is not all we're going to eat?" Katherine asked no one in particular.

Obviously it was. Rose disappeared into the hut once more and exited with two more small bowls. She filled both with the greens and passed one to Katherine. She made a move to scoop up some of the white mixture for Katherine.

At Katherine's negative head shake, Rose filled her bowl with both substances, sat back on a log nearby, indicating that Katherine should do the same.

Katherine gave a frowning glance from her bowl to Rose, who was busily spooning out with two fingers the bread-like substance, then dipping it into the hot greens.

Looking up from her food at Katherine still standing in the same spot with the bowl in her hand, Rose commanded, "Eat."

"I need something to eat with." Katherine pantomimed the spooning motion with her hand.

For a moment Rose looked as though she might argue. She let out an exasperated breath, put her bowl gingerly on the log and went inside the hut. She returned with a spoon that had seen better days. Katherine would have much preferred a fork but after gauging the expression on Rose's face, thought it prudent to make do with what she had.

At least it was clean. It was awkward eating with a spoon but Katherine managed. Surprising herself, she ate every drop of the green vegetable that tasted similar to spinach. She wasn't big on vegetables.

Shortly after Katherine and Rose popped the last fingerful of food into their mouths, a half dozen rebels came crashing from the trail. They were lively, animated and perspiring heavily. Shirts and pants were clinging wetly to upper bodies and muscled legs and thighs. They were orderly, however, and when Rose offered them food they declined, though some peered longingly into the cookware.

Katherine realized Jackson was not with this group of men and two females, even as she told herself she wasn't looking for him. She was relieved that N Zee wasn't with this group. Then it dawned on Katherine that wherever Jackson was, N Zee probably was.

More rebels entered the area, crowding around Rose. As Rose chatted with the men and women, Katherine noted that her attention would drift to the trail as if expecting someone else to step through the bush.

One of the men drew Rose aside, speaking quietly. She smiled encouragingly at him and leveled a finger at the man lying on the platform. Some of the men went to stand over Victor, speaking to him quietly. From where she was positioned, Katherine saw his lids flutter open, then his lips move. The men gestured excitedly to the others who went to crowd around the prone man.

In all of the activity Katherine wasn't at first aware of someone sitting on the ground beside her log. Finally, conscious of the presence beside her, she swung around to face the same man who'd leered at her earlier, now grinning up at her from a kneeling position.

Barely suppressing a shudder, Katherine glared her irritation at the annoying man. "Go away and leave me be," she ordered tightly, snatching her head in the opposite direction. Besides being annoying, the man made her uncomfortable.

The grin stayed in place while the man glanced surreptitiously around him. Rose was in the tent admonishing the men and hovering protectively over her patient. The few women were gathering up the bowls to take away for cleaning. No one was paying attention to Katherine and the grinning man.

Adam leaned into Katherine. He spoke unintelligible words in a guttural-sounding voice near her ear. One hand held onto the circumference of the log while the other dropped to his groin area. He rubbed himself suggestively and his wide grin turned menacing.

Disgusted and angry, Katherine shot off the log and well away from the man. She was afforded a little satisfaction when the log toppled over on his foot. He sprang up and advanced in her direction. Biting her lip, Katherine held her ground. If this man was stupid enough to attack her in front of the others, she might as well face him. Besides, there was no other place to go. The dense forest was at her back and sides and the man's wide body blocked her path forward.

"What are you doing, Adam?" Rose asked sharply, coming up behind the man.

The man named Adam turned to Rose, his large protruding eyes full of innocence. Lifting one shoulder, he grinned.

"Leave her be," Rose ordered shortly to his sneering grin.

"The American woman wants me." Adam smiled wider, a confident light in his eyes.

Snorting in blatant disbelief, Rose eyed her

comrade in mild contempt. Adam was a good fighter but Rose had never trusted him completely.
There was an arrogance and self-centeredness
about him. And because of his skills, prowess and
family background, he thought every female found
him irresistible. Simply put, Adam, good qualities
aside, was a troublemaker.

"She does," Adam insisted when he saw that
Rose did not believe him.

Rose's attention fell on Katherine, who was eyeing them warily while she struggled to make sense
of what they were saying. Thoughtfully regarding
the lovely, willowy American in silence, Rose found
Adam's boastful assertions hard to swallow. Still,
she mused, anything was possible.

"She is not to be harmed in any way. Those are
Jackson's orders," Rose warned Adam.

"It is not harm I have planned for her." Adam
grinned widely in Katherine's direction and turned to
Rose for her to share in his jaded joke. Katherine
didn't understand what he was saying but she knew
well the look he leveled her way. She glared meaningfully at both the man and Rose. They were discussing her in a language she neither spoke nor
understood.

A thunderous expression marched across
Rose's brow. "The woman is not to be touched in
any way by anyone in camp. Dare you defy

Jackson's orders?"

All humor vanished from Adam's face and the corners of his thin lips twisted. "Who is Jackson saving her for, himself? Does he plan to have every woman in camp?"

Shocked at the disrespectful tone and jealously Adam exhibited, Rose had no ready comeback for him. If Jackson or Kimya were here, he would not dare speak as he had. Her face clouded with uncertainty. To her knowledge Jackson had been with none of the women in the camp. Not even the sultry, voluptuous N Zee who threw herself in his path at every opportunity.

"Leave us, Adam," Rose commanded tersely. "The American is to be left alone. I have work and you have training to complete." She swiveled away, giving him her back. She reached out and hauled a willing and relieved Katherine to her side to help gather up wooden bowls and large shells.

Katherine made the mistake of glancing over her shoulder and got an eyeful of Adam rolling his pink tongue over reedy, wet lips while leering at her. Jerking her head back, she snatched her hand from Rose's hold to gather up the containers. The man made her angry and nervous all at once. Added to that, he made her feel unclean. Instinctively she knew to steer clear of him until she left this place.

Following Rose through a narrow lane leading

away from the clearing, Katherine didn't chance another visual encounter with Adam. She allowed the crunch of receding footsteps to fade away without turning back.

Quiet engulfed them and piquant smells assaulted them from all angles, though Katherine couldn't see very far into the thicket. From time to time the path was cloaked in dense shadows, yet Rose stepped as smooth and sure-footed as if they traveled in wide open spaces with a clear sky and bright light overhead

Craning her neck, Katherine squinted off into the trees and brush. Occasionally she sensed something in the thicket staring out at them but she couldn't see a thing. She was completely and totally lost. Jackson and his crew needn't worry about her trying to escape, she realized derisively. She wouldn't make it twelve steps from camp without being turned around.

Still, it didn't hurt to have some sense of direction. To at least know if they were going east, west, north or south. "East. At least I think it's east," Katherine thought as Rose broke through the trees and stepped onto the bank alongside a small, clear stream.

Her dropping the containers carelessly on the ground drew a sharp reprimand from Rose but Katherine didn't care. She fell to her knees on damp soil, heedless of her skirt, holding her head back as a breeze brushed over her damp skin. The trees overhead slanted on both sides of the bank, some so close they entwined together.

She wanted to dip her sore feet into the shallow water whose bottom she could easily see. Rocks and stones were imbedded in sand. Out of the corner of her eye she caught sight of fish swimming within inches of where they were standing.

"What the heck." Slipping off the thongs, Katherine inched forward until she was only a few inches away from the water. She dipped her hands in and came up with a palm full of water.

"Uum sweet," she intoned in approval and scooped another palmful, bringing it to her mouth.

Unimpressed with her surroundings and Katherine's antics, Rose meticulously rinsed out bowls and shells with a dull brown bar of soap. She didn't ask for Katherine's help and Katherine didn't offer. Instead she slipped her feet into the stream and immediately wished she could ease her entire body into the refreshing water.

Finished with her chore, Rose pointed to the clean containers Katherine was to carry and traipsed back the way she'd come.

Once she realized that Rose would not wait for her, Katherine hurriedly slipped on her shoes, scooped up the bundle and followed Rose, but not before lightning splintered through the trees and thunder vibrated the forest floor. Not long in coming, large drops of rain pooled on the leaves and dripped down .

By the time they made it back to camp, a light mist had formed. Rose went to check on Victor, leaving a damp Katherine seated on the log. She prayed that by tomorrow she would be ensconced in her hotel room.

Chapter Eleven

*J*ackson's expression was set in concentration as he stared into pitch darkness. He was some distance from the main campsite, alone without light of any sort. Night sentries were in the vicinity but the only sounds he heard came from the insects and night creatures.

He didn't have to look at the face of his illuminated watch to know that Kimya was way past his time. He should have arrived yesterday. Because of his delay, everything had been put on hold. Something was wrong. Jackson curbed his impatience. If anyone but Kimya had gone into Nairobi and was way past due, he would worry. N Zee had proven to be rash, much too impulsive. His friend Kimya, whose name meant quietness, would not do anything to jeopardize himself or them. Whatever was keeping him, Jackson would stay awake to find out.

It was well past one a.m. when Kimya entered Jackson's hut. Jackson looked up at his friend as he stepped through the door. He had on the same clothes he'd worn away from camp two days ago. In the lamplight Kimya's eyes were blood red, his thick braids matted and teeming with debris. One side of his square chin was swollen, his shoulders were slumped with fatigue and his clothes were disheveled, stained with a dark residue that looked suspiciously like blood.

Without saying a word, Jackson poured Kimya a cup of the coffee he'd reheated minutes ago. He filled a bowl with clear liquid with bits of meat floating on top and waited until his friend ate and drank his fill.

While Kimya ate his meal, Jackson listened at the door to the second room. Katherine was moving about. He'd banished her and her incessant questions to the room before midnight, but she stubbornly clung to wakefulness instead of sleeping as he'd insisted.

In fairness to her, he could not blame her. She was anxious to be with her family and away from them—him. He read the message loud and clear in her face every time he came near her. Black brows drawn, he turned his attention to his friend. Hopefully, in the midst of whatever had happened to delay Kimya, he had good news about Katherine's return.

"The American embassies were bombed in Nairobi and Tanzania," Kimya stated without preamble. He finished with his food and pushed the empty bowl aside. He topped off his cup once more and with bleak eyes cradled his chin in his hand.

In disbelief Jackson listened to his friend recount the details of the devastating blasts that had rocked their homeland. "Many were killed, many, many more injured. I was less than three-fourths of a kilometer from City Center, Nairobi, where I was to meet Peter, our contact, when the bomb exploded. I ran toward the blast. Death and destruction were everywhere. And when I thought it could not get any worse, another blast taking more innocent lives brought me to my knees."

Kimya's voice was steady, his brown eyes tortured. Unshed tears glittered in their depths. He faced Jackson and the pain was so deep and vivid Jackson laid a comforting hand on his friend's shoulder.

"I could not walk away despite the threat to my safety. I could not," he repeated bleakly. "There was too, too much...," he spread his hands wide, "so much to do. So many needing our help.

Betty...," Kimya paused, swallowed. Now it was he who placed his hand on Jackson's shoulder. "I dug Betty's body from the rubble."

Jackson shoved from the table to stand. Before leaving Kenya to attain his doctorate, he had convinced his uncle to allow his youngest daughter, Jackson's cousin, to work at the Ufundi Cooperative House. Sweet, pretty, outgoing, Betty was desperate to live in the city, to gain her independence and get away from her father's ever-present eagle eye. The building where she worked was adjacent to the American embassy. Jackson had helped her get there, and now Kimya was telling him that the building was no more, that Betty was dead.

He shrugged off Kimya's hand. His golden eyes were fiery with pain and fury, willing Kimya to admit he'd made a mistake. But Kimya's next words confirmed the worst.

"They had to sedate your Aunt Wilma. Your uncle arrived at the scene and had to carry her away in his arms."

Guilt dragged on Jackson's chest, dipping down into his stomach. His legs and arms were lead. Betty's girlish, teasing laugher clamored in his head. Her bright smile sharpened in his vision. Because of him neither would be seen or heard again.

Kimya took a step toward his friend. This time it

was he who stared Jackson down. "The bombing was not your fault. Do not blame yourself. You know as well as I that Betty would not want that. She wanted that job, Jackson, was determined to have it, no matter what the cost."

Holding Jackson's glare, Kimya dropped his raised hand to his side. The steel in the square jaw confirmed that his words were falling on deaf ears. Jackson would have to work through his self blame on his own.

"Who did this?" Jackson demanded hoarsely.

Shrugging wearily, Kimya replied, "No one knows at this time. When I left the rescue, things were in a state of chaos. I helped as long as I could in the confusion and disorder. We worked hours and hours, nonstop." He touched a couple of fingers gingerly to his swollen chin and winced. "I'm not sure how I got this. I wasn't aware of it until I was enroute here.

"During that time I was hoping to get word to Katherine's family to let them know that she is alive, and would be returned unharmed. But too many of Biwott's men were arriving in the area. My time was rapidly running out before I would be discovered. I would put no one here at risk.

"Americans were among those injured but I learned a few names and none of them was Wellington. The woman's father is with the World

Bank. He wouldn't have had a reason to be inside the embassy at the time of the blast."

"I could find out nothing about the Americans who attended the dinner party at the president's residence. No one is asking for the missing woman. With everything that has happened in the past twenty-four hours, I suspect the government wants to keep the information from the public, especially the U. S. public, for as long as possible."

"Her family must be seeking her. The bombing will only make them more desperate to find her," Jackson stated with conviction.

"I know," Kimya agreed, "but there is no way to get word to them at this time. Security is like a vise around foreigners, especially Americans. Our contact cannot infiltrate at this time."

Rustling on the other side of the door distracted Jackson momentarily. "Katherine must be returned to her family at once," he stated in a steely voice.

"I know the problem her presence has caused between you and N Zee—"

"N Zee has nothing to do with it," Jackson replied in a tight, hard voice.

Kimya studied his friend closely, seeking a reason for his mood. He noted the tenseness in his shoulders, the purposeful glitter in his eyes, the tight set to his lips. He believed he understood the situation better.

"It isn't safe in Nairobi for any of us. Our contacts have left the city. Biwott's men are like disease; they are everywhere. They can inflict serious damage on the pretext of searching for the person or persons responsible for the bombings. We do not have the necessary shillings to spread around to get information and keep mouths shut." N Zee had seen to that by nearly emptying their coffers to bribe guards during Katherine's kidnapping. Kimya saw no need to remind Jackson of this. "In a couple of days if the government has some idea who planted those bombs, maybe one of us can go back. Until then..."

"I'm surprised they're not blaming us for the bombing," Jackson stated grimly. It would be foolhardy to go against Kimya's assessment. Still, the logic did not sit well with him.

"It is early yet," Kimya surmised fatalistically. He raised his hand to Jackson's shoulder. "You will be okay, my friend?" He let his hand fall back to his side.

Instead of answering, Jackson's brows set in a straight line and he poured the last of the lukewarm coffee into his cup and swallowed it down. Kimya wasn't surprised at his lack of response. The man he'd known all of his life was intensely private. The times were infrequent that his true emotions were visible to others. He would keep the loss of his cousin close to his heart. There were times Kimya felt Jackson kept too much inside, bottled up.

"Where are you going?" Jackson asked as Kimya gathered a change of clothes from the peg on the wall and made preparations to leave the room.

"To wash off this blood and grime and then to sleep," Kimya answered, about to exit the room.

Brushing the answer aside, Jackson spoke in a voice that did not leave room for disagreement. "You will come back here to sleep. You have had a hard few days. You will rest undisturbed in this room."

"Where will you sleep?" Kimya was weary and despondent after all he had witnessed.

Offering an indulgent, smile Jackson answered, "Don't worry about me. It is you who deserves to rest."

After Kimya left, Jackson remained in the same spot. It was very late and he should be preparing himself for sleep but too many thoughts were surging through his mind. All of their activities had been put on hold because of Kimya's delayed return, but his young cousin's death weighed most heavily on his mind.

Katherine entered the room wearing a loose-fitting, shift-like dress to find Jackson entrenched in deep thought. He didn't acknowledge her presence.

"I didn't hear voices any longer," she said by way of greeting. The look of expectation on her face pulled Jackson's full lips taut.

Katherine involuntarily dragged her tongue across dry lips. Nervously, she stared into the lion gold of Jackson's eyes, her round chin lifted high, her slender spine stiffening with determination. Jackson would not intimidate her.

Earlier he'd banished her to the small airless room, insisting she sleep, as though she were some recalcitrant child. How did he expect her to sleep when she was waiting for news of when she would be reunited with her uncle? She'd been on pins and needles waiting for the man Jackson called Kimya to return to camp. As she'd listened to the male voices, she knew without understanding the words they'd been discussing her.

"Well, when do I pack my bags?" she asked flippantly. Her heart pounded as her lips curved into a smile.

"You should be sleeping, Katherine," Jackson replied flatly.

Katherine's heart fluttered. She tried to read Jackson's face. It was impossible. "Who can sleep at a time like this? Especially when I'm ready to travel. Now, this instant. Just you say when." Irked by Jackson's aloof manner, Katherine struggled to hold onto her temper.

"Say when, Jackson."

"Go back to bed, Katherine." His eyes met hers disparagingly. He was ready to dismiss her like some jungle gnat.

"Say when, Jackson," she uttered again around a clinched jaw.

Jackson made a move toward her, but Katherine held her ground. Her breathing sharpened as she stood chest to chest with him. He stared at her and she wanted to laugh out loud. She was more afraid of not leaving here than she was of him. "Say when, Jackson," she repeated with dogged determination.

"Not tonight, Katherine."

Fear caught hold. She fought back the tremors. "Tomorrow? Morning, evening, night?"

"No."

The word was like quiet thunder. Nails bit into tender palms. Katherine kept her eyes level with Jackson's. "What time of day or day of the week do you plan to get me back to civilization? All I'm asking for is an idea."

Jackson skimmed Katherine's face. He read the fear, desperation and anger vying for dominance in her eyes.

"I cannot give you an answer tonight, Katherine. Not tomorrow or the next day. Now please go to bed." The pain in his voice went unnoticed by her.

Just like that. He expected her to obey. She had been a pretty good hostage as hostages go but there was a limit to everything. Something snapped inside Katherine. Jackson was treating her as if she were some brainless idiot. Go inside indeed! This wasn't her home. Her home was in the U. S.

"I am not going anywhere until you give me an answer," she resisted stubbornly.

Wrapping his hands around Katherine's upper arms Jackson backed her into the doorway of the other room. "People are sleeping. There is no reason to shout."

"I don't give a damned about anyone sleeping," Katherine snapped, then thought she had pushed Jackson too far by the harsh look on his features.

As he continued to back her into the room Katherine was nearly on her tiptoes. She had to hold onto his arms to maintain her balance.

"What are you going to do now? Gag me and give me knockout drops to keep my mouth shut? Well, you'd better, buster, because I intend to nag you all night long until you tell me the truth about getting out of this place."

To her surprise, Jackson released her. He lit one of the two ever-present candles. As he began to undress, Katherine folded her arms across her chest, forgetting her initial dispute, and eyed him malevolently. "Now what are you doing?"

Jackson's full lips twisted in a cool smile. "Preparing for sleep."

"You are not sleeping in here," Katherine insisted in strident tones.

"My friend needs his rest. Your actions and endless questions deem it absolutely necessary that I remain here to curb your restless tongue." Opening the last button on his khaki shirt Jackson slid it from his broad shoulders. Next went his boots and khaki slacks.

Incapable of speech, Katherine opened and closed her mouth several times. Her pulse started that wild, rampant skittering she usually got in Jackson's presence. The candle he lit was small and the light was poor, for which Katherine was extremely happy. She saw more of Jackson than she was happy with, however. As she drank in his near-naked state, her palms sweated and a buzzing started somewhere far off.

"I knew it. I knew it," she squeaked. "You're trying to manipulate me into bed with you."

Cutting her a narrow look, Jackson replied sarcastically, "You American women give yourselves too much credit."

Stung, Katherine retorted haughtily, "Some of us deserve it despite what others pretend to the contrary."

With an impatient sigh Jackson held out his hand. "Let's get to bed, Katherine."

"Not on your life, dude," she replied silkily. "You'll answer my questions or I'll wake everybody in this damned camp and keep you and the rest of them awake the entire night." She threw her hands on her curved hips concealed beneath the loose-fitting shift.

Jackson felt world-weary and sad—sad because of his cousin's death, and weary from his battles with the Kenyan government and with this headstrong American. He inhaled deeply and closed the short distance between them.

You don't scare me, Mr. Warrior Man, Katherine challenged silently as she met Jackson's belligerent stare. She could hold her own against anyone. She didn't shrink from the warm contact of Jackson's bare chest brushing her braless, cloth-covered breasts but neither could she stop the tingling sensation racing across her body.

She moved not a muscle when his calloused palms skimmed down her arms, firmly grasping both wrists. She stiffened as he shifted her arms behind her back in a tight, one-handed clasp. His warm breath stroked her face and chest. She could feel his steady heartbeat while hers galloped. He stooped low.

Panicked and unable to keep quiet any longer,

Katherine demanded breathlessly when Jackson lifted her off the ground, "Put me down!"

Laying her on the narrow bed, Jackson joined her, settling behind, his powerful arms wrapped around her waist and stomach. Katherine felt every mahogany-colored, firmly-muscled fibre of him, from the width of her shoulders to the bend of her knees, all the way to her toes.

She squirmed restlessly on the hard platform bed. Jackson tightened his hold, spooning his body more closely around hers. "Keep still, Katherine," Jackson warned close to her ear. His warm breath blew across neck and shoulder. Nerves jumped in her belly and her thighs clamped tightly together.

Blinking into the near darkness, she stared wide-eyed at the wall. A voice of survival signaled that she was in some danger here. But she didn't have many options. None, if the truth be told. The tremors and tingles in her stomach spread to her chest and arms. My God, how was she supposed to sleep?

Closing his eyes, Jackson held the trembling form less snugly and spoke words of comfort in a low, soothing voice. While he spoke, a nagging doubt hovered. All he'd intended to do was quiet this stubborn, headstrong woman, get his belongings and find another place to sleep. He was in no mood to deal with her just now, but the second she entered the room, he deemed it an impossibility to ignore her. Despite her predicament, Katherine did not scare easily. "Ssh," he soothed, stroking her arm.

With all of her heart Katherine wished he wouldn't do that, no matter his intentions. "Don't," she protested, folding her body inward. Jackson inhaled sharply.

"Katherine!" He couldn't shift back any further or he would be on the floor. Which might not be such a bad idea, considering.

Jackson's voice, vibrating with thick tension, was enough to render Katherine immobile. Her body was a tight ball curved snugly into Jackson's male body. There was nowhere for her to go except the floor, where she would gladly sleep this night if Jackson would just release her. But he held her firmly. What in the world could the man possibly be thinking?

Their breathing filled the space in the small room. The sound of it was like a distant drumbeat on Katherine's temple. Her thoughts were random, scattered. The moment they settled, she became uncomfortable with the direction they took.

She was scared. Not that Jackson would do her physical harm. She was beginning to believe that he would remain true to his word. She was afraid of the emotions stirred up while in this stranger's arms.

They were way, way too deep and confusing.

Jackson lay behind her, naked except for briefs, with strong arms circling her waist. The fact that their immediate situation was keeping her quiet was of little matter to her. What mattered was her leaving. "When am I going back to my family?" Edgy desperation laced her voice.

"Ssh. We will sleep now, Katherine," Jackson urged softly, so soothingly Katherine could not muster the righteous anger of seconds before. Before she was aware of what was happening, she was drifting to sleep in Jackson's hold, something she had thought impossible.

Chapter Twelve

Katherine awakened slowly in the shadowed room. She could tell early morning was close at hand by listening to the same distinct noises she'd heard her first two mornings here.

It amazed her how deeply she'd slept without dreaming. Jackson lay still behind her, all warm muscles encased in smooth flesh. His arms were still around her. She was vibrantly aware of every part of him, of every deep breath he took that slid across her neck and down her shoulder. Squinting into the lightless room she made out the shape of his arm curved across her stomach. Tentatively, she brought her hand to the long fingers curled around her waist.

Jackson knew the exact instant Katherine awakened. The rhythmic pattern of her breathing changed, indicating she was no longer asleep. He'd been awake himself long before the monkeys began their early morning calls.

She made an attempt to remove his hand by grabbing his thumb and forefinger. He willingly obliged, allowing her to lift his hand, only to drop it back into place when she let go. Katherine blew out a frustrated breath. The man was persistent, even in his sleep.

Intuition made her suspicious. She twisted her head over her shoulder. His hold was firm, his long body relaxed and his eyes closed. "Jackson?" she queried softly. The only response was deep, even breathing. Twisting her head back around she said a prayer for deliverance. "God, please get me out of here."

"It is too dangerous to move you to the city at this time."

A gasp escaped Katherine at the unexpected sound of Jackson's low voice. In reflex, her fingers tightened around his.

"Why?" she asked around the obstruction in her throat.

"Kimya went into Nairobi to pave the way for your safe passage, but there was trouble."

"What kind of trouble? What does it have to do

with me getting back to my uncle? Why are you holding me in the first place? How long am I to remain a prisoner here?"

Caught up in distress Katherine did not note the tenseness in Jackson's body. His voice was deceptively soft when he spoke, though his grip made her wince. "Your uncle?"

"Let me go, Jackson, you're crushing my fingers," Katherine demanded.

Easing his grip, Jackson pressed Katherine flat on the bed and curved his body over hers. Katherine stared up at him through the gloomy light entering the room. "Tell me, Jackson. What do you want from me? Money? Some kind of public recognition for your group in the U.S.? I assure you my uncle can get you what you want. We need only to get word to him, let him know that I am well." Katherine was ready to promise Jackson the world if it meant her freedom.

Her uncle loved her. She had never doubted that for a moment. He didn't express it often to her, but she knew he would do his best to get her out of this situation, if he knew about it. Abra, on the other hand, would throw whatever obstacle she could in his way.

The silence was deafening in the room. Katherine became aware of Jackson's rigid form. She'd made some tactical error though she was unsure what it was.

"Who is your uncle? What is his name?" Jackson asked quietly.

"Julius Wellington," Katherine answered calmly, realizing it would do no good to hide the truth. He's just been appointed one of the directors with the World Bank."

"And your father?"

Puzzled, Katherine stared up at Jackson. "What about my father? He died right after I turned thirteen. I lived with my uncle until I went away to college."

"What are you doing in Kenya?"

"What kind of question is that?" Katherine retorted sarcastically, her patience waning.

"Why are you in Kenya?" Jackson persisted.

"What is this all about, Jackson?"

"You answer my questions and I will answer yours...as best I am able."

Because it was the first concession he had made since her arrival, Katherine relaxed and decided she would answer his questions, as best as she was able. Which would be much easier to do facing away from him. She tried to pivot away from him but was held still by a restrictive hand on her shoulder.

The contact from Jackson's hand was like the rest of him, vibrant and warm. Katherine forced herself to remain calm and turned her mind away from the parts of his body that were glued to hers.

"What are you doing in Kenya, Katherine?"

"I...uh...," she cleared her throat. "My uncle asked me to come, sent for me really, to join him and his family. He has been appointed one of the twenty-four executive directors of the World Bank, the first African American to have that distinction.

"Kenya has asked for monetary aid and has been denied the loan by the bank unless Matoi devalues your currency. Matoi refuses do so. My uncle is here to gather as many facts about the situation as he can."

For a long time there was silence. Katherine stared up at the stern face, wondering what was going on in that mind of his.

"For once, Matoi has made a decision that will benefit our country. But it is impossible to believe that he will stick to his guns."

Puzzled by the skepticism and derision in Jackson's voice, Katherine asked, "How can his refusal be a sound decision?"

"The previous devaluation of the Kenyan shilling has caused many citizens to become jobless. Property is worthless, and many people have suffered. The citizens' faith in the government is virtually nil." Jackson paused as an idea hit home. "Too many of our people are already unhappy with the way things currently are to risk adding another yoke around their necks. The possibility for insurgence against the government will become greater. Which explains Matoi's refusal."

Katherine liked listening to Jackson speak. The low melodic sound had a hypnotic quality to it. His faint accent drew her close without her realizing it. They were lying on top of an object that passed for a bed, she on her back, he on his side. Though she noted their positions, she did nothing to change them. He wore a pair of briefs, she a thin shift dress with only a pair of panties underneath. They spoke in quiet, intimate tones, casually, calmly. One of his hands was above her head while the other rested on her hip bone. With every second that passed, Katherine realized she was becoming comfortable with Jackson. He, on the other hand, seemed immune to it all.

"What does any of what you've told me have to do with my being here?"

"Does your uncle have children, a daughter?" Jackson asked.

"Why must you answer my questions with questions of your own?" Katherine retorted in frustration. "Uncle Julius has a son and a daughter. They are in Kenya also, so is his wife."

There was no need for Jackson to ask if the daughter was in attendance the night of the dinner party. It was of little matter now. For whatever reason N Zee and David had taken the wrong woman. Jackson's jaw turned to granite. There was no telling where this fiasco would lead or end.

"I don't know what this is all about, Jackson. My uncle is probably beside himself with worry by now." Her slim hand swept the room. "Please know that he loves me very much and will do whatever it takes to get me back."

Behind the confident boast was a trace of wistfulness. He shot her a penetrating look. "What of this fiancé of yours? Will he not do what it takes to get you back? Does he not love you as well?"

"Yes, he does," Katherine flung back. She threw Jackson's hand off her. "Now tell me what my kidnapping has to do with my uncle?"

"It would be unwise for your uncle and the World Bank to loan money to our government at this time."

Confused, Katherine struggled for understanding. "I thought—you sounded like—you and the bank are in agreement, aren't you?"

"If the World Bank and I are in agreement, it is for entirely different reasons."

"I don't care about reasons or motives. I want to be with my uncle. When are you taking me to him?" Katherine demanded bluntly. If she sounded selfish, she didn't care. She'd played cat and mouse with this man long enough. Whatever battle he was fighting wasn't hers or her uncle's.

Jackson noted that she spoke of a desire to return to her uncle, but no one else.

"When, Jackson?" Katherine was unable to keep the quiver from her voice.

"The American Embassy was bombed in Nairobi and Tanzania two days ago. It is not safe to go into the city."

Katherine tensed. "My uncle?" she questioned in a thick voice.

"We don't know if he was inside. Would he have had a reason to be?" His thoughts immediately went to Betty, who had been nearby.

Katherine spoke in a shaky voice as uncontrollable tremors started in her hands. "I don't know. Maybe. The American ambassador was at the party for my uncle. My uncle knows people who work at the embassy. He may have been near or inside the building to report me missing." She lifted her eyes from her tightly clasped hands to meet Jackson's eyes.

"I have to get back, Jackson. I have to know that my uncle is okay."

"Katherine?"

"Please, Jackson. I don't know what your fight is about. I do know that you are not a cruel man. My uncle is all I have in the world."

That she did not include her fiancé was not an

omission overlooked by Jackson.

"Take me back, Jackson, please." The tears that were standing in her eyes threatened to overflow.

"I cannot, Katherine," Jackson said quietly, pressing his lips to her hair. His fingers moved across her cheeks, drying tears spilling from her eyes. "Don't, Katherine," he urged gently. His hand smoothed over her stomach to her rib cage. "My contacts are seeking news about your family as we speak. As soon as they can, they will get word to me." Jackson saw no need to mention his tragedy. It would only intensify her worry over her uncle. Besides, it was his grief to bear alone.

"How long will that take?" she asked around the fear and tears clogging her throat.

"Kimya speculates three to four days, a week, maybe sooner. I will go into Nanuki in a few days to learn what I can."

"I should be with my uncle if he's hurt," Katherine replied in distress. It was hard picturing her aunt caring for her uncle if the need arose. In her own way Abra might care for him but she didn't have a nurturing bone in her body.

"It is too dangerous, Katherine."

"For me or for you?" she spat icily.

"For all of us," he answered honestly.

Katherine swallowed back her sobs. For one

intense moment she hated this man called Jackson. The tremors that had been slowing surged anew through her body. Jackson tucked her to his chest, his large hands covering her trembling ones. Later, she would tell herself it was the distress of finding out about the bombing and the fear for her uncle's safety that made her respond to him.

His lips brushed over first one brow, then the other. He held her hands up to his face, rubbing her knuckles across his cheek and chin.

A new kind of tension entered her body. Inhaling deeply, Katherine's lips parted to issue a verbal rebuke, only to be consumed by Jackson's warm, moist mouth. She raised an arm, to push him back or pull him forward, she would never be sure. It dropped across his shoulders while Jackson plundered her lips at will. Her tongue was swept inside his mouth where he suckled gently, his hunger escalating, becoming demanding.

Desire slammed through Katherine's system. A delicious tugging started in her womb. She crossed one long leg over the other to trap the feeling inside and moaned softly when it went unfulfilled.

Sliding a hand down the length of her leg, Jackson drew the shirt aside and caressed the soft flesh of her inner thigh. He slowly, torturously, retraced his route, paused and teased at the indention in her stomach, moving up to curve around her breast. He thumbed the peak, rolling it between two fingers. Dragging aside the material, he dropped a kiss on the throbbing nipple.

Moaning deep in her throat, Katherine arched forward. Jackson kissed her deeply, hotly. Trailing fiery kisses from her lips, across her chin and cheek to her ear, he spoke her name in a throbbing, husky tone. The sound of her name on his lips elicited an answer in kind from Katherine.

"Jackson." Cupping his face in her hands, she pulled him to her for another soul-destroying kiss.

Shouting from some distance away advanced quickly, threatening to shatter Katherine's erotic haze as Jackson plundered her lips like a man who had been without sustenance for a long period.

His large, very capable hand squeezed her breast gently while suckling on her lower lip. Katherine's arm slipped up around his broad shoulder, her fingers into in his crisp, black hair.

"Eeiii!"

There was that irritating sound again. Katherine thought she recognized where it was coming from, or better yet, who. She pushed at Jackson's chest but he held her firmly.

Angry shouts and words Katherine could not understand penetrated her haze. She made a stab at rising. Despite everything, she had succumbed to this man's lovemaking. Worse still, she was pulsating, in a state of suspended arousal.

Her glare didn't carry much heat. Disgust whipped through her. There was no excuse for her losing control the way she had. Not only was she being held against her will by Jackson, she'd made a commitment to marry another man. Wouldn't Abra love to see her now? She'd think herself justified in accusing Katherine of immoral conduct over the years. The thought of her uncle's wife was enough to invoke her strong will. "Let me go, Jackson," she hissed.

"Where is Jackson, Kimya? Why isn't he here instead of you?" a furious voice from the outer room demanded.

"Stay where you are," Kimya ordered crisply. Astonished at N Zee's brazen audacity, he rolled from the mattress on the floor to an upright position. Lighting a candle, he slipped on his pants in record time.

"He'd better not be with that American." N Zee seethed with mounting rage, the bowl of food in her hand forgotten. Her eyes flew from Kimya to the door behind his back. Privately she admitted she'd made a mistake bringing the woman here. It hadn't taken her long to come to that conclusion or to know that she wanted her gone. That Jackson could lie with that skinny bag of bones when she herself had all but thrown herself at him was too much to bear.

She would pay!

"Jackson does not owe you an explanation concerning his whereabouts or who he spends his time with." Kimya's tone was coolly disapproving, his eyes on the furious woman.

N Zee was beyond reasoning. "I will separate her head from her body," she threatened, "but not before I scratch her eyes out of her head." She made a move in Kimya's direction, the bowl raised.

"You will take your food, leave and not come inside this room again without my permission." Jackson walked through the doorway barefoot and without his shirt. His features were composed, the look in his eyes anything but. Kimya faced his friend, cautiously stepping aside.

N Zee lifted a hand to her racing heart. "Jackson?" She perched the bowl precariously on the edge of the log and approached him. "I came in and did not see you sleeping here and became upset. I thought—" Her eyes shifted to the closed door behind Jackson and back to his sculpted chest.

"Do as I command, N Zee." The biting edge to Jackson's voice drew two pairs of eyes his way.

Fear knotted inside N Zee. A disturbing thought entered her head: that Jackson might banish her from his life. He was truly angry with her, of that she did not doubt.

"I will leave you two to talk." Sliding his arms inside his shirt, Kimya was about to enter the back room when Jackson's voice whipped out.

"You will not go in there. You will remain here." Kimya stared at his friend for long seconds. There was no mistaking the hostility in his voice.

Kimya was able to ignore Jackson's irrational antagonism; however, the expression of painful realization on N Zee's face was not so easily ignored.

"You have slept with the American," she accused in a broken voice.

"I will not ask you to leave here again. When I return, you will be gone." Jackson gave Kimya a look that only he was able to interpret and was gone from the room.

N Zee's cheeks grew hot with humiliation. She stood still in the tiny room, her eyes unable to hold Kimya's. The pity she read there only increased her shame and anger.

Each time she blinked, she visualized the American in Jackson's arms. Her rightful place! From the first day she'd caught sight of Jackson Shugaa she'd promised herself that he would be hers. She meant to have him still.

"Come, N Zee." Kimya curved an arm through hers and guided her outside to the still sleeping camp. She bent her head to his shoulder to hide her tears from his all-seeing eyes. Rubbing her face across the coarse shirt material, she scrubbed away all traces of moisture before the sun splintering through the gaps revealed her devastation.

Tipping her head back, she could easily read Kimya's emotions. He wasn't as good at hiding his feelings as was his friend.

In his own way Kimya was as handsome as Jackson. He was courageous, trustworthy, committed to the death to helping his countrymen live a better life and loyal to a fault. Kimya was in love with her. She had known it for a long time. But he wasn't Jackson. She was shrewd enough, however, to realize she could use his love for her to her advantage.

Standing on tiptoe she pressed a kiss to the side of his mouth. Her tongue snaked out, tracing across his lips before turning away, but not before witnessing the flare of longing and desire in his eyes.

Chapter Thirteen

*G*athering her wits about her, Katherine watched Jackson silently as he laced up his boots and buttoned his shirt. His eyes were on her, intense and brooding, while he dressed. She'd bet her bottom dollar he was regretting his near seduction of her earlier. Well, so was she. It only proved what she'd suspected all along but was too scared and too stubborn to admit. She was attracted to him—strongly. No matter how she berated herself for her own eager reaction, her emotions remained unchanged.

Oh, Alex... How could she in good conscience marry him when she had these conflicting feelings about another man? There had never been any serious competition for her affection before. And though it was laughable to imagine Jackson vying for her attention, her feelings for him were more than she could cope with or even define.

"Good grief, stop staring at me like that," she retorted, irritated that he made her nervous. She backed away when he took a step in her direction, her breathing accelerating. She would fight him this time. His caresses and his unexpected gentleness would not lull her into easy acceptance of his unwanted attentions. Not this time. She moistened her lips, drawing his eyes to the motion of her pink tongue while she fought off the memory of his devastating kisses.

She was at the wall with no place else to go. "I thought you didn't want me," she mocked, throwing his words back at him in a rush when Jackson lifted his arm over her head. Her chin was up, her eyes flashing fire as she waited for his next move.

Jackson pulled a camouflage cap off a peg inches above her head, letting the wind out of her balloon. He boldly surveyed her from her feet to her head before resting his gaze on her mouth. "I think we've both disproved that theory, don't you?" The softly spoken statement held a hint of self-mockery.

Breathing normally at the moment was impossible with Jackson standing over her. The pleasure of his nearness stabbed her and wound its way through her body. For good measure she crossed her arms and scowled up at him, then stared hard at his broad back as he left the room without further words.

Collapsing on the low bed, she was cognizant of the fact that she needed to relieve herself. When she was around Jackson, she tended to focus on him only. The man was dangerous, in more ways than one.

Voices in the next room brought back the memory of angry words in the front room a short while ago. N Zee's shrieks of rage had burst Jackson's sensually spun web, thank God, Katherine asserted, conscious of the heat crawling up her chest to her face. She blushed at the disturbing images, pushing them aside to ponder the question at hand. What in the world was the woman's problem now? Katherine had an uncomfortable notion it had something to do with her and Jackson sleeping in the same room together. "Well, join the crowd, girl-friend, I had a problem with it too, for all the good it did."

Rose's soft tones interrupted her musings. Jackson said something to her in their tongue and uncharacteristic giggles burst forth from the woman. Katherine's ears perked up when Rose responded, drawing deep answering chuckles from Jackson.

Unable to stop herself, Katherine opened the door connecting the two rooms in time to witness

Jackson smiling down at Rose. The woman was glowing brighter than a neon sign. Katherine's heart and breath caught. There was no getting around it. The deep smile transformed his brooding face.

He lifted his head to her standing in the door-way, impaling her with his golden gaze. Katherine's breath trembled over her lips as she fought an unwelcome surge of desire. The smile left his face, replaced by a frown. Dipping his head, he spoke quietly to Rose and vanished.

"Come." Rose approached Katherine and pressed her fingers into her back, indicating she was to follow her outside. Katherine reached out for the woman's arm, indicating as best she could that she needed to go relieve herself. Rose held a fore-finger to her lips and seemed to be asking Katherine to wait.

Understanding dawned instantly. A repeat of yesterday's activities was being enacted as men and women prepared to leave the campsite in an orderly fashion. Before leaving, some of the men and women disappeared into different sections of the thicket, returning moments later. Katherine knew what was going on. She would wait her turn. She had no desire to encounter one of these strangers while she attended to a private matter.

The man who had made lecherous advances

toward her yesterday had his back to her talking to a group of men. Katherine quickly shifted to the other side of Rose's diminutive body. She had no desire to deal with him today.

Taking furtive peeks over her shoulders, she managed to convinced herself she wasn't seeking out a pair of wide shoulders and slim hips. That is, until a flash of deep brown skin and tawny eyes snared her attention. Her heartbeat sped up. The man was an extraordinary male specimen. Katherine couldn't recall seeing him before, but he wasn't Jackson.

Blowing out a frustrated breath from her cheeks, she called herself all kinds of idiot and trained her eyes on the weapons of destruction each individual carried. These people were doing something against the law. Why else would they be hiding out in the jungle?

And Jackson—whatever his last name was-with his ever present commanding air was their leader. The leader of this lawless band of rebels.

Men and women filed past her. Today, for some reason, Katherine could not face them head-on. She made an about-face to return inside the hut, her private needs put on hold, and encountered N Zee poised in front of the door of the shelter eying her.

Icy hatred distorted her beautiful features and

carried a punch, piercing Katherine to her bones. Katherine no longer questioned where the woman's enmity stemmed from. Jackson was at the core. She would wager her freedom N Zee held her responsible for Jackson spending the night with her.

But there was not a thing she could do about that now, was there? Katherine held the baleful stare. Sliding narrowed eyes away, N Zee drew her sandy braids up in a compact knot in the center of head. Withdrawing a hat identical to the one Jackson had put on earlier from the back of her khaki pants pocket, she slammed it ruthlessly down on her head. She brushed past Katherine, bumping her hard.

Katherine threw out both hands for balance and managed to regain her footing. She glared at the retreating back and arrogant swaying hips. "Bitch," she muttered under her breath. Unwittingly she had made a dangerous enemy. Using very colorful and descriptive language to express what she thought of Jackson, she went to relieve herself. She would place the blame squarely where it belonged, at his feet.

"Now!" Jackson's large hand sliced through the air, falling sharply near his taut thigh.

The loud crack of handgun, rifle, and pump action shotgun fire rent the stillness. Jackson repeated the hand communication again and the cracking noise echoed in rapid succession as the second row of male and female sharp shooters, then the next, down to the last row, aimed and fired at targets on tree trunks situated some distance from them. The rebels were in a recently cleared area located two miles from the main encampment.

The logs and trunks Jackson's rebels used as targets came from the small trees they had felled in the area. Saplings, bush and vines had been cleared to make the area reasonably workable for a practice area. High overhead the leaves and branches of hundred-foot trees gave them the protection they required from prying surveillance helicopters.

Jackson surveyed the scene before him. Men and women were engaged in fierce hand-to-hand combat. The women were good fighters, some on a par with the men. His eyes sought N Zee. She was the best of the women fighters, relentless in her desire to win, to be the best in everything. Even in her pursuit of him, she did not hesitate to let it be known that she meant to win him. His blood chilled. She wasn't in sight. He went in search of Kimya at the far end of the compound.

This morning, after he'd explained to Kimya

Katherine's true relationship with the man David and N Zee had assumed was her father, he'd sworn Kimya to secrecy. It would do more harm than good if N Zee learned the true identity of the American.

His personal life was his own; he did not justify it to anyone and wasn't about to start. But Katherine! Katherine's safety was at stake. Never in their decade-old friendship had he given N Zee a reason to hope that they could be more than friends. Still, she fancied herself in love with him and ignored his friend Kimya, who watched her every move with longing and caring in his eyes. Both men were aware that despite her attributes N Zee could be vengeful when she was thwarted.

∞ ∞ ∞

Katherine was just about bored silly. After cleaning up and helping Rose prepare, cut and chop vegetables, there wasn't much left to do. She had been relegated to her stump stool, left to twiddle her thumbs or go back inside the shelter and stare at the wattle walls. She'd already tried that. In less than fifteen minutes she was back outside. Hours passed and from the smell wafting her way from the large metal pot, Katherine guessed it was time for the noon meal.

She silently congratulated herself on how fast

she was adapting to her environment and dilemma. She continued to be wary and cautious but had put her initial fears aside. Except for a few surreptitious glances her way, she was ignored. She did not have to guess where the order to leave her alone had come from.

Although she could not abide the porridge, the rest of the food tasted much like what she ate in the states. Already her stomach was growling in anticipation of the noon meal.

She pulled at her fingers and rubbed her hands along her arms. She needed something to do to keep her mind off brooding thoughts of her uncle. There was nothing around to read. It would probably be in Kiswahili anyway.

It seemed unusually dark and still and she felt melancholy envelop her as her thoughts drifted to her uncle. He had stepped in immediately when she lost her parents. Katherine had never doubted his love for her. He often told her that through her, his brother lived. The times she needed him most, he was always there for her. He, too, was the one connection she had to her father.

Before the tears had a chance to form, she looked toward the few huts before her. Maybe a little exploring was due. With some luck she might come upon a map or something that would lead her out of here.

Rose wasn't in sight. Obviously confident of Katherine's inability to navigate outside of this clearing, she'd left; her food was simmering over a low fire. She was probably somewhere with one eye on her but Katherine didn't care. She'd made up her mind; she would explore. Who knows, she might find something that would come in handy.

She emerged from the first low slung hut empty-handed and squelched the shriek on the edge of her tongue as N Zee appeared from nowhere. The snorts and growls coming from the woman almost made Katherine smile. Almost but not quite. Katherine instantly realized that the woman was spoiling for a confrontation. When N Zee raised a fist, aiming for Katherine's face, Katherine effectively blocked it with an arm. Too late, she saw the large rock gripped in N Zee's other hand coming toward her.

The blow caught her temple and cheekbone. The sight of the gleeful expression on Nzigunzigu's face would be the last thing Katherine would remember for days afterward.

"Hapana [no], N Zee!" Jackson shouted as N Zee drew her arm back to strike again.

"Hapana [no]!" He jerked the rock from her hand, and sent it sailing through the trees.

The brute force of the action pitched N Zee backwards. She emitted a moan as her bottom and back smacked the packed earth with a wallop. Pulling up on both elbows, she did not get up. The expression on Jackson's face held her to the spot.

The cold fury on his face was enough to sear through her clothes. He stood wide-legged, towering over her like some powerful, ancient African ruler. Eyes slitted, his face was a mask of stone. His long fingers stretched wide, slowly coming together in a fist. The whimpering noises coming from her throat only fueled his anger. If he so much as touched her, he would kill her with little regret.

The truth stunned him, angering him more. He gave N Zee his back as he fell to his knees beside an unconscious Katherine. Blood flowed freely from the deep cut above her cheek. A bruise near her temple was already red and swollen. Placing an arm under her legs and head, he gingerly lifted her limp body, marveling at how light she was. However, she had the courage of a lion, courage he secretly admired. He stared into her slack face and icy fear knotted around his heart.

"She was trying to escape, Jackson," N Zee insisted desperately, inching to his side. "I ordered her to stop but she didn't." The hand she laid on Jackson's taut arm was roughly shaken off as he held Katherine's inert body tightly. He advanced toward N Zee, the expression on his face lethal. She backed up and out of his path.

Staring after his retreating back in dread, N Zee realized she had gone too far. Jackson was beyond angry with her. Behind her panic and fear was a feeling of desolation. Helplessly, she watched him enter his shelter. Too late she admitted to herself that her action had been hasty and stupid.

"Katherine!" N Zee spat contemptuously on the ground. Up until now she'd refused to use the woman's name to avoid giving her an identity. But today she'd seen that the woman was all too real. And somehow, someway, in the span of two and a half days she'd used her wiles to ensnare Jackson.

Chapter Fourteen

*W*hat is it? Where is Katherine? Why are you here, N Zee?" Rose eyed her comrade suspiciously, alarm filling her. It was no secret that N Zee had taken an intense dislike to the woman she'd brought into the camp.

Her fellow fighter was capable of creating all sorts of mayhem if someone got in her way.

Why Jackson put up with her antics was beyond Rose's comprehension. If she kept up her self-serving ways, she could seriously endanger their mission. Looking closer at N Zee's face, Rose wagged her head. There was definitely something in the wind.

"I need you, Rose. Come quickly." Rose started when Jackson appeared in the small doorway.

The quiet urgency in his voice spoke volumes.

Barely sparing N Zee a glance, his voice dropped even lower. "Leave my sight at once, N Zee." He pivoted back into the room, and Rose followed him inside.

"Jackson, what is it?"

"Katherine is—she is injured. Maybe seriously," Jackson supplied in a tight voice. He moved away so that Rose could see Katherine lying motionless on the platform bed. Her eyes were closed, and her breathing was shallow and uneven.

Rose knelt beside the bed and noted the dark bruise on the American's temple. A bloody rag, obviously used to stem the flow of blood, was pressed against her face. Gingerly, with probing, knowing fingers, Rose removed the soiled rag and assessed the damage, conscious of Jackson's unblinking scrutiny. The cut was superficial and would heal without scars to the beautiful skin. "Nothing is broken," she offered without glancing up at Jackson.

The wound at the temple was more serious. Her brow knit with concern. "Who did this to her?" The image of N Zee's fear-filled eyes flitting from her to Jackson materialized.

"N Zee," came the terse reply. Jackson described what he had witnessed, appearing in time to see Katherine being struck savagely across the

face with the rock. Somehow Rose was not surprised at the turn of events. N Zee had been spoiling for a fight since her return with the American.

For a panicked moment Rose wondered if
Jackson blamed her for what happened. For a brief
period she'd left Katherine to gather more firewood
for her pots. She never thought the American would
be in danger from anyone in camp, especially after
Jackson's instructions to leave her be. But in the
span of minutes, her life had been placed in jeopardy. Rose pushed herself up, her eyes on
Jackson. His were on the woman on the bed. "I will
get my things. I will return quickly."

Jackson's eyes briefly met hers before returning
to Katherine.

Jackson stood over Katherine's unconscious
body. She looked so slight and pale to his sharp
eyes. There was blood around and behind her ear.
He frowned. He thought he had done a thorough
job of wiping it all away.

He dumped the bloodied water in the bowl out
the window and refilled it with water from the jar on
the log. He dipped in another piece of cloth and
carefully wiped the remaining blood from
Katherine's ear. Finished, he left the rag in the bowl
and set it out of the way.

Leaning within inches of her face, Jackson softly called her name. Receiving no response, he

caught both slim hands in his large, warm ones. His thumb caressed her under her chin. "Katherine," he whispered insistently.

Her eyelids flickered a few times and opened. Jackson's hand tightened around hers. Katherine's breathing accelerated and she stared—unseeing. Her lids closed and her breathing slowed. Jackson repeated her name several times more, to no avail.

When Rose returned carrying pouches and a dark liquid in a clear jar, Jackson was upright, grim-faced, watching Katherine from near the tiny window.

"I will tend to her now," Rose said briskly.

"How is Victor?" Jackson asked, seemingly unwilling to leave.

Efficient hands set to work as Rose answered Jackson. "He is fine." Her tone clearly stated that she wanted him gone.

"I will go see him before returning to practice." Jackson paused at the door, his back to Rose. "I know you will do your best for Katherine."

After he left, Rose felt the urge to go after him and apologize for her sharpness. He didn't know that Rose had feelings for him. It wasn't his fault that he did not think of her in those terms. But even as Rose prepared to make the American well, she wished her miles from this place, thus from Jackson's sight and mind. It was probably too late for such wishful thinking. She'd seen too many women vie for Jackson's attention and fail to get it. Now, this one had done so without trying. She hunched her shoulders in resignation.

ᗧᗧᗧ

Jackson was returning to the campsite, pleased with what he'd seen. It was a slow process but Victor was healing nicely. Rose had wonderful healing hands. Surely under her ministrations Katherine would fare well. Once she was well, he would return her to her uncle. Her uncle! What a joke!

David and N Zee had made a serious tactical error. Added to that, N Zee had attacked the woman she and David had mistakenly kidnapped. If they had investigated thoroughly, they would have learned that the American's daughter wasn't in attendance at the dinner. And none of this would have happened!

N Zee wasn't in the campsite when he left Rose and Katherine. He would have banished her from the camp for a long period as punishment for her cruel actions if she had been in his sight. It was best for all concerned that she had vanished. Jackson had lost all patience with her.

Although Kimya marched ahead of the rebels who were returning to the encampment for lunch, their muttering reached his ears when they didn't see a sign of Rose, or detect the smell of food in the air.

Kimya ordered the rebels to remain where they were and went in search of Rose. After speaking with her, he went in search of their leader, his mind filled with worry.

Kimya met Jackson coming from Victor's sickbed. The two men walked shoulder to shoulder on their return to the encampment. "Rose told me N Zee attacked Katherine," Kimya stated bluntly, his bass voice laced with questions and concerns.

The grumbles and complaints from the hungry rebels reached Jackson's ears as he and Kimya stepped into the clearing. It was one more strike against N Zee. The men and women had worked hard this morning. They looked forward to and deserved a meal after such an intense workout.

"N Zee has overstepped her bounds," Jackson stated with cool authority.

"Where is she?" Kimya scanned the area and saw no signs of her.

Hunching a muscular shoulder, Jackson answered curtly. "I do not know but if she were here now I would banish her."

Lines of worry creased Kimya's forehead. That Jackson had reason to be very angry was understandable. N Zee and David had made a terrible mistake in bringing Katherine here. And for N Zee to turn around and attack her in such a vicious manner? Without cause? Or was there a cause? He eyed his friend, considering his response.

"What reason did N Zee give for her actions?"

Jackson turned an angry glare upon his friend. Kimya withstood it without flinching. "She said Katherine was trying to escape," he said through gritted teeth.

The same disbelief in Jackson's eyes was mirrored in Kimya's. Only a fool would try to escape the jungle if they were unfamiliar with it and its unforseen perils. The American had courage but she didn't appear foolish.

There wasn't a need for further discussion. They both knew why Katherine had been attacked. Jackson had spent the night in the room with the American. Kimya had been too tired to care what had gone on between his friend and the pretty American, nor would he ask now. N Zee, however, was convinced she knew. The knowledge that Jackson had spent the night in the room instead of sleeping alone made Katherine a threat to N Zee, a serious one. But banishing N Zee from camp was

a harsh punishment to carry out because of someone they had known for less than a week.

"I promised Katherine that I would leave tomorrow for word of her uncle. I cannot leave now until
I am sure she will be okay."

"I will go," Kimya stated simply.

Though his golden eyes were filled with gratitude, Jackson gave a negative shake of his head.
"We will see. One of us must relieve Rose so she
can finish preparing the meal." Not to Kimya's surprise, Jackson was the one who entered the hut to
seek out Rose.

After listening attentively to Rose's instructions,
Jackson dropped down on the ground as close to
the bed as possible. Rose had prepared the immediate area for illness. The marercws and mataihi
leaves were spread about, already their pungent
scent permeating the air. She had boiled water for
the muthign and green heart tree leaves which left
a taste of fire in one's mouth but which cured many
illnesses.

Already it looked as if the swelling were going
down on the right side of Katherine's face. Or was
it wishful thinking on his part? He leaned over and
peered into her face, waiting for some sign of life.
He spoke her name once, twice, half a dozen times.
Her eyelids did not flutter. As before, he held her
hands in his for a length of time before neatly fold-

ing them across her abdomen. His fell to his sides listlessly, his heart thudding dully.

The weight of the events of the past week rested heavily on his shoulders. His cousin's untimely death, Katherine's capture and subsequent attack. He could only wonder what was next in store.

∞ ∞ ∞

Slinging the blinding tears away from her face for the last time, N Zee entered the village like so many others on the outskirts of Kenya. This one was important to N Zee because it was the home of Frank Kimani, a sorcerer.

Diviners and sorcerers were a part of life in some villages. Frank Kimani had been born with the mystical powers of a diviner. In general, a diviner's duties were to combat evil, but somewhere along the way, he had chosen to use his gift to cause harm to others.

N Zee was in desperate need of a diviner's power. She needed something or someone to make Jackson forgive her, to make him understand that everything she'd done was for him. To make him love her the way she loved him.

Sidling up to the canvas door, N Zee paused, indecisive on how she was to enter.

"Hodi [hello]?" she greeted in a low whisper.

Her brown eyes darted wildly from side to side, seeking movement from the other villagers.

There was a long beat of silence until finally a deep raspy voice spoke. "Karibu [welcome]."

Nearly jumping from her skin, N Zee brushed the flap aside and entered. She waited for her eyes to adjust to the darkness. From somewhere within the hut she heard the striking of a match. A small flickering spurt flared, providing illumination.

"What is it you want?"

The voice was deep, scratchy sounding, as if had not been used in years. Resolved not to be swayed from her purpose N Zee squinted into the weak light and outlined the reason for her visit.

She wasn't asked to sit. The sorcerer kept his head bowed and asked, "Do you have the opportunity to speak to this man whose affection you wish to obtain?"

"Yes," she answered, peering down from her height at the tightly-curled hair.

"Is there someone who stands in your way to this man's heart?" The sorcerer tilted his head back. With shrewdness that stripped away some of N Zee's confidence, he watched her from faded eyes.

What could she say? She was the reason for Katherine being with Jackson. She had brought the American to him and Katherine had ensnared him.

She would not have him! "Yes," she answered simply.

The sorcerer reached into a pouch tied around his neck, extracting a small dark brown root. He held it in his arthritic palm and began to speak softly in the Gikuyu language. Pausing, he indicated by sign language that N Zee was to kneel in front of him. After she knelt, he began to chant, intoning magical words over the root in his palm. N Zee was instructed to repeat the intonations in ritualistic order.

She did, dropping her eyes from his incredibly wrinkled skin. When she finished, the sorcerer carefully wrapped the root in a square piece of white cloth and placed it in N Zee's hand.

Before rising to her feet, N Zee made an attempt to press some shillings into the sorcerer's hand. He recoiled from her touch, speaking harshly. Pushing to her feet, she nervously laid the money on the ground beside the candle.

Now all she had to do was get Jackson Shugaa alone and seduce him. When she kissed him, she would transfer the root from its hiding place under her tongue to his mouth. Its powerful magic would flow into him, causing him to love her as she did him.

She stepped cautiously until she was well away from the hut. Breathing long and deep with relief, N Zee retraced her route to the campsite.

Chapter Fifteen

*L*aying the semi-automatic weapon carefully on the log, Jackson rose to his feet and paced the area. Kimya continued to clean his gun, while keeping half an eye on his restless friend.

Darkness was approaching. What light there was seeped through the gaps in the trees, striking Jackson over his dark head and grazing his broad shoulders.

"I will leave for Nakuru early in the morning. I'll find a ride from there into the city," Kimya said.

Nodding absently, Jackson continued to pace. Kimya eyed his friend closely. "She is going to be well. Rose assures it."

"I want her well before she is returned to her

uncle. Why hasn't she awakened yet?" Swinging around, Jackson stared at his friend as if seeking an answer. Katherine was still unconscious for a second day, though Rose had been tending to her closely. Whatever free time Jackson managed to get was spent at her bedside. If he was aware that N Zee was back from her mysterious disappearance, he wasn't saying, nor did he act as if he cared.

Kimya knew N Zee was anxious to get back into Jackson's good graces and expected him to pave the way for her. Kimya was certain of that. He asked himself if it was possible this time. Jackson seemed in no mood to forgive her. His anger was easily aroused at the mere mention of her name.

Jackson's attention shifted to Rose, who was exiting the shelter. She came to them, her eyes on Jackson. Her slim shoulders were drooping, her smooth skin lined with fatigue. Grim-faced, Jackson stood like granite with his fingers curled into fists as he awaited her words.

"She is awake."

Without waiting to hear more, Jackson left Rose and Kimya staring after him and entered the shelter. Rose's tired legs carried her to a tree to rest against its massive trunk. Closing her eyes, she rested her head in the crook of her arm. She was very relieved that the woman had finally begun to respond to her ministrations. Glad for the woman and yes, even glad for Jackson.

"You did a good job, Rose. Jackson is always thankful for your efforts." Kimya settled his hand gently on shoulders that sometimes carried a heavy burden.

Rose opened her eyes and stared across the campsite to the door Jackson had entered. Kimya read love as well as despair in their soft brown depths. He was well aware that his words of consolation were inadequate.

She gave Kimya a cheerless smile, pushed herself up from the tree and slowly made her way back to her shelter.

∞∞∞

"Katherine?" The name rolled slowly off Jackson's tongue. He stared into the lovely honey brown face illuminated by candlelight, frustration marring his features. Her eyes were shut. If she was awake, she wasn't responding to his entreaty. He called her name again.

"Katherine."

Thick black lashes fluttered. Jackson pressed closer, willing them to open. They did. He slid to a knee, staring deeply into the whiskey-brown depths. His fingers skimmed across her cheeks and her forehead. Katherine's eyes drifted shut at the soft caress. They opened again when Jackson's fingers stilled on her collarbone. Jackson was pulled into their smoky depths.

"How do you feel?" he asked softly. His lips did not smile but his expression was gentler than Katherine had even seen it.

"Sore all over," she replied in a raspy voice.

When a smile crossed Jackson's rugged features, Katherine's heart bounced around in her chest. The light shaped the sharp angles of his features. Even in her tormented, bone weary state, that face set her pulse to fluttering. She shut her lids again, this time to conceal her emotions from the man intently observing her. In her weakened state he would clearly see how vulnerable she was and how much she had come to care for him.

Strong fingers massaged rounded shoulders, slipping across silky arms to a narrow waist. The palm of Jackson's hand brushed over her flat stomach, very lightly stroked over her breasts and up to settle comfortably against her cheek. He studied the multi-colored bruises on her other cheek and temple.

"You have been lying without movement for two and a half days. It is understandable that you are stiff as well as sore. We will have to exercise you back into shape."

"What do you have in mind?" Katherine asked throatily through unused vocal cords.

Though the question was innocently asked, the air around the couple became electrified. Katherine's breath hitched in her chest when Jackson's eyes swept across the smooth expanse of flesh visible above the neckline of the loose-fitting dress, then shifted to the rise and fall of her breasts. A pulse began to beat erratically where neck met shoulder. Long, calloused fingers smoothed it.

Katherine ran her tongue over parched lips. She had never witnessed this side of Jackson, this gentle, indulgent side and wasn't sure how to handle it or him. Her flesh tingled everywhere his fingers touched. And the way he was looking at her... Her tongue slid back over dry lips, once, twice, three times.

Jackson's golden eyes fell on the moistening motion of her tongue and deepened to a tawny shade of brown. His eyes locked with Katherine's. He was going to kiss her and she was going to let him. Lord, how she ached for him to!

When his soft full lips claimed hers, Katherine was unaware of her sigh of relief. She gave in to the slow, thoughtful, commanding kiss, her own lips opening, allowing his tongue entrance. Shivers raced from the bottom of her feet to the ends of the hair on her head and every point in between. She made a noise deep in her throat. Jackson abruptly pulled away, anxiously watching Katherine. He held one of her hands in his.

"Did I hurt you?" he whispered.

Moving her head from side to side, Katherine lifted a hand to stroke the clean-shaven face, tugging him closer. He dropped a kiss on the throbbing pulse in the hollow of her throat, moistening the spot with his tongue, before sliding it across her collarbone to the rise of her breast and back up to his starting point. Katherine's fingers tangled in his crisp black hair as she twisted her body forward, allowing him easy access to her throbbing flesh.

Eyes squeezed tightly shut, Katherine's fingers gripped Jackson's head to her as she breathed his name. She couldn't be sure if she said it loud enough for him to hear.

Raising his head, Jackson inhaled deeply. His fingers were steady when they touched Katherine's brow, his eyes a deep shade of brown. "Are you hungry?"

At first Katherine had difficulty interpreting the question. It was some seconds before her befuddled mind cleared enough for her to ask herself how Jackson could think of food at a time like this. She'd even forgotten the pounding near her temple in the onslaught of his lovemaking. Surprisingly, her stomach growled in answer to his question. Both smiled at its persistent rumbling.

"I will see that you get something to eat."

Thinking that Jackson meant Rose would bring her the food, her eyes stretched when he returned with a bowl of roasted meat and rice.

Her attempt to sit up fell short of its mark when lightheadedness stalled her effort. Easing a strong arm under her head, Jackson placed the bowl on the log and fed her the strong tasting meat and rice with one hand.

There was an intimacy coupled with Jackson's actions, the way their heads were nearly touching. The way he watched each spoonful she took, following the chewing motion of her mouth. Katherine was so flustered that halfway through the meal she was swallowing rather than chewing until Jackson admonished her to slow down.

At last finished, Katherine rested her head on Jackson's arm. Jackson continued to keep his eyes on her. She observed him in silence for long seconds. Her voice was puzzled when she spoke.

"Why did N Zee attack me?"

Jackson's expression turned hard as he spit out his answer. "N Zee is a spoiled child. She will not hurt you again. I have left word for her to be sent from camp."

Amazement did not begin to describe the effect

of Jackson's statement on her. She strongly suspected that N Zee was in love with Jackson. She had no inkling what Jackson's feelings were towards N Zee.

While it was true she had been attacked for no reason, to send away someone he had obviously known for some time in favor of someone he'd known less than a week was a radical step to take, in her estimation. However, she was glad she would not have to see the woman for a while. Unsure of what it all meant, she spoke hesitantly. "Will she be allowed back?"

"N Zee is an excellent fighter. Some of the men and women have spoken for her return. Whatever, she will not be allowed to hurt you again."

Katherine tried her best to decipher a hidden meaning behind Jackson's words. He was doing what he was so adept at doing, concealing all of his emotions. His expression was a total blank.

"Before we came to the forest N Zee was taken into police custody. She was beaten to make her speak of my whereabouts. She did not utter a word against me, nor did she lead the police to me. After she regained her health, she joined us here and has fought as bravely as any man."

A twinge of jealously gripped Katherine. The woman Jackson spoke of was a complete stranger to Katherine. There was caring and admiration in

Jackson's words. She quickly wiped it away, telling herself she had no business being jealous of any woman in Jackson's life.

"She will probably be allowed to return eventually. If so, things will be different. She will not come near you at any time." Jackson's arms tightened imperceptibly and his eyes iced over. "You are to tell me immediately if she or anyone else comes near you to try and do you harm."

Katherine's eyes locked with Jackson's. The events going on around her were varied and strange. Here she was literally craving the touch of a man on the run from authorities. What she knew could surely get him and his followers thrown in jail, or worse, killed. Yet she had been as relaxed in his arms as she'd ever been in Alex's. Where this would all lead, she knew not; but the ending would not be a happy one, of that she was sure.

A part of her was afraid. She did not trust N Zee to abide by Jackson's order. That she-devil seemed to have a flagrant disregard for rules, even Jackson's. Once she returned to the campsite, Katherine would have to be on her guard. She did not intend for N Zee to get the upper hand again.

Foremost, she must be on guard regarding her rapidly growing feelings for Jackson. It would be disastrous for her to fall for this man.

"I need a bath," she announced. She swung her

legs to the floor, fighting off the dizziness that assailed her. She averted her eyes from Jackson's all knowing eyes.

"You need to wait another day before you start to move around, Katherine." The velvet- edged voice allowed no room for debate.

With flashing eyes, Katherine rounded on him. He was sounding like his old autocratic self. A self Katherine could deal with. "Jackson—"

"No, Katherine. Tomorrow is soon enough." He rested a hand on her tight fists nestled in her lap.

"I said it before, I'll say it again. You are a bully!" she snapped, trying to shake his hold off. "I don't see how your people can stand you." She was irritated by the cool shield he could pull over his emotions as easily as he breathed.

"I force no one to join me, despite what is said to the contrary. Once they do, they cannot easily leave. And all must accept and abide by the rules. Without rules there would be chaos." Jackson's tiger eyes bored into hers.

What was he trying to convey? Katherine's heart thumped painfully. The only words she keyed in on were the ones about not leaving easily.

"I'm not one of your fighters or warriors or whatever it is you call them. I will not freely or willingly abide by your rules."

A smile eased the severity of Jackson's features. "Tell me about it."

Successful at suppressing an answering smile, Katherine raised her chin. "What do you expect? I'm not here by choice."

The compelling eyes were unfathomable. Without responding, Jackson rolled to his feet. Katherine glared up at him.

"At least give me my one change of clothes." She glanced at the dried blood around the neck of the shirt and grimaced in distaste. "I've had these on since N Zee banged me unconscious with that rock."

Because Jackson's back was to her, Katherine didn't see the flare of anger or the tightening of his jaw. "I will see to it," he replied curtly and left the room.

Katherine wondered at Jackson's unpredictable moods. He was as prickly as a bear. But she didn't care. At least she could change out of this clammy, wrinkled shift even if she couldn't bathe.

A female Katherine didn't know by name brought her another wrap-around skirt and scooped neck blouse. Sighing loudly, she took the clothing from the woman and thanked her. The woman stared at her blankly before leaving the room.

After changing into the clean clothes, Katherine felt somewhat refreshed but was still weak from her ordeal. Her mind rebelled against lying down, though she knew it was probably best for her. She had too much time on her hands as it was. What other reason could explain her thoughts continually straying to Jackson? She didn't want to remember his devastating kisses or be stirred by them, but she was. Lord help her, she was.

With a jolt she realized she did not know his last name. "What's happening to me?" She was totally dismayed that she had allowed herself to be captivated by him. A man a part of her feared.

She blew out all the lights and stretched out on the bed. The drone of male and female voices outside the hut did not penetrate her consciousness as she conjured up one way after another to get out of the forest, only to quickly discard each.

She was on her stomach, in a deep sleep, when Jackson entered the room and lit a candle. He was weary beyond belief, mentally and physically. His attention unerringly fastened on the sleeping American. He held the flame over the bed and saw that the swelling was completely gone from her face but the dark bruises and scar on her cheek remained. Obviously Katherine was not vain like some women of Jackson's acquaintance. She had not asked for a mirror to examine her face one time.

His eyes slowly traveled over the rise of her hips, where her skirt was bunched in disarray over her long limbs. Jackson sucked in a deep breath and was slow to release it. One smooth, brown hip was revealed clearly in the feeble light. Katherine's underwear was missing! He turned away but the golden brown skin beckoned him. He took a step toward the bed.

As though sensing his appraisal, Katherine mumbled in her sleep and turned on her side, pushing the skirt down her hip in the process. Jackson released a sigh of relief and disappointment that she was now covered. His brows knitted when Katherine winced and grunted as if in pain. Her hand found the bruise on her cheek and temple and rubbed.

Jackson's lips compressed into a straight line as he undressed. For nearly two hours he had listened to arguments for N Zee's return to the inner ranks. That she was in the forest he was already aware. That she wanted to return, he did not doubt.

Most of the men and all but a few of the women, Rose included, spoke of her returning. Strangely, the one individual he expected would speak in her behalf was silent. Kimya. Jackson could have refused to listen to them and left N Zee exiled but in the end he'd allowed a vote. The vote ended as he expected. N Zee would return, but with conditions, and in a reduced capacity of leadership.

N Zee was once a very good friend. Her willful ways had never been a major problem before. It was only when she began to want more, much more than he was able to give, that the problems started. He would allow her this one last chance.

Easing onto the bed behind Katherine, he draped an arm above her head and the other over her flat stomach. He listened to her steady breathing a long time before pressing his nose into her shoulder, inhaling her scent. His arm tightened across her waist and he forced his fingers to relax on her abdomen, lest he further mar her beautiful skin.

There was no way he could lead a rebellion and be this woman's keeper. She was fiery, stubborn and fought him every step of the way. He had to find a way to get her back to her family soon—for her sake and his.

Her side and hip were going numb. Katherine made a move to flip to her back and bounced into a solid wall of warm flesh. Her heart lurched until the identity of the person in the bed with her hit home.

"Jackson," she breathed huskily. "What are you doing here?" Her pulse leaped. Her hand found its way behind her; except for his briefs, Jackson was naked. His body was intimately glued to her backside. She tried not to think of what was in those briefs, pressing into her derriere.

At the sound of her voice Jackson's eyes opened. It was impossible, still Katherine could swear that she saw a golden glow in the dark room. "Making sure you rest well through the night," was his husky reply to her question.

Goose bumps dotted Katherine's arms at the sound of his deep, accented voice. His warm breath fanned over her sensitive flesh, increasing her uneasiness. She swallowed heavily, wanting to tell Jackson to leave her, but no words would pass her throat.

"Go back to sleep, Katherine. Sleep and get well." Jackson's lips feathered over the shell of her ear, down the length of her neck. One hand smoothed over her hair while the other settled on her hip. The soothing motion soon had her eyes heavy with fatigue, despite his disturbing closeness.

Before she fell asleep, Katherine decided that she and Jackson would have a discussion the next day about his coming uninvited to her bed. Well, it was her bed if her stay was to be extended. Even as the words drifted through her mind, she was settling more fully into Jackson's embrace to drift into a dreamless slumber.

Chapter Sixteen

A cool draft at her backside awakened Katherine. Jackson was gone. Exactly when he'd left, Katherine didn't know.

She did have a hazy recollection of him pressing a kiss to her lips. It didn't take much effort to visualize his long, male body wrapped around hers, every hard inch of him. Or to remember his buttery soft kisses, meant to soothe. Reliving all of it set her pulse to galloping. Katherine folded a fist and held it to her quivering stomach.

Swinging her legs around to the ground, she sat up and slipped into the thongs. Standing, she tested her equilibrium and was happy to find the light-headedness had passed. Her headache was barely a dull ache and tolerable. But her bladder was on overload.

She exited the rooms and walked into Jackson's arms, literally. He was standing just outside the opening, his eye on the entrance.

Grunting with the impact, Katherine bounced off Jackson's chest. His arms snaked out to catch her, keeping her upright. Speechless, she stared up into his distinctive features. His eyes were fastened to her face.

Pushing out of his arms, she glanced around the campsite. Everyone was gone. "What time is it?" Her calm voice was at odds with the triple beating of her heart.

"Past eight," Jackson answered smoothly, his eyes still scrutinizing Katherine.

She had truly slept a long time. Thankfully, she felt rested. She took note of Jackson's attire. He wore a gun on one side and a small bundle tied through a belt loop hung from the other.

"Would you like to take a bath now?"

Fighting through the cobwebs in her brain, Katherine dragged her focus from Jackson's sidearm. She offered him a weak smile, "Yes."

"Come." He held out his hand for hers.

"What?" Confused, she stared at Jackson's outstretched hand. "I have to uh...uh...you know...use it first," she supplied in embarrassment. "I'll bathe after I finish." Gathering her thoughts, she scanned the area in front of her. "Where is Rose? She always goes with me."

"Rose had other things to do. I will go with you," Jackson offered languidly.

Katherine's eyes flew to Jackson. She slammed her hands on her slim hips and stated with finality, "Oh no, you won't! Don't you have some rebelling to do or something?" She stared pointedly at the handgun strapped to his waist.

Exhaling a breath, Jackson clasped a hand around Katherine's wrist and tugged her forward. "Don't fight me on this, Katherine."

Resigned to the belligerent fire in her eyes and her resistance, Jackson deftly scooped Katherine up into his arms and started in the direction of the trail she and Rose usually took in the mornings.

Deciding not to give him the satisfaction of saying a word, Katherine settled her arms across her breasts and stared straight ahead. Nearing the area she used each morning, she sneaked a peek up at Jackson through thick lashes. She longed to knock that smirk off that handsome face. No one deserved it more than he!

"I will wait over there." Briskly setting her on her feet, Jackson disappeared into the thicket of saplings and brush. Casting a suspicious eye at the spot he vanished in, Katherine grimaced. If there was one convenience she sorely missed, it was indoor plumbing.

The moment she finished, as if by magic, Jackson emerged from the underbrush. Katherine watched his approach with skepticism, unable to determine by his expression if he had seen anything. For her own peace of mind, she would give him the benefit of the doubt.

Jackson led her into an area of saplings and wild brush so prevalent that he had her wait while he made a path for them. They had to bend low to avoid low hanging vines and thorny branches growing out of small trees.

"Where are we going, Jackson?" Katherine demanded. Her headache was back full force. "Are you taking me some place to do me in and dispose of my body? And I'm such a willing victim. Trailing happily along behind my cap...ump."

She hit a solid wall and the breath swooshed from her lungs a second time that morning. A thorny leaf scraped across her uninjured cheek, stinging her skin. Slapping it away, Katherine's eyes lifted to Jackson's black expression.

"Goodness. I was only kidding. Can't you ever take a joke?"

Obviously not, Katherine surmised as Jackson gave her his back without a word. He moved with long strides through the undergrowth. "Well, that and much worse has been known to happen to hostages," Katherine grumbled under her breath. "It happens in Kenya and all over the world. Moody, irascible man!"

After enduring the sting of unknown insects one time too many, Katherine had had enough. "Look, Jackson—."

"We will be there shortly, Katherine."

"Well, fine!" Katherine clamped her lips together, stomping the spongy ground with each step. If looks could do damage, Jackson would have a hole in his back as big as the Space Needle.

Katherine became so engrossed in their surroundings, she failed to see the fallen, rotted log Jackson deftly threw his long legs over. Before she knew it, her foot snagged the wood and she was pitching forward. Only Jackson's quick reflexes saved her from meeting the insect-laden forest floor. He spun around and caught her up in his arms when she yelled in surprise.

"Are you all right, Katherine?" Jackson asked, as he scanned her face closely.

Her arms were wound around his neck and she was staring back at him, drinking in his striking, dark features. She nodded, unable to tear her eyes away. She didn't want to be attracted to this man, this rebel. But heaven help her, she was, very much. As sure as her name was Katherine Rene Wellington, it would all lead to heartache and disappointment.

"Tell me the truth." Jackson took note of Katherine's distressed expression. He believed he'd caught her before she did damage to herself. But the headstrong American might be in pain and just not tell him. Enough had befallen her at the hands of others already. Maybe she was still reacting to her earlier injuries, though Rose swore she would have no lingering effects. Had he pushed her too hard, too far, by allowing her to walk this distance? It probably was not wise, however much she seemed healed.

She was a handful, this one. Argumentative, opinionated and very vocal in her wishes. Yet there was something about this American. Arms snug around his neck, she stared resolutely ahead, refusing to answer him.

"We're almost there." The rich timbre of his accented voiced created a flutter in Katherine's stomach. True to his word, Jackson pushed through the foliage to a tree-laden bank and stopped. All of Katherine's senses were assaulted simultaneously. This spot was different from the one she'd come to with Rose. Like soft fingers, the air caressed her skin. At that moment, she became aware of just how fast she'd adapted to the density and dimness of the jungle.

Trees on both sides of the bank shielded a wide,

shallow stream. Large algae-covered rocks rested on the bottom. As far as Katherine was able to see, the water curved through small trees, wild bush and large palms in both directions. The current before them was steady but the distant rushing noise drew Katherine's brows together in a frown. She tilted her head toward the sound, straining in concentration.

Jackson made a move to set Katherine on her feet and she nimbly scampered out of his embrace, embarrassed to have lingered so long. Her feet touched the ground and she wobbled. When Jackson would have held out his hands to steady her, she stiffened her arms out in front, holding him at arm's length. "I'm fine. You don't have to respond to every little misstep."

Reacting to the coolness in her tone and demeanor, Jacksons hands fell to his sides. Katherine turned from him, failing to notice the thinning of his lips or the flash of rejection in his eyes.

"You may bathe here." Katherine's eyes widened at the statement. She pivoted to voice her objections but Jackson was gone. On the ground rested a bar of the grainy soap and a towel.

Narrowing her eyes, Katherine strained to see through the trees. She moved in closer to the enveloping saplings. "Oh no, you don't, buddy. You get back here where I can see you. I'll not have you spying on me," she sputtered.

Silence met her strident demand. Katherine stood on the bank alone for indecisive moments. Finally the sound and scent of the water lured her. It looked so inviting, so cool and clear. It seemed like months instead of days since she'd had a complete, leisurely bath.

She kicked off her thongs, scooped up towel and soap and inched to the edge to dip her toes, then her entire foot into the water. The shocking pleasure had her humming with joy. Hiking up the skirt, she plunged into the water up to her calves. Then she waded further out until the water was at mid-calf.

"To hell with it." She unknotted the tie from around her waist. Her hands hovered over the gathered neckline of the blouse before snatching it over her head and flinging it to the bank. The skirt quickly followed.

"Okay, Jackson, here I am in all my glory," she challenged. "I guess you've seen it all before anyway, huh? Tell you what, dude. You can look but you'd better not touch." Katherine craned her neck. Still no movement and no Jackson. And listen to her! As naked as the day she was born, thigh-deep in water in an unknown forest, challenging a rebel leader who was a dangerous man. Was she so comfortable with him as to forget her circumstances?

She dipped the soap into the water and began to bathe. The gentle breeze created goose bumps along her skin. Katherine glided further along to the center of the stream until the water was past her waist. Throwing her head back, she closed her eyes and lifted her arms above her head. Water ran in rivulets down her arms onto her breasts.

What she wanted was to remain in this spot forever. With Jackson. She wanted—Aghast at her train of thought, her eyes popped open. Despite everything that had happened, she admitted that a small part of her would relish the thought of staying here alone with him

Suddenly, like some phantom disappearing and appearing at will, Jackson materialized, his magnificent body as naked as hers. During their time together Katherine had seen him only partially undressed and that was always in shadows. Here, the sun was on his tall form, accentuating every muscle, every lean piece of flesh. His eyes caught and held hers.

He waded into the water up to his thighs. With an unerring will of their own, Katherine's eyes fell below his waist. Unwanted excitement surged through her. She dug her toes into the sandy bottom and battled the dryness in her mouth and the trembling in her limbs. "You planned this," she spat, barely loud enough for her own ears. She jabbed an accusing finger at him and tried to summon indignation and anger. Even as she made the futile attempt, her conscience mocked her; she should have expected this turn of events.

Clutching the soap to her chest, she waited for the inevitable. All the words she knew she should say fled from her mind. She knew she should get as far away from Jackson as possible but all she could think of was that he was beautiful! Absolutely and without question, heart- stoppingly handsome.

Prying the soap from her nerveless fingers, Jackson turned Katherine so that her back was to him. He slowly and methodically began to bathe her. Katherine did not have enough strength of mind or body to stop him.

"Jackson." Her voice was a croak. "This setting, these idyllic surroundings. You, me, here alone. A writer couldn't have planned it better," she accused in a stronger voice.

"Don't always look for the why in every situation, Katherine." Jackson's silky voice sounded amused. Katherine hesitated to face him for fear of what she would see on his face and what he would read on hers.

His hands skimmed up and down her back, past her tiny waist and over her round hips. Their warmth burned into Katherine's skin and her mind.

"This is not some story begging for a happy ending, Jackson," Katherine said above the drumming in her ears. She had her wits about her now, mostly. Allowing Jackson to make love to her would be a grave mistake. "You won't seduce me out here the way you almost did this morning. I don't care how well you planned this, or how well you make lo— I don't care about any of that."

"Why do you keep protesting, Katherine? Are you afraid I will not make love to you?"

Inhaling sharply, Katherine spun and snatched the soap out of Jackson's hand. The audacity! The nerve! She was trembling again, this time from anger. Her naked breasts heaved, dragging Jackson's eyes from her face to the brown-tipped orbs. To her acute distress, her nipples hardened under his intense stare.

Before Katherine could speak or move, Jackson's mouth was on hers, warm, open and moist. She made a move to resist and her body stiffened. Jackson's maleness was between them, warm and throbbing. His long fingers stroked the curve of her hips, fitting her perfectly to his body. His teeth nipped a line along her jaw to her slender neck and agonizingly, slowly, back to her waiting mouth. It was a kiss that went on and on, hot and moist, nearly consuming her resistance.

An inner voice persisted in telling her that if she

succumbed to this man, she would be lost forever. From somewhere, she found enough strength to wedge her arms between them and push away. She spoke in an accusing though tremulous voice. "You did plan this."

Smoldering eyes now a deep tawny brown seared her skin. Averting her head, Katherine sought to avoid Jackson's kiss. It was a mistake. His lips landed on the taunt cords of her neck, nibbling, suckling at the soft skin under her chin. He took her wrists and dragged her body back to his so that the tops of her breasts grazed his chest and his enlarged shaft rubbed against her stomach. Jackson slipped a hand down her thigh and up, finding her feminine core. His fingers slid into the tight, wet opening and Katherine was lost.

She emitted a low groan, slumping against him the instant his lips closed over her nipple, drawing it deep into his mouth. Katherine's legs opened to accommodate his questing fingers and her arms reached out to grasp his broad shoulders. The water's low current lapped at them. The wind was cool on their heated skin but Katherine was oblivious to everything but the man holding her up.

Jackson pulled his head back and stared into her dazed eyes. It was long seconds before he withdrew his fingers from her warmth. Katherine's own fingers dug deep into his flesh when he did. In the time it took her mind to clear, she read triumph in his expression. She didn't like it. What she saw said, "Despite what you say, I can have you and we both know it."

But his breathing was as labored as hers and his manhood was as hard as the rocks in the water. The pulse in his throat vibrated wildly. His eyes held Katherine's then shifted to her swollen lips, then down to her turgid nipples. He inhaled deeply and bent over, plunging his arm below the water's surface to gather up the forgotten towel and soap from the bottom of the stream and set them in Katherine's palm.

"Wash my back." He didn't wait for a response but offered Katherine his broad back. She rebelled against the cool command and his indifferent body language. The angry words remained suspended in her throat when she saw the scar zig-zagging from a shoulder to the rise of a narrow hip. Katherine's mind rebelled against thinking how he might have gotten the wound.

Fixated, she was unable to move. She could ask Jackson, but intuitively she realized she didn't really want to know. His shoulder muscles bunched tightly as though he were uncomfortable under the scrutiny.

"Katherine?"

His voice held a note of warning. Who did he

think he was? Who did he think she was? Glaring at his relaxed posture, Katherine soaped the towel. She slapped it hard and loud across the unscarred portion of Jackson's back.

The stinging slap temporarily discolored his deep brown flesh, but Katherine received little satisfaction from the act. She got no joy out of trying to hurt him. It must be because her uncle had taught her better, she reasoned. Something about the unyielding back and accompanying silence made her wish she could see Jackson's face.

Gentling her touch, she swirled her hands over his back, enjoying the texture of silkiness over hardness. Her fingers trailed along the edges of the long scar. A sound from Jackson's throat had her snatching her hand away and saying contritely, "I'm sorry. I thought you were healed."

"I am," he returned evenly, his back to her.

"Well, why did you sound like that, like I'm causing you pain?"

"I said I was okay, Katherine."

Well! There was a definite edge to his voice. It sounded strained—a triumphant smile creased the corners of Katherine's mouth. She was getting next to him. Well, good! 'Cause he surely got next to her. Even now her body hummed in places his lips and hands had touched.

A soft breeze stirred around them but Jackson's

flesh was warm under Katherine's palms. Its silky texture began affecting her in ways that increased her awareness of him and their nakedness.

The thoughts she was having were dangerous, disturbing, and much too much enticing. The towel glided over Jackson's hips and an image flashed in her too-active mind of him poised above her, his buttocks tight and rocking urgently. The towel and soap slipped from her hands into the water.

"Why did you stop?" Jackson shifted around to meet the stubborn expression. His focus dropped past her clenched fists to the towel and soap in the water. Retrieving both, Jackson swung around to Katherine.

From behind her long lashes, Katherine's eyes slid down to his ridged stomach, then down below the water's surface. His large sex was clearly visible. Her eyes flew back to his face to find him watching her in that enigmatic way of his. She wet her lips.

"It's your turn now." His voice washed over her like hot silk.

Katherine lifted her hands in denial. "No more, Jackson," she rebuffed weakly. She could withstand no more of his sexual assault.

Heedless of her words, Jackson wet and soaped the towel and smoothed it from one end of her collarbone to the other. He glided it over the rise of her breasts and in between, leaving a tingling trail everywhere he touched—her stomach—below her navel.

Katherine was a bundle of nerves. She clamped her thighs tightly together. Her face was flushed, her body rigid. She raised her eyes no further than Jackson's wide chest and spoke through gritted teeth, "I will bear this violation until you have satisfied your male lust."

Because her head was averted, she missed both the furious flare of Jackson's nostrils and the calculating gleam that entered his expression. His continued strokes became decidedly erotic. His dark hands slicked over honey brown skin in ways that weakened Katherine's knees and started her frame to trembling.

Still, she was determined to fight Jackson's expert caresses. Biting the inside of her jaw, she lifted her eyes so that he was able to read defiance in their dark depths. Jackson leaned close. She might succumb to his seduction but she'd be damned if she'd make it easy for him.

The cool towel brushed over her left cheek and eye, then performed an identical motion on the other side of her face. Standing back, Jackson took Katherine's hand and set the instruments of bathing in her palm. In amazement, she watched as strong, fluid strides carried him away from her. Unable to believe that his seduction had ceased, her mouth fell open as he waded from the water. Disappointment gripped her. Katherine knew at that moment she could easily hate Jackson!

He faced Katherine as he leisurely dressed without drying off. She was acutely aware that she would have to walk naked to the bank if he remained where he was. And remain he would. Finished with dressing, he lounged on the bank, leaning back on his elbows.

So be it. She had not gone through the hell she'd endured with Abra without developing some backbone. And she didn't want him either, regardless of what he thought otherwise! He and his little games could go straight to hell!

As Katherine came out of the water, Jackson's head lolled to one side. It took everything she had to pick up the towel, dry off the wetness, and nonchalantly dress. Deep frowns drew Jackson's brows together, causing Katherine to wonder what was next in store.

"How do you feel?" he asked cooly.

Katherine searched for a double meaning in his words. Finding none, she answered just as cooly, "Clean."

Jackson's lips edged up in a smile that revealed straight white teeth. Katherine issued a silent order for her heart to remain in its place.

"Come." He held out a hand she was reluctant to accept until his expression said to do otherwise was futile. Placing her hand in his strong, calloused one, they retraced their route back to camp.

Once they were back in the empty camp, Jackson turned to her. "Rose will be here soon to prepare lunch. You must rest after you finish eating."

"Jackson, I am fine," she protested. She didn't want to lie down. Besides she was never one to sleep during the day unless she was ill. And all she did here, it seemed, was sleep.

"Rose will inform me if you disobey me, Katherine," Jackson warned.

And what will you do if I disobey, spank me? Wisely, Katherine kept her thoughts to herself and demurely lowered her gaze.

Suspicion narrowed Jackson's knowing gaze. Katherine had given up too easily. He lifted her chin with two fingers, probing her expression. Pursing her lips, her face all innocence, Katherine folded her hands angelically in front of her and batted her lashes, rolling her eyes side-ways.

For the second time that morning a smile lit Jackson's golden gaze. Always unprepared for that side of him, Katherine simply stared. She was doubly shocked when his mouth captured hers. Her senses were still in overdrive from the erotic water

dance earlier. She caught fire as the kiss deepened.

They were both so engrossed in each other they
failed to see the hate-filled eyes watching them
through the gaps in the thick branches circling the
campsite.

Chapter Seventeen

*J*ackson was the first to pull back. He scaled a lean finger over Katherine's cheekbone before backing away. Touching her swollen lips, Katherine kept her eyes on him until he vanished in the direction the rebels took each morning and afternoon. Though her body continued to thrill from Jackson's kisses, her heart was heavy. She was in trouble. She was in love with Jackson. It was a hopeless situation, one that would lead nowhere. She was in love with a man she knew next to nothing about, a fugitive, one a woman was willing to maim, maybe even kill for, yet Katherine loved him.

It did not matter that she had a successful, handsome, law-abiding man waiting for her back in the States. She was in love with an outlaw. What a waste!

Her appetite was gone. However, when Rose came, she forced down the mixture of potatoes, beans and ripe bananas mashed together. She wasn't the least bit sleepy, yet Rose did not have to instruct her to lie down. She wanted to escape this place and everything and everyone in it. She entered the room almost eagerly, wanting to shut herself off from reality.

Despite her turbulent thoughts, she became drowsy. Her last thought was that Rose had put something in the flat tasting water on Jackson's instructions. No one ever defied Jackson. No siree, no one.

∞∞∞∞∞∞

Katherine was asleep when Jackson entered and did not stir when he put his hand to her brow or lowered his head to her chest to listen to her even breathing. He sniffed the delicate fragrance of her skin, pleased by the scent.

"She needs to awaken to eat," he said hours later to Rose, his brow gathered in concern. They were sitting outside his shelter, along with some of the men. Some were engaged in conversation while others quietly relaxed. For the past two days they had been pushed hard, mentally and physically. Once again they were preparing to strike Nakuru with hit and run attacks. They must press and gain an advantage, strike while the government was otherwise engaged.

"The American will awake when it is time," Rose ripped out, and clamped down on her lower lip at the look in Jackson's eye. Contrite, she worked to erase the concern from Jackson's expression. "Do not worry, the sleep is healing for her body. It will be a long walk back to Nakuru and the more rest she gets, the better. It will build her strength. She is slight and not used to stress and her endurance is not as great as ours." Rose could only hope that she was right.

Chuckling inwardly, Jackson doubted that there was little Katherine could not conquer, but he kept these private reflections to himself. His back braced against the hut's wall, he listened to a group of his men humming in harmony. Tension eased from his body. Another dip in the cooling waters would wash some of the tiredness from his body. An image of honey-brown skin blurred his vision and abruptly had him on his feet.

Kimya, sitting a short distance away, stared

after his friend, puzzled. What put that look in his eyes? What caused him to stand rigid as if ready to strike at an unseen force before disappearing into the dark. Was he aware of the curious pairs of eyes on him? Did he care?

Did he know of the questions asked about his absence from the morning drill? A first for their leader who never missed a drill if he was in camp. N Zee was lurking about the fringes of the camp, desperate to regain entry. Was he aware of that? Did he not know that Kimya, his friend since child-hood, was in love with her, a woman who did not know he was alive unless it benefited her? Did he know that sweet reliable Rose was at this moment watching the spot he had vanished from with her heart in her eyes? Where had Jackson's mind been as he stared off into the darkness beyond the camp minutes ago? On the pending raid or on the beau-tiful brown- skinned captive lying in his bed?

With a fatalistic wag of his head, Kimya rose also. It was with a heavy heart that he acknowl-edged that he and Jackson were traveling the same path—the road to unhappiness.

Moonlight poured through an opening where a tree had fallen long ago. It cast a silvery glow on the tall, lean man standing naked in the cooling water. He resembled an ancient warrior, tall, dark and powerful with striking looks and golden eyes.

He scooped up water with his palms and splashed it onto his chest from which it ran unchecked to meet the water near his waist. He did this several times, then tilted his head back as if enraptured by the moon showering his body with soft light.

If he was conscious of the eyes running hungrily over his body, he did not reveal it. He gave himself over to his thoughts while methodically and mindlessly washing the day's sweat and labor from his skin.

N Zee carefully folded back the ends of the cloth she carried, took a small piece of the harmless-looking root from it and inserted it under her tongue. Quietly, so as not to startle Jackson, she eased from her hiding place to the spot where Jackson was bathing himself. Swallowing around the bitter root, she began to take off her clothes.

Thankfully, he was too absorbed in his thoughts to notice that she had dared to follow him to this idyllic spot. She knew about it but this was her first time here. It was ideal for what she had in mind, and Jackson couldn't have been in a better position.

Swallowing, her eyes drank in his naked splendor. He was hers! No one else would have him.

Her heart beat a little faster. This morning he had kissed the American woman. Had she been to this spot with Jackson? She lifted her head to the hanging moon as if she could find the answer she sought.

Fastening her eyes back on the man before her, she watched the way light danced over his broad shoulders and chest. Ripples stirred when she eased her bare feet into the cold water. Slight though they were, they were enough to garner Jackson's attention.

Spinning around, he poised to lunge for the handgun lying on top of his pants. Anger stiffened him when he recognized N Zee. "What are you doing here?" He glared his annoyance, struggling to keep a lid on his temper.

As naked as Jackson, N Zee's brown breasts jutted forth arrogantly. The water had yet to reach her upper thighs. She glided slowly Jackson's way, moonlight shimmering down her shapely body. She was beautiful to look at, Jackson conceded emotionlessly. As with any man, his body reacted to her, but on an emotional level she failed to move him.

"I want to speak to you." N Zee continued to close the distance separating them. When there were only inches to spare, she tucked the root more securely under her tongue and spoke around it.

"I want to come back and fight. You need every

man and woman. I am good at what I do." She stroked her hands up his arms and slanted her head at a provocative angle.

There was an undercurrent of desperation in N Zee's voice that Jackson could not ignore. Nor could he ignore the fact that she had disobeyed his orders to stay away until further notice. Not only had she followed him, she was in the water with him, nude! This one was much too bold and disruptive. This combination would eventually lead to a bad end.

He sighed wearily. The words she spoke were true. He needed her and despite everything, he admired her courage. N Zee knew better than any of them how to infiltrate security ranks and manipulate the police force. The votes had indicated all but a few wanted her back in the ranks. He, however, did not want her as she wanted him.

Standing here, both of them unclothed and her so close, he could feel the heat from her body. He was in a state of semi-hardness, while his mind was elsewhere. Yes, he could use N Zee to appease this gnawing hunger; she was eager for him. He would not do it, however. Too much was at stake.

"I will give it more consideration and have an answer for you soon." As an afterthought he asked, "How are you faring? Are you eating well?"

A jubilant smile crossed N Zee's lips. He cared

for her! He was just too stubborn and proud to admit it. She would see to it that he loved her as she did him. He most assuredly wanted her. His hardness bobbed in the water in the tiny space separating their bodies.

Her own flesh heated at the smooth texture of his skin under her fingertips as she continued to stroke his arms lovingly. Even if she could not see his eyes, she was confident that in their depths was the same hungry gleam that lurked in other men's eyes when they were on her, including Kimya's when he thought she was unaware. But N Zee was always aware of the effect she had on men and her power over them. Jackson was no different from the others when it came down to desiring a woman. He was just more adept at concealing his emotions.

Instead of answering his query, N Zee dragged her palms further up his arms until they rested on his shoulders. Leaning forward, her naked breasts grazed his chest. "I am not as well as I could be. If I had you, I could be very well," she whispered throatily. Standing on her toes on the soft wet bottom she boldly thrust her lower torso into his, grinding against his manhood.

Thrusting his hands below water level, Jackson clamped firm hands around N Zee's waist and shoved her from his body. "If you continue, I will not allow you back, no matter how much we need you."

His voice was heavy with censure.

N Zee's heart crashed and burned. Her countenance turned vicious. "Have you slept with the American?"

Disgust twisted Jackson's full lips. His light gold eyes became hooded. He'd had all he was going to take. "Leave, N Zee, now! Turning his back dismissively, he glided further into the water until it was at his stomach. He threw water into his face, hoping to cool his anger.

As best she could, N Zee stalked from the water. The root was useless if she couldn't get close enough to Jackson. Angry tears blurred her vision while she dried off.

She looked out across the stream at Jackson, who was so sure she would obey him, he faced away from her and continued leisurely bathing. For long seconds N Zee remained where she was, taming her temper as best she could.

He didn't fool her. Jackson wanted her. She'd had her proof when she leaned into him,   no matter how he protested otherwise. She wasn't through with Jackson Shugaa. And no one, absolutely no one, had better get in her way!

Most of the rebels were asleep when Jackson

returned to the campsite. Few lights were visible in tents, small huts and amidst trees. Entering his shelter, Jackson lit a candle and noted that there was no sign that Kimya was going to spend the night here.

Very well. He would look in on Katherine and sleep in this room. A warning nagged at him that N Zee might try to hurt Katherine again. He knew she'd been skulking around the fringes of the camp before coming to him tonight.

Reaching the room, Jackson paused at the foot of the platform bed. Katherine was talking in her sleep again. An arm was stretched out languidly, her fingers curled into a lax fist. Jackson inched nearer just as she turned onto her back. She seemed to be constantly revealing a tantalizing amount of skin while she slept, he concluded ironically, his eyes on the long brown leg exposed by the split in the skirt.

Opening her eyes halfway, Katherine peered up through sleepy lids. She held an arm out. "Jackson," she mumbled softly before it fell limply to her stomach.

Thoughts of sleeping in the other room evaporated. Dousing the candle, Jackson put it away, stripping to his undershorts in the dark. Lying on the small bed behind Katherine, he extended one arm above her head, and the other he slipped possessively around her waist. She scooted back, snuggling into his embrace. Her soft curls tickled his nose. A smile crossed his face.

Once Jackson thought he heard his name when Katherine spoke indistinctly in her sleep. He touched his lips to her shoulder, leaving a light kiss there. Kissing her earlobe, he lingered, enjoying her scent. "I will keep you safe, Katherine," he promised softly, sliding a hand down her bare arm. Drifting off to sleep, he added, "I must."

Chapter Eighteen

*A*n empty rumbling stomach brought Katherine to wakefulness. She lay still for long moments as memories of a hard body seared to her backside washed over her with astounding clarity. Her skin tingled even now.

After she rose, Rose brought maize and my ama cloma [barbequed goat meat] to her, insisting she eat a few bites, even though she had no appetite. Afterwards, she aimlessly wandered around the campsite.

The rebels returned in early evening and the sound of their laughter and voices distracted her for a while. Sitting in the doorway of the hut, she spotted the tall, broad-shouldered man Jackson called Kimya quietly observing the men and women. At first, Katherine had thought the taciturn man disliked her. Now she wasn't so sure. Since N Zee's attack on her, he'd always nodded to her when he was in her presence. As with Rose, she could detect no animosity from him, and she was beginning to feel at ease around him. Though he made no attempt to communicate with her, she suspected he knew English.

It was that other rebel, the one she'd met when she first entered the encampment, who gave her an uneasy feeling whenever he was near her. Like now. He was staring at her like a scavenger ready to pounce. Goose bumps rose along her arm in the warm evening air. Too nervous to sit any longer, she abandoned her seat and escaped inside.

Once there, she paced the tight area, asking herself the question uppermost in her mind since the rebels had returned. Where was Jackson? All day she'd anticipated his return, wanting him here with her more than she'd wanted him gone.

Finally, exhausted with disturbing thoughts and emotions, she collapsed onto the bed. The last coherent thought in her mind was that she was doing too much sleeping in this isolated place.

Sometime during the night she gradually became conscious of a hard body draped over hers. She attempted to sit up until a steel arm clamped around her.

"It's me, I am here Katherine," Jackson's deep voice informed her as she tried to lunge from the bed.

"What are you doing here?" she demanded in a reproachful tone. While it was true she'd wanted him to return to camp this evening, crawling into bed with her was quickly becoming an irritating habit of his. A dangerous one. Already her heart was galloping and her skin was beginning to tingle.

Long fingers spread over her hip, gently rubbing. Soft lips lightly touched behind her ear when he spoke. "You were sleeping restlessly. I wanted to be close if you had need of me during the night."

Katherine's senses leapt to life at the implication behind Jackson's words. Her hands clamped down on his for the purpose of removing them. Something intrinsic was telling her that if she gave in to this desire that was stalking her she would be lost forever.

"Jackson." Slender fingers lifted long, unresisting ones.

His lips grazed the slope of her shoulder. Desire shot to Katherine's very center. Her fingers curled around the hand she'd wanted to remove.

He palmed her round breasts and kneaded the sensitive nub with thumb and forefinger. "Jackson," Katherine moaned again, this time to urge him on. She pressed her buttocks back and Jackson's hot hard manhood pushed through his briefs against her hips.

A hand slid underneath her clothing, seeking the warm, moist, hidden treasure between her thighs. With her back still to him, Katherine lifted a leg to accommodate the knowledgeable hand and sighed in bliss when a finger slipped inside the tight opening. She reached a hand around her and grabbed his thigh, pressing tightly against him.

His finger moved inside her and Katherine was unable to stifle the moan in her throat. Her hips moved in tempo with his finger but she wanted more. She faced Jackson and wound her arms around his neck, drawing his head to hers. He claimed her lips, crushing her to him. His tongue delved deep as his hands did wondrous things to her body.

Drawing away, he made quick work of discarding their meager clothing. Katherine's hands boldly scaled Jackson's broad back, pausing to gently examine the healed scar. She wished it was turned toward her so that she could kiss it. Instead, she circled her soft hands over his tight buttocks. Jackson made a low moan in his throat before his lips closed over her nipple.

Katherine arched up off the bed, offering Jackson her breast, which he greedily took and suckled. The erotic action created an intense, almost painful constriction of her womb. Katherine was feverish, restless, burning up with desire. Her hand reached out for Jackson's maleness but he held both her hands to her sides as he paid identical homage to her other breast.

Nearly beside herself, Katherine's head thrashed back and forth on the bed. Her body had a mind of its own, she couldn't remain still. Jackson pressed kisses along the narrow, healing wound at her side. At last his mouth reclaimed her lips. Katherine drank in his sweet kisses and acknowledged that this was beyond mere seduction. Her mind and her body were on fire.

Even as her body reveled in Jackson's mastery over her senses, a small part of her resented him for it. But there was no time for recriminations. Jackson rose up and slid between her waiting thighs, eliciting a long sigh from Katherine. Biting her lips, she helped him ease into her tight opening.

His body jerked in surprise and she felt him staring down at her. Aware of the questions on his mind, she raised her hips high, offering him what they both wanted. As he inched further and deeper inside he called her name. "Katherine?"

She nodded to his unspoken question, then answered him verbally upon realizing he probably could not see her nod. "I'm all right, Jackson." To prove it, she scaled her long legs up his hips to

wrap around his waist. With slow seductive, circu-
lar movements, she showed him just how all right
she was as her lips sought out his.

Jackson moaned into her mouth, grinding her
hips down into the platform bed. Katherine hugged
him close, confident that he was experiencing the
same mind-blowing desire she was. Her legs
locked at the ankles, holding his pounding hips
close.

Thoughts flew from her mind. Her captivity was
forgotten. Every part of her body was alive, vibrant,
in tune with the man above her. Her inner thighs
started to quiver and Katherine had to bite her lips
a second time to keep from calling out as the soul-
destroying climax started to overtake her. It worked
its way to where she and Jackson were connected
and for one second her legs fell wide, so intense
was the emotion, and just as quickly they grappled
his thrusting hips.

Jackson's hands slid along her hypersensitive
body, grasping her hips as his lips closed around an
engorged nipple. Katherine felt as if she could not
bear any more of his sensual onslaught. Yet, her
mind resisted the inevitable culmination the
moment their bodies stiffened and the frenzied climax exploded between them, thrusting them both
over the top.

Jackson dragged Katherine's spent body atop

his, where she collapsed, breathing shallowly. His hands caressed the sides of her breasts down to her waist and hips. He kissed each cooling shoulder and finally her forehead, which was nestled under his chin.

Curled in Jackson's embrace, Katherine was as content as a well fed cat. She absolutely felt like purring. Any words used to describe what had just transpired between them would be too trite, too much of a cliché.

"Uuummm." Good Lord, had she just purred? Too spent to care, her eyes closed.

"Do you and your fiancé not make love?"

"What?" Katherine's eyes popped open.

"I said," Jackson repeated as though speaking to a child, "do you and that American fiancé of yours make love?"

For long seconds Katherine was speechless. How dare he bring Alex into this after she'd done such a good job of putting everyone of importance in her life to the back of her mind. Her temper flared. "None of your business." She tried to roll off Jackson's chest but was hindered by the hand at her hip.

Undaunted by Katherine's tone and stiff form, Jackson spoke thoughtfully. "I only ask because your body is not used to making love."

"Oh, and you're such an expert?" Katherine

replied sarcastically. Her inability to suppress the shivers in her stomach when Jackson's hands grazed over the round smoothness of her backside to settle her more firmly atop him fed her annoyance.

"I did not say that," the low voice rumbled lazily near her ear. "But I do know when a woman is versed in the art of making love. You were not and you were clearly surprised by the things happening to your body. Not only that, you have not made love often."

Searching for an insult in Jackson's statement, Katherine leveled him a stare in the darkness. Finding none, she failed to find his cocky assumption comforting. While it was true she and Alex didn't have sex often because she found it sorely lacking and a bit untidy, it wasn't anyone's business but her own. And besides, Alex never complained.

A hand nudged her shoulder. "Admit it, kipenzi changu [my love]."

"I'll admit nothing of the kind. And what did you call me?"

Instead of answering. Jackson slipped a hand behind her head, dragging it close so that his lips could capture hers in a heady, drugging kiss. His hand unerringly sought out her warm haven. In the midst of the fire spreading through her loins, she berated herself for responding so mindlessly to this arrogant man's ministrations.

Of course she didn't know a lot about amour. How else could Jackson bring her body to a fever pitch in the blink of an eye so soon after their intense lovemaking? Her own hands glided up his sides to wrap around his shoulders as her head dipped to capture one of his nipples in her mouth. She would not remain inexperienced for long, she thought as Jackson's moan reached her ears. Her legs fell on each side of his raised hips, grinding against that hard, boneless flesh, eliciting a tense hiss from deep within Jackson. Before succumbing completely to the erotic cloud, she promised herself that though Jackson could work wonders with her body, he would never know her complete mind. And she would enjoy the ride for all it was worth.

The camp was in deep sleep when N Zee entered. Snoring and intermittent groaning punctuated the damp air as her stealthy footsteps tramped the packed earth. "Oh yes, Jackson Shugaa has met his match," she intoned to the quiet, early morning.

While everyone was asleep she would slip into his bed naked and seduce him. She snickered confidently, thinking it would not take much seduction. Not after seeking him out at the stream earlier tonight. Jackson wanted her, no matter how hard he tried to deny it. A shiver of longing and anticipation coursed through her. He would be hers as she was already his. All that was needed was one kiss! She once more tucked the root under her tongue.

Why had she not thought of a plan such as this before? Her answer was quick in coming. Because the opportunity had never arisen. She'd been too fearful of Jackson's wrath and possible rejection. Rejection didn't sit well with her because the shoe had always been on the other foot. She'd been the one to do the rejecting. But now she was desperate. An inner voice urged her to make her move quickly.

She strode quietly into the shelter, allowing her eyes to become accustomed to the darkness before cautiously moving further into the room. There was no one sleeping here. Her heart thumped loudly in her ears. All indications were that Kimya was spending his hours of rest elsewhere. Where was Jackson spending his?

Apprehension eroded her earlier confidence. She fought the implications of Jackson's absence from the room. The man she knew would not break tradition to be with the American. He would not!

Standing in front of the lopsided door, N Zee was struck with a rare case of nerves. If her heart would only settle, she could concentrate on what she was about to do. Praying, she shuffled closer to the door.

What was that? Movement, voices? Jackson speaking soft, indistinguishable words? N Zee pressed a fist to her open mouth and leaned as close to the door as she dared. A soft murmured reply from a woman, the American! Then N Zee heard the tell-tale moans coming from man and woman.

Shock forced her back until she was at the entrance. Hot tears scorched her face, blinding her. Her teeth bit into her knuckles so hard the skin split. Unmindful of the pain, N Zee whirled out of the door in despair.

Nooooo! she soundlessly screamed. Ye ye ni wangu [He is mine]! Ye ye ni wangu [He is mine]! Rage literally consumed her, shaking her frame. She must go into the city tonight. She must stop this before it was too late. "You will not have him!" N Zee spewed furiously as she left the sleeping camp behind. "He is mine! I will see you in hell first, American!"

∞∞∞

There was no need for Jackson to glance at the watch on his arm to know that it was nearing early morning. Time for him to rise soon. He was the leader. He didn't have the luxury of taking days off. Today would be no exception.

Except that Katherine's curvaceous body was draped over his. A long leg nestled between his corded thighs, slender fingers were curved over his shoulder and supple breasts were pressed into his chest. Though deep, even breaths signaled that she was asleep, Jackson stared down into the outline of her lovely face.

He curved an arm over her back, snuggling her to his lean form even as a frown rumpled his brow. The endearment he'd uttered in the aftermath of passion loomed large. Katherine had not understood the Swahili words but demanded to know what they were. He had successfully distracted her. People said all sorts of things when they were making love, he reasoned. He brushed that concern away to grapple with another.

Had someone been in here, outside the door earlier? He'd been too enraptured with Katherine to pull himself away to investigate. Kenya needed him. He needed Kenya. Nothing and no one had ever kept him from his duty before. Irritation furrowed black brows. He was a warrior and a rebel first and foremost.

When he shifted, Katherine instinctively burrowed deeper into his chest. He was a man who never yielded to desire when matters involving his country were at stake. His lips feathered over her cool forehead; his nose inhaled her feminine fragrance. Katherine stirred, purring his name, her arms reaching for him in her sleep. He would get up, he promised himself. Just a few more minutes of this thing called indulgence.

∞∞∞

Easing onto her back, Katherine stretched long limbs like a sated feline. Slowly her eyes focused on the trail of weak light forcing its way through the hole—she could not call it a window—in the wall. Smaller shafts of light beamed through the cracks in the wood.

Jackson had left the bed long ago. It was probably late, but at the moment Katherine didn't care. She wanted to lie here and luxuriate in the emotions that had overwhelmed her earlier. Her mind burned with the memory of Jackson's touch, arousing her, consuming her.

Her body reacted immediately to the seductive, vivid recollection and her heart raced. A stream of longing swept over her. On the heels of desire a warning rang in her head. To indulge in such meandering was not good for her peace of mind.

Throwing her legs over the bed, she sat upright, dragging fingers through her tangled strands. The mass needed a thorough shampooing. Maybe she could convince Rose to take her to the small stream of water where they washed dishes. The thought of Rose taking her to the stream where she and Jackson had bathed never crossed her mind. Instinctively she knew that the place was off limits to others in the camp.

Untangling the strands as best she could, she twisted her hair into a thick knot at the base of her head. Slapping her palms briskly on her thighs, she stood and dressed. She was hungry, starved. She was willing to eat almost anything Rose put in front of her this morning.

A shock greeted her when she reached the outside. The camp was empty. Rose was nowhere in sight. It was much later than she had assumed. She and Jackson had rested little after he'd come to bed, and when she finally was able to sleep, she'd slept deeply.

"Well." She settled her hands on her hips and gazed unbelievingly around once more. They were truly confident in themselves and their surroundings to leave her alone. After indulging in 'what ifs,' Katherine shrugged a shoulder. She wasn't going anywhere. She knew it and so did Jackson. She wanted to leave but she wanted to reach Nairobi intact.

Food was uppermost on her mind. She returned inside, hoping she had overlooked something in her rush to get outside. She spied the covered bowl resting on the log in the corner. It was still warm. The efficient Rose had been in earlier.

Katherine took the bowl outside with her. The animal sounds were dying away. At that moment Katherine was cognizant of how alone she was. It was unnerving. Her appetite had diminished but she was able to eat some of the porridge. She smacked her lips trying to identify the sweet taste. Honey? It was the first time she'd eaten it since arriving here. The honey made the boiled cereal somewhat palatable.

She was of a mind to go in search of Rose but squelched the notion after realizing she had a chance to do some exploring on her own. There were so many trails leading in so many different directions it was downright confusing. What if she stumbled upon some dangerous, uncharted territory—at least for her.

Her attention was caught by the trail along the side of the hut. The packed earth yielded up many foot prints disappearing into the thicket.

Her mind was made up. She hurried along the path before she was missed and someone came along to stop her. She wanted to see with her own eyes what it was everyone did each and every morning. What Jackson did.

"Head up!" Jackson feinted to Adam's left before taking a quick, deceptive step back. The heavily muscled rebel charged, his expression menacing, his arms folded, elbows thrust outward to ram into Jackson's chest. Crouching low, Jackson threw a strong leg between the charging warrior's own. Adam went tumbling forward as Jackson agilely stood and brought the butt of the SKS 56 up under his chin, knocking the smirk from his face.

The blow landed hard enough to knock the rebel onto his back. Blood flowed from the cut under his chin. Crouched over Adam, Jackson's cold eyes pinned him to the ground.

"That was a foolish move," he growled, unrepentant for the pain he'd caused. A move like that in battle would get the man killed. "You must watch your enemy at all times. Do not underestimate a cornered man or woman. Never become overconfident, no matter how much of an advantage you think you have!" The curt voice continued to lash out at the prone man. "A cornered animal will fight to the death to escape, to be free. So will most humans."

A tense silence reigned as dozens of pairs of eyes watched their tall, lean leader straddle the hapless rebel. All could tell Adam wanted to rise but was held steadfast by the look in Jackson's eyes. Sweat coursed down the sides of his face and over his wide forehead to mingle with the blood flowing onto the neck of the army green shirt. His rifle lay useless on the ground by his side.

Speaking calmly, Kimya entered the semicircle of rebels gathered around the two men. "You have learned a valuable lesson today, Adam. Take it to heart." Kimya stuck out an arm to drag the rebel to his feet. He leaped up quickly, retrieving his rifle. "Wash your face. Think on what you've learned. In twenty minutes come back ready to conquer the enemy."

With as much bravado as he could muster, Adam shrugged from under Kimya's helping hand. He cast a belligerent glance somewhere in the area of Jackson's chest but quickly turned away, unable to withstand the glacial glare directed at his bowed head.

"Break time," Kimya interjected. Sighs of relief could be heard as small groups of men and women huddled together speaking in hushed tones, surreptitiously eying the pair in the center of the fighting area. Quiet, nervous laugher reached Jackson's and Kimya's ears.

"Is something wrong?" Kimya watched his friend with open concern. He was unusually tense and spoiling for a confrontation. None of the men would accept the challenge. Jackson was a lethal and deadly fighter.

Struggling to find an answer, Jackson averted his head from his astute friend. This morning during their practice sessions he'd made several slips with his opponent. That they were so minor only he noticed was of little matter. The fact was that in battle a miscalculation or misstep, no matter how trivial, could be the cause of instant death.

He'd been distracted, his thoughts not on current events. There was a craving inside him that was raging out of control although his sexual appetite had been appeased, momentarily. He never should have touched Katherine! Not giving his undivided attention to what was happening in front of him angered him to the point that he was determined to get back his momentum.

He'd fought each succeeding opponent methodically, coldly ferocious and without feeling. He'd disposed of each one of them in less time than it took to assume an attack stance. Adam was the last rebel brave enough to come forward to challenge him.

"Is it the American? Is Katherine not well?" Kimya inquired after Jackson failed to answer. The look Jackson gave him would have humbled a lesser man. Kimya was not intimidated.

"Katherine must be returned."

Lifting a brow, Kimya folded his arms across his massive chest. That fact was a moot point. "Our sources have already told us that her uncle is making frantic inquires as to her whereabouts. He is also requesting additional help from his state department. In a day, maybe two, she will be returned as discreetly as possible."

"I will return her," Jackson replied sharply.

Kimya did not argue. He wagged his head, wondering if the captive was at the root of Jackson's attitude. He regarded his friend closely. A jolt rocketed through Kimya. Jackson was sleeping with the woman! It was so against everything they believed in. Apprehension filled him. His concern ran deeper than Jackson's sleeping with Katherine, much deeper.

"I will return shortly." Abruptly Jackson left his friend standing alone as he stomped off into the trees. He didn't know where he was headed, only that he needed to get away to think, to clear his head and devise a plan to get Katherine to her family without incident. That was what was uppermost in his mind: Katherine!

Katherine was lost. Inexplicably lost. She'd been wandering around in uncharted areas for an hour, two? She'd lost track of time long ago.

Fool! What did it matter how long? She didn't know where she was, had no idea how to get back to camp and would probably remain lost. The animals and insects would have a feast on her body. She cringed at the thought, then threw back her shoulders in an attempt to muster some of that Wellington courage.

Nosiness had gotten her into this fix. Pure and simple. She had wanted to find out where Jackson and the others went each day. At first she followed the many footprints without a problem. Then, without warning, the path literally disappeared. Wild brush and saplings grew everywhere, plunging Katherine into a gloomy darkness.

Before Katherine knew it was happening, she was too deep into the brush to find her way out. She made a couple of aborted attempts that led her nowhere. Everywhere everything looked the same. She couldn't find any distinguishing marks to tell if she'd been in an area before.

"Circles." The soulful Atlantic Starr tune played over and over in her head. An hysterical giggle bubbled forth. She slammed her hand over her mouth lest she draw the attention of some wild animal lurking in the underbrush. True, she'd not encountered one during her stay here, but what were all of those strange noises she heard each morning?

Something was crawling up her naked leg! Katherine yelped and jumped as if she were standing on hot coals. Eyes squeezed shut, she batted at the thing sticking to her skin. A tiny furry body brushed under her palm. Shrieking in disgust and terror, she knocked it loose and spurted into a wild run. She wasn't easily intimidated but when it came to crawly things, she was a coward.

Branches and vines clawed at her, scratching her skin. She didn't care. Tears of frustration filled her eyes when she felt a slimy textured insect stinging her arm. Katherine furiously batted it away, and immediately the spot began to itch. She tensely inspected her body from head to foot to make sure nothing else was hiding on her. Once she was sure she was critter free, she took stock of her new surroundings.

Chapter Nineteen

Because of the nagging feeling he'd had that something was wrong with Katherine, Jackson had slipped away from the practice site a few minutes earlier than everyone else. When he entered the campsite it was unusually quiet and Rose was nowhere to be seen. His temper soared. Rose had been given explicit instructions not to wake Katherine but to keep an eye on her. Surely she was up by now. He looked inside the shelter.

On his way out, he spied the empty bowl on the ground. Was Katherine with Rose? N Zee's attack loomed large in his mind.

"Where is she?" Jackson barked just as Rose stepped into the clearing.

"Jackson," Rose breathed nervously. Dismay darkened her eyes and she swallowed convulsively. She had hoped to locate that willful American before their leader's return. How had she managed to rise and slip away so quickly? Rose was only gone long enough to assure herself that Victor was resting well after an unusually restless night.

Resentment filled her even as fear quaked her bones at the scowl Jackson wore. If he'd allowed the American to be awakened at a reasonable hour instead of insisting she rest as long as she wanted, Rose could have taken her with her while she tended to her other tasks.

After all, she was only one woman with only two hands! None of these thoughts Rose spoke out loud. "I had to leave for a short period to see about Victor. He did not have a good night last night," she explained, despising the tremor in her voice. "I returned to find the empty bowl and the woman gone."

Without waiting to hear more, Jackson's rapid strides carried him beyond the shelter in the direction of the thicket. Rose sped after him, anxiety causing her to stutter. "I went to...to the stream where...I took her to bathe...to bathe thinking she may have found her way...way there." She was running to keep pace with Jackson's long legs.

"Stay here in case she returns," he instructed

without breaking his stride or glancing her way.

"But I need to gather the food for the noon meal. And Victor," she protested.

"We will not starve if a meal is late," he snapped, "and you recently returned from Victor."

Color and movement caught Kimya's attention a heartbeat before he lifted a powerful leg to step over a fallen tree. His eyes widened at the sight of Katherine staring as if in shock at a small sapling a short distance from her.

Her state looked worse than the day she'd first entered camp. Her clothing was badly torn and plastered to her body from the brief but heavy downpour that had pelted the forest less than ten minutes before. Her wraparound skirt hung from her waist, its back hem dragging the ground, and her thin blouse sagged in pieces off her shoulders. Her hair hung about her face in wet clumps. Her expression was one of misery mixed with sheer terror.

Kimya took in the situation at a glance and eased into the path of clearing. When he was within inches of Katherine, he spoke her name softly.

Katherine was paralyzed into immobility. She had come within a hair's breath of clamping her hand down on a snake blended into the dark branch of the small tree, its slinky lower body entwined around its fragile trunk. Its head was raised, as if ready to strike. A cold, reptilian eye was fixed on Katherine while its black, forked tongue worked its way in and out of its mouth, testing the air.

Kimya beckoned with his hand and instructed in heavily accented English, "Move slow to me. It more afraid of you than you of it."

Terrorized, Katherine took no notice that this was the first time Kimya had spoken directly to her or that he was using broken English. Her throat muscles convulsed and her doubt showed on her face when she chanced a sideways glance at Kimya. Inhaling deeply, she gathered courage and obeyed his instructions. Inch by inch, Katherine slunk out of striking distance of the snake that kept an unblinking eye on her. Apparently tiring of its vigil, the snake glided down the tree to the ground, submerging itself under the loose leaves and noise-lessly slithering away into the brush.

Katherine lunged into Kimya's arms, unmindful of the long, curved knife at his side. "Oh God. I thought I had seen the last of you all. Never thought I would be so glad to see the face of one of my cap-tors again." She curved her arm around Kimya's wide shoulders and held on for dear life. Hesitatingly, Kimya's arms circled her waist, absorbing the tremors racking her body.

"I got lost trying to find out where you all go every day. Before I knew it, I was walking around in circles. You know the song "Circles" by the R & B group Atlantic Starr?" Leaning away, Katherine peered up into Kimya's puzzled expression.

"No, you don't." She laughed, on the verge of hysterical relief. Hugging Kimya close, she babbled once more. "I kept seeing green. Have you noticed that the color green is everywhere? If I never see a shade of green again it will be too soon. Nosey. That's what I am. I got hot and sticky. There was no room to breathe. Little creatures were crawling all over me, sliming me, biting, stinging." She shivered and raised her arm, endeavoring to peer at the still itching flesh of her underarm. "See here." Dropping her arm, she didn't give Kimya a chance to look. "I hate it here. I thought I was going to die. Lost forever until the animals devoured my very bones."

Filled with wonder at the incessant chatter, Kimya ran his hands lightly over Katherine's back to assure himself she was fine. The slight-looking American had a firm grip around his neck, holding on for dear life. He would allow it until she came to her senses. Shivers continued to rack her body. He could only imagine the terrible images rampaging across her mind at the prospect of not being found. How on earth did she get away from Rose?

"Katherine, Kimya."

The quiet, cool, unexpected voice propelled Katherine deeper into Kimya's arms. Both heads swivelled in Jackson's direction as he entered the clearing with a rifle slung across one shoulder and a look on his face that had Katherine shrinking in Kimya's hold.

Though Kimya did not immediately release Katherine, his hold around her narrow waist loosened. Katherine's arms continued to cling tightly to him.

Jackson's eyes were expressionless, but his sensual lips were thinned into a narrow line as he closed in on them. Kimya eased his arms from around Katherine, firmly setting her away from him.

Uncertainty lit her dark brown eyes, as Katherine stared at Jackson. She couldn't tell if he was glad he'd found her with Kimya, unharmed or what. The way he was looking at her she thought she might be better off staying with Kimya.

"Cover yourself," Jackson ordered roughly. He slammed the butt of the gun on the ground near his legs. With a swift movement, he shrugged out of his shirt, leaving him in a damp tee shirt, and shoved it at Katherine, who grasped it with shaky fingers.

Only now as she slipped the big shirt on was

she conscious of the way her clothes hung off her. Embarrassment caused her to cringe at the way she'd clung to Kimya. She held up apologetic eyes to him. After all, he'd been nothing but comforting. He faced Jackson, speaking in Swahili.

"I became concerned when you slipped away without a word. I came in search of you in case you needed to talk." Kimya's tone was calm, unhurried. "I discovered Katherine lost on this path, trying to locate our practice site. She was terrified of a snake when I found her and soaking wet. I believe she is unharmed."

Jackson ran his eyes over Katherine from foot to head. The wariness on her face as she shrank back and watched him with large eyes caused his lips to tighten and his expression to darken. It did not help his temperament to know he'd put that look there.

He'd never experienced a relief so great as when he spotted the beautiful American with his friend. The other emotions that rode fast upon the heels of relief were alien to him as well. Unwilling to accept and acknowledge anything but anger, he lashed out in English.

"Katherine, that was stupid thing for you to do, to leave camp without any idea of where you were going or how to return. You're one arrogant woman, with a head made of solid rock. You have no concept of the trouble you cause others." Jackson's impudent stare dared Katherine to dispute his assertion.

Seething with self-righteous indignation at the condescending tone, Katherine countered icily, "I may be a lot of things in your estimation, but stupid is not one of them. After I located you I was going back to camp. How was I to know that your foot-prints would disappear like...like..." As her voice trailed off, her shoulders reared back proudly, her chin jutted mutinously, and she folded one arm over the other, glaring her distaste at Jackson.

"I will see you back at camp, Kimya," Jackson addressed his friend, his penetrating glance leveled on Katherine.

Kimya watched the pair in silence for long seconds. His attention shifted to the slender American. He had no doubt she could take care of herself. Neither one was aware of him leaving the area.

"Don't call me stupid, Jackson," Katherine said tightly.

"You were foolish to leave camp alone for any purpose," Jackson amended slightly. He closed the distance between them and Katherine flinched, yet stood her ground. Jackson's eyes narrowed at her reaction but otherwise he spoke in a normal voice. "You are unharmed?" The hand he raised to Katherine's face fell to his side as she stepped out of his path, answering him stiffly.

"I am."

Jackson slung his gun onto his shoulder and gave Katherine his back. What if N Zee were lurking somewhere in these woods? He could not bear the thought of what could have happened to Katherine. His rage was self-directed for not taking better care of her.

Scowling at Jackson's rigid back, Katherine stuck her tongue out. The gesture was childish but it afforded her some satisfaction. As she stretched her legs to keep pace with his long strides, she knew he had reason to be angry with her, though she'd never admit it to him. Still, his coldness stung.

∞∞∞

No more. Not another step. It was like walking on the trail with N Zee and David. Katherine would not go another step. She was too tired to care if she made it back to camp before nightfall. If this was Jackson's punishment for her leaving camp, he was succeeding all too well. He had been merciless in the way he'd pushed her in the past hour.

She had to run to keep up with him along the narrow trail. If she slowed, he did not decrease his pace. He never assured himself that she was behind him, though he knew she must be from the noise she made.

He broke branches, snapped limbs and cleared the path he traveled. Still, vines and limbs tore at her tender skin. Well, this girl had had enough! If Jackson was upset at her, fine. But she'd be damned if she'd walk any further at this pace without taking five.

Right here she would remain, in this relatively clear spot. As the thicket swallowed up his wide shoulders, she waited for Jackson to return for her. She knew he would. He was too contrary not to come back and punish her some more.

She wasn't disappointed when he tracked back within seconds of missing her. Legs wide apart, he shot Katherine an accusing glance. Before he could launch into an angry tirade, Katherine struck a relaxed pose and asked in a sultry voice, "What's your hurry, big boy?" She knew by the expression on his face Jackson failed to find the humor in her question.

Losing the nonchalant air, Katherine retorted, "You're killing me, Jackson. I can barely keep up. How can you be so cruel, so unfeeling?" She was amazed at his callousness, especially after all that they'd shared. "Especially after..."

Raw emotion shook her voice. Jackson had been so tender and loving when they made love that the remembered passion they'd both shared caused her stomach to churn. He looked at her now as if he'd never seen her before.

"Especially after what, Katherine?"

Especially after you made me melt in your arms again and again, she intoned silently. The silky cadence in his voice didn't fool her. I mean nothing to you, nothing! And she was a fool to wish or think otherwise. All she was, was a means to an end in this isolated place. "Go slower, please." Her eyes held her appeal.

Long strides brought him to her side. He stood so close Katherine felt the heat from his body. Golden brown eyes scanned her face. He touched a palm to her damp brow, stroking over high cheek-bones to firmly grasp her chin in his fingers. Katherine wanted to remain unmoved but her insides turned over.

"Are you unwell?"

"No, but I will be if you keep up this pace." She gave him a brief, ironic smile which he did not return.

Shifting the rifle to his shoulder, Jackson picked Katherine up in his strong arms before she could protest. She was nestled against his expansive chest and could feel his muscles ripple as he moved. Her eyes were liquid brown pools. "You intend to carry me all the way to camp?"

Instead of answering, Jackson stared down at

her skeptical expression.

Swinging around in the trail, Jackson began the lengthy trek back to camp. His features remained grim all the way. Exhausted, Katherine wasn't about to look a gift horse in the mouth.

Chapter Twenty

ackson and Katherine reached the campsite after the rebels had returned to the afternoon drill session. Rose and Kimya were quietly waiting to greet them. Katherine squirmed out of Jackson's arms the second they hit familiar ground. Rose was the first one to speak.

"I'm glad she is back unharmed." Her expression revealed immense relief. She touched a cool, impersonal palm to Katherine's forehead. Satisfied, she stared past Jackson's chest to his face, which had lost some of its harshness.

A spurt of jealously shot through Katherine at the woman's soft expression. Katherine was so surprised at the unexpected emotion, she averted her face. She heard Rose speaking from far away and knew she was being scolded. "What are you saying?" she asked no one in particular, turning a cautious eye to the diminutive woman.

"She said it was a foolish thing you did," Jackson answered succinctly.

"What else?" Katherine snapped, not liking the woman's description of her but resigned to it.

"That it is a good thing it was me who came to look for you."

Ears attuned for smugness or conceit, Katherine glared her hostility at the pair.

"I don't need another lecture—from either of you. In English or Swahili," Katherine responded, hackles raised. With a jerky motion she pulled off Jackson's shirt that was full of his scent and thrust it at him.

"I got enough of a tongue lashing and cold treatment from you back there. What I would like is a bath, preferably hot, and to be left alone."

Fire, pure and golden, lit Jackson's eyes. It did not matter if Rose did not understand most of Katherine's words. She understood body language. This audaciousness would not do.

Katherine held her ground while inwardly cringing at the searing look in Jackson's eyes. Stomach quaking, pores sweaty, Katherine compressed her lips, wisely refraining from speaking. It was true she was a captive but she wasn't a robot. She was no shrinking violet either.

The sound of Rose sucking her teeth gave Katherine a chance to pull her eyes from the scorching draw of Jackson's. She read Rose's expression as well. It said, "Don't push it."

Leveling his unblinking stare at Katherine, Jackson spoke in a blistering, rapid tone to Rose. Whatever he said caused the woman to blanch and drop her eyes to the ground. Finished, he left the two women standing before the shelter.

Despite her circumstances, Katherine's heart went out to the tiny woman. It was plain to see she was struggling with her own pain from whatever Jackson said. And it was obvious from the way her eyes trailed after the retreating back, she was in love with him.

Confused about her own response to Jackson, Katherine held out a tentative hand to Rose's shoulder. Whatever her own feelings were about Jackson, they couldn't be everlasting. She was soon to leave this place. She shoved her stupid jealously aside, admonishing herself that she had no reason to exhibit any animosity towards Rose. Though not friendly, the woman had treated her like a human being.

Avoiding the gesture, Rose gave a negative shake of her head. Her chest heaved with a long sigh. She pointed toward the shelter, indicating that

Katherine was to go inside.

She didn't want to go inside. Katherine wasn't sure what she wanted at that moment. Sensing resistance, Rose tugged on her arm. "Inside, go. Inside!"

Katherine decided to give up the battle before it began. She had caused the woman enough problems for one day.

Inside, she slumped down on the platform bed. She drifted off to sleep and dreamed of the jungle. Of being lost in it and of being chased by a cheetah, powerful, and deadly. She was running, running away from danger to safety always just beyond her reach. Somewhere along the endless dense trail, a lion joined in the chase.

Chancing a hurried glance over her shoulder was her undoing. The look in the lion's golden eyes impaled her. Her palms started to itch and her heart to thunder. He would get her, the lion's eyes promised. No matter how far or how fast she ran. She would be his to devour as he wished. Already he was rapidly gaining on her.

Her heart in her throat, mouth open wide in a scream of protest or capitulation, Katherine woke on the narrow bed, sweating profusely. Holding a hand to her pounding chest, she jerked up with relief.

Someone had lit a lamp in the room. Jackson?

Was that a tub standing near the wall? Katherine approached the metal object. It was the same small tub she'd bathed in her first night here. And it was half-filled with water.

Bending, Katherine dipped two fingers, then her entire hand into the water. Not hot, but pleasant to her skin. There was that sweet smelling soap on top of a towel which sat on a pile of clothes on the log. A plastic comb with a few missing teeth was included also.

Katherine didn't take the time to question the origin of these simple items but stripped off her drenched clothing and got into the water. Unable to lean back comfortably, her head lolled forward as she washed her hair as best she could, then soaped her body, reveling in the cooling moisture on her skin.

Male and female voices reached her ears. The rebels were back. Which meant it was evening. This day was practically shot. The sameness of the days was beginning to fray her nerves.

Vestiges of the dream echoed in her mind. An image of Jackson, dark, disturbing and persistent, chased away whatever calm she'd managed to summon.

Finished with her bath, she got out of the tub, dried off and dressed. She sat on the low bed and began to comb her hair. Katherine luxuriated in the feel of the tangles coming undone, at the smooth silkiness of the strands sliding between her fingers. She was at last beginning to feel human.

Jackson entered the room as she was combing her hair. His eyes flickered from Katherine to the stroke of her arms in the air above her head. The lamplight danced over her skin, highlighting the slant of her upturned breasts that pushed the thin fabric away from her chest. His eyes roamed down her arms, across her breasts, past her hips, sliding down her outstretched legs to her naked feet propped up on the bed.

What had started out a pleasant task became a torturous ordeal with Jackson standing there, looking at her the way he was. Katherine wished that he would say something, anything to ease this tension he brought into the room with him. He finally broke visual contact and crossed the small space to rummage in the burlap sack. She wanted to tuck her legs but didn't. Jackson made her as nervous as a cornered cat but she refused to show it.

She watched him from under her lashes. He was an imposing man. And he was sexy, sexy, sexy. That was it in a nutshell. Katherine doubted he had a clue to the effect he had on a woman or if he even cared.

She could almost hate him for his indifference in all things. In an instant her emotions shifted gears.

She could feel a lot of strong emotions for Jackson but never hate. If he had turned to her at that moment, Jackson would have seen what was in her heart written on her face. But he barely acknowledged her with a backwards glance as he left the room. It was then that Katherine realized she had been holding her breath. She quickly braided her hair in one long plait. All of the enjoyment had gone out of the act.

Two male rebels came into the room to get the tub. One of them was the man who had rubbed himself in the obscene manner two days ago. Katherine was uncomfortable in his presence and her guard immediately went up. He blocked Katherine's rush to exit the room by innocently stumbling in front of her and sloshing water from the tub as a deterrent.

His partner struggled to right the tub, snapping at the leering man. His tongue rolled suggestively across his thin lips. Katherine swallowed her disgust, contempt showing on her face. She couldn't let this man know how much he bothered her. He would never leave her alone. He was as much a threat to her as N Zee.

She waited long after the two had left before venturing outside. The camp was a bustle of activity and excitement permeated the air. Candles and lamps were lit in every shelter. Men and women were clustered in small groups speaking in animated tones. Katherine became conscious of something else. Instead of relaxing and removing their practice clothes, they were still dressed in them and all had weapons of some sort at their sides. By now Katherine was accustomed to the guns and knives each carried, though she was uneasy at their significance.

Intermittently one of the rebels would glance her way, then back to Jackson who sat huddled with Kimya far enough away that Katherine could not hear their conversation.

Both dark heads were huddled together in intense conversation. Katherine couldn't tell anything from Jackson's sharp profile but Kimya's usually staid features were visibly upset.

"Either let her back in with us or dismiss her. Don't leave her wandering aimlessly in the jungle." It wasn't often that Kimya expressed his displeasure so vocally or strongly.

In heavy silence Jackson contemplated his friend's words. He was right. He had to make a decision concerning N Zee's time of return.

Their funds for bribery were depleted. They needed someone who could distract the guards in town before the raid. N Zee was that person. He shifted his focus from Kimya to Katherine, who happened to be looking his way at that moment.

Their eyes caught and held. Something passed between them that Jackson refused to acknowledge. He answered, his focus remaining on Katherine. "She can come back," he conceded. "She may go to Nakuru with the others to participate in the raid." He chuckled dryly. "I am sure she is already aware of all of the details." His vivid eyes flashed a warning. "If she causes more trouble, she will be banished, forever. And," he added ominously, "she will suffer the consequences if she injures anyone."

The blunt admonition rang loud and clear in Kimya's ears. There was no mistaking the meaning behind it. He followed the direction of Jackson's gaze. That anyone was the American, Katherine. N Zee must be very careful. Her jealously would be her undoing if she continued this one-sided war with Katherine. He would personally see to it that she caused no more mischief. His heart beat with relief and he could not hold back the pleasure that lit his eyes. She would be back!

She must give up this obsession she had of capturing Jackson Shugaa and look for happiness elsewhere. He would see to that also. His days of patience were nearing an end. N Zee would be made to realize that loving his friend was useless.

The small light burned bright in the campsite and men and women buzzed around in a casual fashion. Katherine watched some of them disappear into the forbidding foliage, piquing her curiosity, while others went into their tents or one person huts.

As she watched the rebels, the fine hairs suddenly stood up on the back of her neck. Pivoting to the left she looked into the insolent eyes of that worrisome man, Adam. He was sitting across from her on the ground, his legs resting close to her log. His eyes were constantly on her when he was in camp. Katherine shivered. Instinctively she knew he was trouble.

Maybe she should say something to Jackson about the man. Her eyes shifted from him to Jackson who was paying attention to something Kimya was saying. She chanced another glance at the man who, surprisingly, dropped his eyes and was pretending interest in the gun in his lap.

Katherine immediately saw the reason why. Jackson's eyes were concentrated on her once more. His eyes stroked her, initiating fresh sensations to spiral up and down her spine. She found it increasingly difficult to concentrate on anyone or anything but him. She couldn't even conjure up a picture of Alex, though she tried.

She was struggling against her desires, her

longing and it was a battle she was losing, badly. Unable to bear the train of her thoughts, honest though they might be, she twisted her eyes away from Jackson's compelling hold. Misery filled her being. Her abduction was not some TV script for a movie of the week, where the handsome, dangerous hero seduced the beautiful, irresistible heroine into loving him and everyone lived happily ever after. This situation was all too real with very real, dangerous players destined to a doomed conclusion. She believed that to the bottom of her soul.

Abruptly she stood, bobbing the heavy log and drawing Jackson's curious eyes to her slim figure. She went inside, refusing to acknowledge him any more tonight.

Weary at heart she settled on the bed and closed her eyes. She didn't expect to sleep, especially when she couldn't banish Jackson from her thoughts. As she tossed and turned, Katherine realized this was a fight she was sure to lose.

∞∞∞

Jackson's impatience was growing but no one could tell it by looking at him. He listened as Kimya discussed details for the impending raid, leaning on his elbows, his long legs out-stretched. His eyes fell on the map his friend drew in the dirt, then shifted back to the spot Katherine had recently left. He answered all of Kimya's questions lucidly, responded to his comments with statements of his own and made a major change concerning the entrance of attack.

Concluding for the night, Kimya announced that he was going for a late night swim. It was the only way to work off some of the tension, he added. Jackson surmised that he meant to seek N Zee out and let her know of Jackson's decision. He'd come to the conclusion that his friend was in love with the willful woman and silently wished him luck.

He remained where he was until the activity around him came to a standstill. There was an explosive desire simmering within him that, instead of taking him to its source, held him rooted where he was.

The door to the shelter was standing wide, the inside dark. He'd waited in vain for the flicker of flames after Katherine's hasty departure. What was she doing in there in the dark? Unable to resist the lure of the American woman any longer, he rolled to his feet and entered the shelter.

Long legs took him to the foot of the bed in the shadowy darkness. A weak flame cast light along her legs and thighs. He listened to her breathing. Uneven, erratic, followed by deep sighs. "Katherine?" One step took him to the head of the platform. His ears picked up movement, the rustle of clothes. He was conscious of eyes on him, traveling up and down his tall form. He would have thought it impossible a day ago, but his body hardened under the probe of those eyes. Longing made his limbs heavy and the desire he'd kept at bay all evening leapt to the forefront.

Propelling herself onto her back, Katherine continued to stare unabashedly into Jackson's face. With little light in the room, he still had the power to capture every one of her senses. She couldn't tear her eyes away until his strong, dark body was free of clothing.

Desire pierced her to the bone. It spiraled through her, creating emotions so intense it was hard to breathe freely. Why pretend? She wanted Jackson so badly she ached. She would fool herself no longer. This man was a part of her and thousands of miles away he would be a part of her for the rest of her life. Intuition warned her that their time together was drawing to a close.

Pushing herself up on an elbow, she pulled the blouse over her head. Her skirt was next. She pressed down on the mattress, long limbs spread slightly. "Jackson." Her sultry voice rang out with longing laced with need. She held out an arm.

Breath escaped from Jackson's lungs and he fell to a knee. Katherine's female scent assaulted him, pulling him in. His lips fell upon hers, hungry, demanding, devouring. She opened up to him like a flower seeking the rays from a morning sun, greedily absorbing all he had to give.

Her tongue stroked along the strong cords of his neck, across a wide stretch of shoulder, back up to work its magic in his mouth, while his long fingers teased a nipple with thumb and forefinger. Katherine arched off the bed, moaning into Jackson's mouth.

The kiss took them deeper, deeper inside one another and still they could not get enough of it or of each other. Jackson's hands whispered across her flesh, eliciting another moan. She had to break away, if only to breathe!

He watched her as she inhaled deeply. His own breathing was heavy and erratic. His eyes, burning hot, were golden brown slits. A hand caressed her chin and a calloused thumb brushed over her soft lips. Katherine's tongue tasted the salty tip and sucked it into her mouth. Jackson's tongue replaced his finger, and soon there was nothing left but the moist, uneven texture of tongue and mouth driving her out of her mind.

Her hands reached for him to pull him into the bed but he wasn't finished whipping her body into a frenzy. His fingers sought out her wet, tight womanhood, sinking deep as his tongue swirled around and around her nipple before sucking the flesh into his mouth.

"Jackson, ooooh Jackson." Katherine's hoarse cries were urgent, pleading. Her fingers dug in his shoulders. He was driving her, driving her.

She spoke his name in a way that made his blood boil. Her beautiful face was contorted with need and her soft flesh contracted under his touch. Every part of her hungry body submitted to him. She was a slave to his desires. He wanted her desperately. So much so that he would not, could not, wait any longer.

Easing onto the small bed, he guided his engorged shaft into her womanhood. When he slipped inside her tight warmth, a sigh of pure bliss purred over his ears. He moved slowly, savoring the heat, the exquisite way she sheathed him, squeezed him.

Her legs came up to his thrusting hips, guiding him. Was that her husky timbre demanding that Jackson increase the pace? She wanted, she wanted more, and, she wanted this to go on forever. She gripped his shoulders, her rounded nails digging into his flesh, breaking the skin.

A moan escaped his lips. He couldn't call it back, nor did he want to. He buried his face in her neck and shoulder, breathing her name over and over until it became a litany. And she pulled him deeper inside her as they moved to the melodic tempo of their bodies. Twin cadences drummed through them, simultaneously building to the age old dance. Jackson's strong hips pumped, Katherine's slender thighs met his thrusts. The crescendo was building, building inside her. Swallowing her scream on a hot kiss, Jackson released another guttural moan into her mouth.

Tomorrow. Tomorrow would bring with it questions, doubt and enough heartache to last a lifetime. But tonight was magic, electrifying, and it was theirs.

Chapter Twenty-One

The couple lay in a tangle of lethargic legs and arms. When one exhaled, the other inhaled, absorbing each other's breath. Jackson, settled comfortably between Katherine's thighs, smoothed fine beads of perspiration from her brow. Katherine caught his fingers and kissed them lightly. His hand curled around hers, then rested on the rise of her breast.

There was no pressure, only a deep, deep satisfaction and—love? Fear sliced along her spine, spread, lodging under her heart. Her body stiffened at the unbidden acknowledgment.

"What am I going to do?" She was so full of sudden hopelessness she wasn't aware of speaking out loud until a thumb rubbed lightly over her lips.

Jackson lifted up on an elbow to light a candle. When he was able to see her face, he asked, his eyes intent on her, "Do about what, Katherine?" The whisper of her name from his lips and the warmth in his expression cut through her fear. His arms settled possessively around her waist, then his hand smoothed a rhythmic pattern back and forth over her naked skin. Katherine's skin tingled at the intimate contact. Jackson, gold eyes warm with satisfaction, waited for an answer.

"Do about you," she answered honestly. She wasn't prepared for Jackson's reaction.

The gold in his eyes deepened and his full lips tilted upwards in a smile, transforming his brooding features.

"What do you want to do about me?"

Shrugging a slim shoulder, Katherine's lashes swept her cheek so that Jackson could not read her true expression. "There is nothing I can do." The truth of their situation wiped away all pleasure of the intimacy shared before. Her heart began to hurt just a bit.

"You're thinking of your fiancé." It wasn't a question but a flat statement. Jackson's visage changed, his strong jaw clenched. Ice splintered his words and his eyes glittered, but with what emotion Katherine could not discern.

Shivering slightly, she averted her eyes. While it was true that Alex had crossed her mind fleetingly, as an afterthought, going back to him was out of the question. She would not delude herself into believing she could ever think of him as anything but a dear friend from this moment on. No other man could touch her after Jackson. It was beyond consideration, and she knew it would always be this way. But there was no need to let Jackson know just how important he'd become to her.

His eyes were intent on her face. "You will not be happy with him. He does not know you as I do. He does not know how to please you and will only leave you feeling incomplete." She had silently admitted as much but Jackson's challenging smugness infuriated Katherine.

"And I suppose you do?" she retorted. A laden silence was her answer. Scowling at him, more so because what he said was true, she searched for some way to burst his bubble.

"You think I would be happier with you?" she asked sarcastically, searching his face closely.

His expression turned flat, unreadable. "I did not say that. I only know how you react in my arms. Not like a woman deeply in love with another man." Katherine huffed up at Jackson's arrogant yet accurate description. He continued to speak before she could interrupt. "At first you were hesitant, unsure of yourself and of me. You were very much surprised at the pleasure a man and woman can give each other. Once you overcame your shyness, you melted and became like putty in my hands."

Warmth suffused Katherine even as she nearly strangled on outrage. Became like putty in his hands indeed!

"I know for sure that you will not forget me, Katherine Wellington. You will never be truly happy with anyone while another man is uppermost in your mind."

Katherine blinked. Talk about conceit, the nerve! A stinging rebuttal was on the tip of her tongue. She could tell by the look on Jackson's face that he expected it. As she continued to hold his look, insight guided her tongue.

"It is you who will not forget me, Jackson. No other woman can take the place of me, of what we've shared. When I leave this place I will always be in your head no matter if we are oceans apart."

The hard eyes flared with emotion before a cool smile tilted the sensual mouth, wiping it away, along with Katherine's meager hopes. "Which one of us here can forget the spirited, defiant American? You leave a lasting impression on those who come in contact with you."

It wasn't what she was seeking, what she needed to hear. She raged without words as she gave in to the lure of those soft lips and hard hands. She knew this man could never give her what she wanted even as he fed her soul. But for now, this moment, she would receive the essence he gave and resign herself to future unhappiness.

∞∞∞∞∞

Katherine awoke to a drone of voices outside the shelter. Dressing quickly, she went out—side to meet a gray mist already shrouding the dense forest floor. She came upon some of the rebels preparing to leave the campsite. As usual, they glanced her way in silence, then continued with their preparations.

Squinting through the dewy moisture, Katherine sought a familiar face, preferably Jackson's. She hugged her disappointment deep inside. He was always leaving her.

After making love, Jackson had held her snug in his strong arms. During her rest, she had thrashed about in her sleep until he spoke soothing Swahili words in her ear, immediately calming her. An extremely light sleeper, he left her side long before the others awoke.

A sudden chill invaded Katherine. As she watched the rebels leave, she crossed her arms, clamping them around her waist to drive back the unbidden panic building inside. "What is wrong with me?" she muttered, perplexed.

"Katherine?"

The deep voice nearly shot her out of her thongs. Katherine's eyes flew over her shoulder to find Jackson standing close, keenly observing her.

Dousing her joy at his appearance, Katherine rounded on him, lashing out. "Why do you do that? You want to see me drop dead from fright?"

Jackson closed the meager distance, a black brow tilted inquiringly. "What is it? Tell me what is wrong, Katherine."

Misery engulfed her like a steel weight, Jackson's intuitiveness notwithstanding. She rolled her palms up and down her naked arms, throwing him a hostile glare. "I'll be glad when I leave here is what's wrong with me. I've never been so sick of a place in my entire life!" She threw the words at Jackson like heavy bricks.

She wanted to be gone, today if possible. And God help her, she didn't want to leave Jackson. She was in love with the man; a week, a year, it didn't matter. She loved him to the point of desperation. Closing her eyes to shut her misery inside, her fingers dug into her side. The healing cut stung but she took no notice. The thought of not seeing Jackson again made her ache.

Something was building inside of her, something she was unable to stop. She raised her head and glared up at him. Why did he have to touch her? Why couldn't he have left well enough alone, let her remain just a captive until he returned her to her uncle, her heart intact?

Concern melted from Jackson's dark features like hot wax. For an unguarded moment which Katherine was too distressed to notice, pain glittered in the tawny depths of his eyes. It was wiped away, replaced by white hot anger. Long fingers reached out and dug into Katherine's soft upper arms, pulling her close to his body.

"You will stay in camp until I return," he commanded in a quiet, icy tone. "I have too much to do to spend my time searching these woods for you. Remain here. Is that understood, Katherine?" Jackson sucked in a breath and shook Katherine when she failed to respond to his demand. The expression on his face had her recoiling in fear.

Swearing long and low at her withdrawal from him, Jackson loosened his hold but did not remove his hands. "If you do not promise me this I will lock you inside."

"You wouldn't," Katherine replied, half-believing he would.

"I would," he responded succinctly. Posture relaxed, he patiently waited for her answer.

"I promise," came the resentful response.

Narrowed eyes scanned her face for truthful-
ness. Satisfied with his observation, Jackson drew
his warm, work-roughened hands away from her in
a caressing motion.

∞∞∞

Sweat ran off rebels' faces in rivulets as they
fought their opponent, each shrewdly gauging the
other for a weakness that could be used to advantage.

Many of the men had long ago discarded their
shirts and their dark bodies gleamed with perspiration, and their limbs ached with fatigue. Still the
practice went on.

Jackson's keen eyes swept over the men and
women engaged in intense mock battle, some with
weapons, some with only their hands. Hard bodies
hit the solid ground with powerful grunts as the air
was forced from lungs.

There was little conversation, and whatever
pain or discomfort the rebels experienced was
theirs to suffer alone.

Except for the misstep made earlier, when an
overanxious and nervous rebel accidentally cut him,
Jackson was pleased with the conditioning of the
majority of men and women and with the way they
fought. The dull ache in his shoulder did not deter

Jackson from raising his hand to signal the young man who had joined him several months ago. The cut in his shoulder wasn't serious, despite the way it had bled. The bandage Kimya had supplied kept the stinging sweat out.

The young man hesitated as he reached Jackson, who had taken a fighter's stance. His eyes went to the white bandage on Jackson's naked shoulder. He'd done that to Jackson Shugaa! What on earth could he have been thinking to make such a stupid mistake? And now Jackson was ordering him to face him again. Jackson would destroy him in the blink of an eye. "But...I mean...your shoulder."

Jackson's expression hardened. "If I were the enemy, would you stand there worrying over a wound you had given me?"

Determination filled the young face. He struck fast. Jackson deflected the intended blow, but he knew the rebel got the message.

Three hours later Kimya came to Jackson and said, "You must let Rose tend your wound. Blood has soaked the bandage through."

Jackson had forgotten about the cut. He looked at it now and saw that what Kimya said was true. Blood was seeping from under the bandage. Jackson tore it off and accepted the towel from Kimya before tossing the soiled cloth into the foliage.

"Go," Kimya insisted. "We're finished here. All that is left is to clean up and put weapons and equipment away. We will be along as soon as we're done."

∞ ∞ ∞

Rose and Katherine were alone. The woman nodded at Katherine, then went about her tasks as she did each day. Katherine was glad she was being ignored but knew that after yesterday, the woman had antenna out on her every movement.

She wanted to go somewhere, curl up in a ball and cry her eyes out. Not ever in her life had she come close to crying over a man before. But she had never been in love before, not even close.

She prayed fervently that every moment Jackson spent away from her was miserable for him. Totally and completely. She had not asked for this predicament or to fall in love with her captor. Now look at what a mess she was in.

∞ ∞ ∞

Katherine couldn't hide her pleasure when Jackson returned to camp ahead of the others. He'd scarcely paid her any attention when the rebels returned to eat at lunch time. Katherine had vanished inside the shelter after finishing her meal, unwilling to watch Jackson ignore her.

He found her with Rose and Victor, planted on a log, listening to the exchange between the two friends.

Victor's wound appeared to be healing without infection. Rose beamed, please to see that her handiwork was taking effect. Her patient was now able to sit in a reclining position and Rose was careful that he did not put a strain on his injured leg. She was unlike N Zee, Katherine decided. Rose was decidedly cool toward her but Katherine could not fail to notice her care and concern for the injured rebel.

Approaching footsteps had both women turning their heads. The sight of Jackson's forceful presence set her heart to galloping. She was cognizant of the fact that he'd made enough noise so as not to startle her this time.

Katherine's attention was drawn to the jagged tear in the shirt of his upper shoulder. She inhaled a sharp breath at the sight of the bright red blood wetly circling the wound. He was gripping a bloody rag in one hand. Sharp fear spurted through her. Jackson had been hurt.

Her eyes flew to his to find him watching her, a grim expression on his face. Before she could say or do anything Rose was at his side, carefully examining the wound. Over Jackson's protests, she raised the shirt to better see the damage to his shoulder, exposing his ridged stomach.

Running her hand around the wound, Rose exclaimed excitedly in Swahili, which elicited a smile from Jackson. Shaking his head on a chuckle, he rotated his injured shoulder, generating a frown and a soft murmur of protest from Rose who surprised them both by gliding her finger tips over Jackson's sharp cheekbones and firm jaw, smiling up into his face before dashing off to secure water and a wet cloth.

Jealously, hot, pure and strong, surged through Katherine. When Rose returned to Jackson, Katherine watched her work diligently over him as if he were a king and she was his subject. Unable to stand the sight or Jackson's intense scrutiny any longer, she wrinkled her nose and angled her chin in the direction of Victor, who regarded the trio in solemn curiosity.

At the sound of Rose's sharp exclamation, Katherine's attention was pulled back in their direction. She gestured in an agitated fashion at long thin scratches across Jackson's shoulder, one traveling way past his shoulder blade. She spoke in a rapid fire, shrill voice. Jackson's answering response was calm and brief. Whatever he said failed to mollify Rose's outrage at the additional marring of the dark smooth skin. Lifting speculative, probing eyes Katherine's way, Rose encountered a guilt-ridden, flushed countenance.

Rose quickly bowed her head to her task. She said something in Jackson's ear before shooting Katherine a withering glance. Jackson's crisp reply brought a flush to the woman's features. Dropping her head once more, she bent to her task without further comments.

Great! Thanks a lot, Katherine fumed at the silent, watchful Jackson. Must he alienate every-one in the camp against her? Rose had assumed accurately who had given Jackson the scratches and probably why. Katherine flushed deeply again. Jackson's dismissive, abrupt manner only made matters worse.

Resigned, Katherine pivoted away at the same instant Jackson stepped upon the platform to talk with Victor. Things were going from bad to worse for her. She couldn't leave here fast enough.

Engrossed in her brooding reflections, she was startled into a loud yell when two dark hands fell across her shoulders. She whipped around. "I thought I asked you not to do that," she gritted out through tight lips, her heart pounding.

The shirt Jackson had on now was tucked into his slacks and tightly hugging liberal shoulders and an equally liberal chest tapering off to a snug waist. The man was lethal and he was standing much too close to Katherine, inhibiting her ability to breathe freely.

"Come with me."

Wordlessly, Katherine stretched her hand into the one Jackson held out. His strong fingers enclosed her slender ones. A familiar sense of awareness danced over her skin. She wanted to chastise herself for her reaction to Jackson but could not. She craved his touch too much. Missed him incredibly when he wasn't in sight.

How was Rose taking all of this? she asked herself. She did not want to hurt the woman but she wanted Jackson more. She tried to peek over his shoulder at Rose as they turned to leave but found her view blocked.

She had to wonder at Jackson's audacity. He entered camp and one woman rushed to attend to his medical needs, then he left with another. Covertly eyeing his profile she couldn't fail to see what Rose, N Zee and probably every woman saw when they looked at Jackson. But the man was a bandit, an outlaw. Yet here she was, following him without question.

Chapter Twenty-Two

Jackson and Katherine returned to the wide lake they had bathed in two days ago. Reaching the incline, Katherine's eyes did a thorough sweep of the area. Of the few places she'd been since coming here, she liked this one best. Maybe it was because more sun was able to get through the trees. Lots of blue sky and white clouds were visible. Water trickled musically over rocks covered with moss. It beckoned, looking delicious.

It was much too idyllic here. It could easily lull her into thinking she and Jackson could have more. Refusing to fall under the spell of the setting or the man, Katherine stiffened her spine and backed away from the water's edge into Jackson's chest.

The impact wobbled her. Before Jackson could steady her, she spun around to face him, hands on hips, a stubborn angle to her chin, waiting for him to make his move. It wasn't long in coming.

"Take off your clothes, we will bathe." Jackson dropped to the ground to take off his boots. Next to go was his shirt, pulling Katherine's eyes to the wound which was not bandaged. Instead, a clear, sticky-looking substance was smoothed over it, covering it completely.

"But it's not night yet!" Katherine squeaked, striving for an aloofness she didn't feel as his hands unsnapped the waistband of his pants.

Jackson's eyes lingered on her in silence. Something close to a smile curved his lips at her defensive stance. "What difference does the time of day make?" As casual as you please, he sprang upright and slipped out of the khakis. His finger was on the band of his briefs when Katherine started inching back.

When he touched her she could not resist him, but at least under the cover of darkness she didn't feel completely vulnerable to him. In the light of day Jackson's male beauty was spell-binding. If she stepped into that water clothed or naked with him, she would not have the will power to resist him. She had no experience in hiding love. Her entire being would be open to him.

She grasped at straws. "What about your wound? You can't get it wet. What about your— aren't you needed back with the others? Won't you be missed?"

Leisurely closing the distance between them, Jackson fingered the collar of the faded blouse Katherine wore. His voice was lowered sensually, his eyes on hers. "I will take care of my wound. Do not worry about it. It is of little consequence." His hand cupped her face, the sure fingers caressing her lower lip and cheekbones while his other hand was busy dispensing with the blouse. "My where- abouts are of little matter. This a period of relax- ation for everyone." The full lips twisted in humor. Warmth, along with another emotion, darkened the gold in his eyes.

A light breeze hit Katherine's skin, letting her know that she was bereft of her blouse. In shock, her eyes dropped to see it hanging at her wrists. With a flick of his fingers, Jackson had it complete- ly off her. Her eyes went wide and her lips formed an attractive "O."

Eyes that had grown darker caressed the turgid nipples jutting out rigidly. Katherine's breathing accelerated, as did her pulse upon recognizing the expression on Jackson's face. Only at times like these did he appear susceptible to some of the same emotions she experienced.

"Jackson?" The question hung in the electrified air.

"We both know where this will end, Katherine. You want me, I want you. It is not something that is easy to fight or win."

He spoke as if he'd been trying to do just that, as she knew she had and should, even now as her lips parted in anticipation of his kiss. Her breasts were crushed to his hard chest and her arms snaked around his waist. His hardness pushed through his briefs at her, probing , seeking. This time she wasn't so shocked to find deft fingers had removed her skirt by the time the kiss ended.

"Come with me into the water," Jackson urged softly, raining kisses along her jaw line to her graceful neck.

Knees weak, limbs trembling, Katherine struggled to find the will to resist the earnest plea, the hot, searing kisses. Skillful hands slipped around and down, zeroing in on her bud of pleasure.

Grasping his shoulders, Katherine held on to keep her knees from buckling. She made a noise deep within her throat as her head fell against Jackson's chest. In a sensual haze, she opened her eyes to witness the passion blazing across Jackson's face. Scooping her into his arms, he carried her to the water's edge and set her, feet first, into it. The water lapped over her thighs, barely cooling her burning flesh.

Jackson brushed her forehead and at last her lips with light kisses. "First we will bathe, then we will seek pleasure," he murmured thickly in her ear. His breath spread over the sensitive skin on her neck, causing butterflies in her stomach.

Bending low, he cupped water into his palms and allowed it to cascade down Katherine's hot skin. She did the same with him, being careful not to wet the wound in his shoulder. She relished the feel of silk over steel under her hands. Turning him, she placed kisses along the long, healed scar as she'd wanted to do since discovering it. The muscles spread out across Jackson's lean body tensed, his hands clutching at air as Katherine's open mouth trailed over his back. His thick manhood sprang forth stiffly when he faced her, leaving little doubt how he intended to seek his pleasure. Rising up on tiptoe, she straddled him, gliding her woman-hood back and forth along his hard member before claiming his lips. She flicked her tongue from one corner of his mouth to the other before plunging it deep inside, all the while continuing the torturous movement with her hips, leaving him little doubt how she wanted him to give her pleasure.

Jackson's large hands clamped down on Katherine's undulating hips to hold her still. "You are trying to drive me insane," he accused, his voice thick with passion. Katherine chuckled seductively and wet her lips with her tongue. The look in her eyes held a challenge. With a sound that was more growl than groan, he snatched her up in his arms, carrying her to where their clothes were scattered and placed her on them. Her arms curled around his neck, dragging him down with her. He settled between silken thighs, which she wound around his hips. She could feel the tip of his manhood tantalizing her entrance.

Thrusting her hips up, Katherine positioned herself to accept that seeker and giver of pleasure. Obliging her silent pleas, Jackson eased inside the tight, wet chamber. Embedding himself to the hilt, he crushed her to him. It was taking everything he had to control himself and not give in to the raging ecstasy threatening to pull him over the top.

"Why can't I resist you?" Katherine's husky voice was laden with desire and confusion.

Capturing her face with both hands, Jackson stared into her eyes. "Why should you be able to resist me, kipenzi changu [my love]? You are in my blood. I can no more than think of you than want you. It is only fitting that you feel the same."

Katherine's senses were too befuddled to stop and question Jackson about the words he'd spoken in Swahili. All she desired now was Jackson where he was, deep inside her. His hips rose, eliciting a gasp from her.

Crying out at the sheer force of the many sensations racking her body and mind, Katherine clung to Jackson, her hips surging up to meet his. She felt like a piece of hot, sweet liquid. Jackson! Jackson! The name drummed itself inside her temple. She could not escape it, nor did she want to.

Never, ever, would she be the same again. No matter where she was. This rebel, this warrior, for better or worse, had changed her life forever.

Content, Katherine lost track of the time she and Jackson spent by the small lake. Yet, at the back of her mind, she sensed that their time together was drawing to an end. She would not question him about her departure, content to leave the spell he wound around them in place. She was in no hurry to leave here, and she sensed, neither was Jackson.

After making love for a second time, with little rest in between, Jackson held her loosely yet possessively in his arms. Snuggling next to him, she reveled in the shared intimacy. She secretly enjoyed the way he held her at any time, whether they were making love or not.

For the first time Jackson asked her a series of questions about her life back in America and how she came to be with her uncle. He grew silent and pensive when she glossed over the ill treatment she'd suffered at Abra's hand. Shrugging the old hurts aside, she changed the subject, became evasive when he questioned her about Alex. He wanted to know what she was going to do when she got home. She wasn't going to marry Alex but there was no need for Jackson to know this. He was too self-assured as it was.

"You will tell me what I want to know before you leave here," Jackson stated confidently.

"When pigs fly," Katherine replied evenly.

"What is this flying of swine?" Jackson questioned, his tone earnest.

Cocking a brow, Katherine noted his serious expression. She explained that it was just one of the many slang terms in the U.S. He immediately demanded to hear others.

By the time Katherine had listed some of the many in the African American community, Jackson's expression had changed time and again from puzzlement to astonishment to shock to outright humor. His laughter was long and deep, mesmerizing her.

A smile did wonders for his face, rendering his brooding features stunningly handsome. She could understand why she might initially be drawn to him on his looks alone. But there had to be something else inside the man to keep her interested, no matter how he looked. There was much depth to Jackson. In fact, there were things there she wished weren't.

Hunger finally drove them from the spot, however reluctantly. The trek back was filled with a comfortable silence, with Jackson intermittently pointing out plants Rose used to make her medicines and those they used for food.

Reaching the main camp, Katherine received a jolt at seeing N Zee standing some distance away from their shelter, as if she'd been waiting for their return. The time she'd shared with Jackson dulled.

Her eyes fell to Rose, who seemed to be working on the evening meal. Neither woman was aware of their entrance until they were in the midst of the campgrounds. Both heads sprang up, two pairs of adoring eyes going straight to Jackson.

Concern etched Rose's features as her eyes flew to him. Straightening to her full height, she watched the American standing by his side. He wasn't touching her but his stance spoke volumes for those willing to accept the truth. Rose did not approach him but spoke to him where he stood. His own response was short and quiet, and Rose resumed her task without further comment.

N Zee's lips curled down in disdain and a fierce look crept across her face as she watched the American by Jackson's side. Inhaling a deep breath, she approached him. Standing close, she touched his arm and spoke in their tongue. There was a seductive quality to her voice that had Katherine's ears perking up, though she could understand none of the words. Jackson's response sounded pleasant enough. However, his expression was one of pained tolerance.

Ignoring Katherine, N Zee tugged on Jackson's arm in an effort to pull him away from her side. Jackson didn't budge.

Katherine's newfound peace was shattered. Reality hit her like a steam roller. N Zee 's return meant trouble. If Jackson couldn't see it, so be it. Katherine could not expect him to go against the woman for her. She was, after all, one of his rebels. The quicker she got out of Dodge, the better. She made a move to walk off from the pair but Jackson's hand around her waist forestalled her.

"Where are you going?" His eyes washed over her, alert and oddly indulgent.

"Inside. So the two of you can talk." She didn't acknowledge N Zee, whose eyes she felt tearing into her. She jerked a finger in her general direction. "She doesn't want me here and frankly, I have no desire to be in her presence."

"It does not matter what you or N Zee wants," he stated flatly. "You will remain here."

The man didn't care whether he hurt her or not. Katherine clenched her teeth, brimming with sudden anger. Her eyes conveyed the fury but none of the pain caused by his callous words. "I am not one of your puppets waiting to do your bidding and hanging onto your every whim. I am flesh and blood and am able to think and feel without being dictated to."

Jackson quietly assessed the anger glittering in the depths of Katherine's eyes. His expression remained bland but his eyes sharpened on the lines of strain around her mouth. They had walked some distance from and to the main camp and had made love numerous times.

"Are you tired?" he probed.

Thrown off by the sudden change of topic, Katherine simply stared. Her limbs did feel lethargic after the arduous lovemaking last night and this morning. But Jackson's astuteness did not make up for his ill treatment. If he was trying to disarm her with false concern, it wouldn't work.

"What I am tired of...is this place." She was about to say you, but something in his narrowed eyes cautioned her not to push it.

Concern fled from Jackson's face. His jaw tightened. "The meal will be ready soon," he stated crisply. "Lie down and later you will return here to share your meal with me."

The man hadn't heard a word she'd said. He was as autocratic as usual. It was as if last night and this morning had not happened. Throwing him a dismissive look, she snorted, "I have no desire to remain around that she devil." She stared fixedly at the glaring N Zee.

There was a distinct hardening of Jackson's eyes as he followed the direction of Katherine's stare. Katherine didn't care if she offended him with her description of N Zee. The woman hated her and would do her harm if she could.

"No one will harm you. They will live to regret any attempt made against you." The dispassionate statement surprised Katherine, as did the fierceness in the depths of Jackson's eyes. A trill of fear curled around her stomach. Whatever his reasons, there was no uncertainty in her mind that Jackson would follow through on his threat.

She backed up mentally and physically from the revelation she'd glimpsed. This man was dangerous. Anyone lulled into believing otherwise, as she'd been while lying naked in his arms, was in for a rude awakening.

A muscle twitched in Jackson's cheek, but his expression remained closed as Katherine spun away from him. His eyes remained on her retreating back as she entered the shelter. He faced a silent Rose poised over the metal pot, ladling stew, his face revealing none of what he was thinking or feeling.

Rose's face was averted and her eyes downcast. He was on the verge of speaking with her when he chanced a glance at N Zee, who was staring after Katherine. Her eyes were filled with hate and her expression registered her disapproval when she faced Jackson.

It was at that moment that Jackson realized N Zee was unrepentant about her attack on Katherine. It was quite clear she'd learned nothing from her temporary banishment. Inwardly, he sighed. He must continue to be wary of her for Katherine's sake.

Dark features detached, he spun around, freezing in his tracks when N Zee would follow him away from the encampment. "Kimya and the others will return at any time. You will be prepared to listen and follow orders. Truphena will lead the raid into Nakuru."

"Truphena?" N Zee repeated, aghast. They were both referring to the quiet, unassuming female rebel who was fierce in battle and able to wield the panga, a long, sharp curved knife, as well as any man.

Vexed that N Zee continued to challenge his decisions, yet wishing to stave off one of her fiery outbursts, Jackson responded to her unasked question as patiently as possible. "You cannot expect to return to camp and take command as if nothing has happened. You know the consequences when you cause serious trouble. Truphena is more than capable of leading the raid."

"She has never done so before," N Zee protested.

"She will when the time arrives," Jackson volleyed back crisply, closing the subject.

N Zee wasn't through. Her brown eyes sniped at Jackson as she sputtered angrily, "So I am to continue being punished like some wayward child?"

Too late, Jackson faced the results of his years of indulging N Zee. Due to their friendship and his reluctance to severely punish her after she had carried out some past mischievous and troublesome acts, including Katherine's kidnapping, she had become more arrogant and uncontrollable with each passing day. More than one man in camp lusting after her only fed her arrogance.

"I will not tolerate your continued defiance any longer," Jackson replied with barely suppressed irritation. "If you do not abide by the rules, you will leave, never to return."

N Zee's lips parted in disbelief. She stared into Jackson's dark golden eyes long and hard. He meant it, every word! He would send her away as if what they'd shared was of little matter. Anguish squeezed her heart and her hands shook as she raised them halfway in a beseeching manner.

"That American has bewitched you," she spat

nastily. "You have become someone else before my eyes." She held her hands aloft as if to ward off whatever spell Katherine had cast as she backed away. When she was some distance away, she spat out the useless root. It landed beside her booted foot with a light thud. Lips snarling, hands fisted at her side, N Zee ground it into the packed earth. Why carry it around when the man it was to be used on would not come within two feet of her?

Chapter Twenty-Three

K imya and Jackson, with their backs to the forest, were isolated some distance from the rest of the rebels, finalizing the plans for the raid on Nakuru's military base and a possible hit on the president's residence, if things went according to plan.   Because of the bombing at the embassies days earlier, there would still be a heavy police presence in the surrounding areas.   They were cautiously optimistic that they would slip through the net.

The president's residence was well guarded, but everyone's attention was momentarily focused on capturing the person or persons responsible for the terrorists' acts. They were aware that the scrutiny focused on the tragedy could very well work to their disadvantage. The police could be overly cautious, ready to shoot at the merest sign of trouble. It was a chance they were willing to take.

Satisfied that they had a workable plan, Kimya leaned back on his elbows and looked at his friend. "How much time will you need to slip Katherine back into Nairobi before joining us?" he inquired. Jackson was adamant about returning the American to her family despite the risk of getting caught and the inevitable consequence—death—if he was.

Kimya was more than willing to go with Jackson to the ends of the earth but a small part of him was relieved that Jackson insisted on going alone to return her. When it came to the beautiful American, his friend was unpredictable and as prickly as the thorny cactus in the desert. If Kimya took her back and something were to go wrong, Kimya would not relish the thought of facing his childhood friend's wrath.

Distracted by his brooding thoughts, some time passed before he realized that Jackson had not responded to his query. He stared at his friend in the lantern light. "Is there something I should know? Have there been changes?"

"I'm not taking Katherine back. At least not just yet," Jackson qualified.

"When then?" Kimya questioned, holding his

alarm at bay. He waited out Jackson's silence. Sometimes it was best to tread carefully.

A defiant light lit the tiger eyes even as Jackson shrugged a broad shoulder. "I cannot say. Not for several days...a week."

"You said that Katherine must be returned to her family with haste to avoid bringing the wrath of the American government down on our heads," Kimya reminded him. "Nothing has changed. The longer we keep her here, the more danger we face. You know this as well as I," Kimya reasoned. He could not read his friend's face. What Jackson did not want you to see, you did not see.

"What you say is true," Jackson admitted smoothly, bracing his elbows on his knees.

"And?" Kimya probed. There had to be more. His expression turned thoughtful. "She will remain for a few more days—a week? Do you think she will be out of your system by then?"

Jackson's eyes sharpened on Kimya's calm, placid features. He searched for mockery and found none. What he saw was concern mixed with understanding. It was the former that had him offering up an ironic smile to ease the tension.

"It's always been you who promised me that some woman would penetrate this 'thick shell' as you aptly put it." He lifted a brow, a bemused glint in his eye. "Katherine is courageous, stubborn and

can be provoking. She wants to return to her family, yet she would not deliberately harm one of us to
do so. She has much heart." He paused, his eyes
in the distant darkness. "I will return her—when the
time is right."

Kimya kept his opinion of Jackson's decision to
himself. "Does Katherine know of your decision?"

All lightness vanished from Jackson's expression. "Why should she? Her knowing changes
nothing." He rolled to his feet, his long legs carrying him into the dark thicket on all sides of them.

In puzzled wonder Kimya watched Jackson's
retreating back. If it were as simple as Jackson
made it sound, why was he suddenly so uneasy?

∞∞ ∞∞ ∞∞

"Jackson Shugaa has changed," N Zee argued
obstinately. "You can see it as well as I." She and
Kimya were sitting outside Kimya's sleeping tent.
Lamplight flickered over them, highlighting the vary-
ing emotions crisscrossing their features.

N Zee had come to Kimya, desperate to talk.
He was no more willing to turn her away than she
was willing to return his love. Though she had
brought it on herself, she was hurt, embarrassed
and feeling betrayed because her command had
been taken away. In many ways, she was like a

spoiled, recalcitrant child. She handled neither her pain nor fall from grace very well.

And though she was further disobeying rules by remaining with him, Kimya could not send her away, not this time. Leaning back into the shadows, he stretched out his legs and spoke in a composed but cautious manner. "What you say is true, to some degree."

N Zee shot him a penetrating stare. "You approve of this change?"

"It does not matter whether I do or not. Jackson has never asked for approval from anyone on how he lives his life."

"It's the woman. She has changed him," N Zee accused hotly. Picking up a handful of twigs, she began tossing them toward the lamp flame. They made a tinkling noise as they hit the glass covering before falling to the ground.

N Zee's outrage, dislike and acute disappointment equaled the truth she spoke about the change in Jackson since his encounter with the American. Wisely, Kimya remained quiet. He would let her talk her anger out until she was calm, then he would send her to bed.

"I cannot wait until she leaves! There have been only problems since we brought her here. I rue the day I set my eyes on that skinny wench." She spat disparagingly into the dirt. "She is weak and afraid. I can see how she clings to Jackson's side." Chuckling nastily, she continued, "She is afraid of me, and well she should be. I would break her in half if I could get my hands on her." Her dark eyes glowed malevolently in the dark. "Jackson does not need someone he has to look after every passing moment, someone who cannot take care of herself."

Bending over from where she sat, she stared into Kimya's face. "What time are you taking her back? When we return from our successful raid I will personally wash down both rooms to wipe away the American's stench." Smacking her lips in satisfaction, she dropped a hand across Kimya's wide shoulder. "I cannot tell you how much I look forward to tomorrow for more reasons than—"

The stillness of Kimya's body stopped N Zee from finishing her sentence. The giddiness she was building to evaporated, like the morning mist above the trees.

"What is it, Kimya?" she asked cautiously, bracing herself.

Kimya would have preferred not to return an answer, but knew instinctively it would be fruitless to avoid the truth. "Katherine is not leaving, not right away."

"When?" N Zee's eyes glittered and her voice dropped dangerously low.

Sitting upright to gauge her reaction, Kimya answered calmly, "In a couple of days... maybe."

It was worse than she could have imagined. N Zee stood abruptly, her face hidden in the shadows as she spoke in a voice that sounded foreign to her ears. "Why the delay? Whose idea was this?"

Fighting his helplessness, Kimya braced his elbows on his knees, turning his palms upward. His gesture said that Jackson had made the decision. Experiencing an unusual bout of irritation, he scanned N Zee's face.

Why could she not accept the fact that Jackson did not love her, that he never would? Why could she not accept that he, Kimya, loved her? If she would put Jackson out of her mind, she might be able to acknowledge and return his love. It was all so very hopeless. Dropping his head, Kimya stared into the burning flame.

"She has bewitched him," N Zee mumbled in a choked voice, bringing Kimya out of his reverie. Her tone hardened and her lips curled in hate. "She will regret the day she set foot on Kenyan soil."

Too irrational and too stubborn, Kimya's mind shouted. Katherine can no more control Jackson's actions and emotions than I can control yours. "Don't do it, N Zee," he warned out loud. "Jackson will not be forgiving this time if you go against his orders and harm Katherine."

A length of time passed and N Zee did not acknowledge Kimya's admonition. Finally, her shoulders slumped and her posture sagged. Sitting down next to Kimya, she reached for his hand and held onto it tightly. A great sadness settled over her. The tears glistening in her eyes tugged at his heart. Gathering her in his arms, he leaned her head on his shoulder, absorbing her deep sobs. She cried, releasing her despair for the wheels she'd set in motion, wheels she could not turn back even if she tried. Finding her in bed with Jackson had sealed the American's fate. Despite the guilt tearing at her, she knew she'd done what she had to do. Kimya's words proved as much. In the end, Jackson would understand that everything done was for him.

As she sobbed holding tightly to him, Kimya mistakenly felt that at last he had reason to hope.

∞∞∞

Darkness shrouded the camp but Jackson had yet to make an appearance inside the small shelter. Movement in the front room earlier had brought Katherine tiptoeing to the door to peek out and stare up into the always solemn face of Kimya.

Brown eyes did not reveal surprise at her entrance into the room. Nodding his head in a for-

---

---

mal manner, he turned back to the gun he was putting together. Finished, he stuck the ammunition into a small burlap sack and quietly left Katherine to wonder about him.

He had not spoken over two dozen words to her during her time in camp, and yet he had come to her rescue the day she was lost and encountered the snake. She was sometimes conscious of his eyes on her but she didn't feel an aversion to him. The rebels listened when Kimya spoke as they listened to Jackson. He was the one person Jackson seemed to laugh freely with and was completely at ease with.

A fleeting curiosity entered Katherine's mind. What did these rebels do to ease their loneliness? Was there someone in love with him, or someone he was in love with? With N Zee? What did it matter? Soon she would be 'outta here,' never to see this place or these people again. At least she hoped so. Her heart thudded with pain at the knowledge that her days with Jackson were nearing an end.

Turning back to the darkened bedroom, she tried to curb her disappointment. The rebels had finished eating hours ago. Where was Jackson? The moment the meal was finished, he'd spoken briefly to Kimya and left.

Back to Nairobi, soon! Away from this lonely

place full of people. Away from these rebels fighting for their cause, whatever that might be. Away from Jackson. She ceased pacing, her heart twisting in her chest. She could and would go on with her life. She must. Jackson would be relegated to her past. Her strange, sometimes bittersweet past.

She would pray for his survival and his safety. How could she not after knowing him? She would gather the pieces of her life and continue. She was a survivor.

∞∞∞

Easing into the silent room, Jackson undressed without hurry. His eyes adjusted to the darkness, spying the slim shape lying atop the narrow bed. Naked, he dropped down onto the platform, molding himself to her soft form. Unable to resist, he kissed her behind her ear. She stirred, murmured and shoved her bottom into his groin.

A harsh breath escaped from his lungs. He felt himself growing hard, gritted his teeth to ease his rapidly growing passion. He couldn't blame anyone but himself for his aroused state. He should have slept in the first room as he'd promised himself he would do upon his return to camp.

Katherine stirred again and the press of her hips burned through the thin fabric of her skirt. He was by no means a greedy man. Had always been a man of patience. But with Katherine. Katherine!

"Katherine." He spoke her name softly, half in hope that she would not answer, half in hope that she would.

"Mmm....Jackson." The throaty response torpedoed blood to the tip of his manhood. In the throes of slumber Katherine reached behind her and massaged his arousal, then caught his hand in hers, bringing it to her breasts. She held his hand in place until her grip slackened, her even breathing revealing her sleeping state.

Discarding the notion before it could take root, of allowing her to sleep, Jackson shifted her in his arms. Quickly he removed the thin barrier of clothing, a small smile curving his full mouth at her sleep-induced pliancy.

His mouth captured her nipple, sucking and nibbling it with his teeth. Running a hand down the length of her leg, he traced a trail to the inside of her warm, soft thigh. When Katherine moaned in her sleep, he let his hands and fingers roam at will until her slender body nearly shook from his ministrations.

"Love me, Jackson. Please love me!" Katherine urged hoarsely, coming fully awake and literally aflame with desire. There was desperation in her plea. And because she believed this her last night in the arms of the man she'd come to love, however improbable it seemed, she held nothing back. There was no hesitation or shyness in her touch. And touch him she did, from the top of his head to his wide chest and flat stomach. She grasped his engorged manhood between both hands, stroking the silken, throbbing flesh, causing Jackson to thrust up his hips and groan her name.

She rubbed suggestively against his hard body, unable to get close enough to him. Whispering seductively in his ear, she urged him to take her, catapulting his need and desire for her to heights beyond his control. His heart thudded in his chest from warring emotions until Katherine uttered his name again, drawing out the sound.

"Yes, kapenzi changu [my love]," he replied thickly. Tomorrow would be soon enough to worry about how she would react to his news. Because you will hate me, of this I am sure. But for now I will love you and hopefully it will sustain me throughout your fury.

Even as he crushed Katherine to him, reclaiming her lips, he knew he would want her just as intensely tomorrow, in the throes of her fury, and in all the days that followed.

Chapter Twenty-Four

Katherine stretched languidly, then rolled to her stomach. The events of the night seeped into her consciousness. Images of her and Jackson entwined together had ripples of tension stiffening her body and nails cutting into her palms. Moaning out loud, she came fully awake and rolled over on her back.

She stared up at the thatched roof. Had she ever noticed how low the ceiling was? Or was she only aware of how Jackson seemed to tower over her, filling the small space when standing in here? She didn't notice much those first days here because she'd been too full of fear.

Now her mind was full of Jackson. However much she wanted to avoid facing the inevitable—

leaving Jackson—it was useless. Not when images of him rampaged through her mind. She swallowed, barely, as memories of the things she'd done to him and he to her assailed her.

Her face burned and she was glad no one was here to see her, for surely they would recognize her for what she was, a loose woman. Heat suffused her body. Had that been she? All arms and legs, teeth, tongue and mouth? She on top of Jackson, riding him with frenzied thrusts, him kneading her breasts, her head thrown back, mouth agape in uncontrollable passion? And Jackson moving under her, thrusting, thrusting.

Moistness which had gathered on her naked body quickly chilled. It would do her no good to continue to dwell on Jackson and the intimacy shared with him. She sat up and swung her feet to the ground.

She would leave him, that much she did not doubt. It would tear her apart inside but it had to be done. What kind of future did she have with him? She knew next to nothing about this war he was waging with his government. During their time together yesterday, for the first time, he had provided sketchy details to her probing questions. Judging from his reticence, he obviously thought she would tell her uncle all once she was back with him. She didn't even know Jackson's last name.

The one time she'd asked, she received a silent stare.

Reluctant to venture outside, she cocked her ears. The few voices she'd heard moments ago were fading away. Dim light guided her to her clothes which were carelessly scattered across the log. She didn't have to ask herself how they'd gotten there.

Before slipping the blouse over her head, she examined the forgotten scar on her side. It was healing nicely. Pain had been nonexistent since her second day here. Her hand went to the healing scar on her face. It too would soon be gone. Rose was definitely good at her job. Whatever salve she mixed together for Jackson to rub on both scars had worked wonders. Katherine blew air through pursed lips. Rose would probably be glad to see her gone too.

Aw hell. This environment wasn't conducive to forming friendships. Katherine smoothed the wrinkles from her clothing as best she could. She was impatient to pitch these rags into the trash and slip into some fashionable, cool summer outfit.

She wasn't hungry and knew why. But Jackson would insist that she eat. It was a long trek back as she so vividly recalled. Her eyes dropped to the thongs on her feet. Would these shoes hold out? She would have to find out.

The campsite was vacant. The usually hovering Rose was not in sight. Katherine went back inside the shelter and spotted the bowl. Uncovering it, she picked it up and peered at the rice and meat inside. It was cold. She had been asleep a long time. She put the bowl, untouched, on the log and went back outside. Curiosity pulled her brows together. Was Rose with her patient, Jackson with his rebels? It seemed unlikely since he was taking her back today.

Wasn't he? She'd assumed he would. She didn't want anyone else. Jackson was a disciplined man. Would her wants and desires matter to him at all?

Once she'd been curious to see what lay beyond this camp; today she wasn't tempted. The trail leading away from camp was as cold as the food and most importantly, she was in no mood to get lost again. Besides, the minute she left, someone was bound to come in search of her, whether they were in the immediate vicinity or not.

It was eerily quiet, so much so she sauntered back and forth waiting for someone to return. An hour passed, two. She was going stir crazy but with nothing else to do and weary from the waiting, she went inside the shelter to sit.

She was only able to sit for a few minutes before she was back outside, her nerves in overdrive.   Squinting through the trees, she was amazed to see that it was well past the noon hour. Where was everyone? Where was Jackson?

Glancing around her immediate vicinity, goose bumps lined her arms from an unexpected chill. Sensing motion, she twisted around to her right, facing the dense thicket, her heart thumping in anticipation. But it wasn't Jackson stepping from the trees. Instead, it was the annoying rebel who kept a covetous eye on her when Jackson wasn't around.

A grin lit his narrow face as he advanced toward Katherine. Unlike Jackson, his smile only served to make him appear sinister.   With each step Katherine took back, he advanced two until he was standing close enough for her to smell the over-powering odor of sweat.

Alert to danger, Katherine's eyes dilated and her body tensed. Surely he wasn't brazen enough to attack her with Jackson somewhere in the area. Or was he?

Before she could speculate further as to Jackson's whereabouts, the man caught her arm in a tight hold, jerking her to his chest. He leered down at her, his thin lips parted to reveal his stained teeth.   His free hand clamped onto her breast, squeezing hard, causing immediate discomfort.

Katherine didn't fight or thrust his hand aside.

The man appeared caught off guard by her lack of resistance. His hold loosened on her arm. Indecision crossed his face before he leaned in, his lips parted.

Something in her eyes warned him of her intent. The leg Katherine raised to thrust into his groin was deflected as the man shifted his body sideways. He twisted Katherine's wrist painfully as he struggled to hold onto her squirming body.

She had pitifully little to fight with, but Katherine was not defeated. She stomped down on his boot-ed foot with everything she had in her. The man grunted, heavily, then chuckled arrogantly in her face. The move stung her more than it hurt him, but it was enough to cause him to loosen his grip.

Katherine raised her free hand and raked it across the man's face, gouging it deeply. Strips of his brown skin clung to her nails. Blood ran down the man's face as he howled in enraged pain, then successfully secured both of Katherine's hands in his. He viciously bent her hands back towards her wrists.

"Jackson!" When she opened her mouth to scream louder, he jerked her to his chest so hard he knocked the wind from her lungs. Snaring both hands in his one, he clamped the other over her mouth, shutting off her yell.

Katherine bit down on the fingers over her

mouth. The taste of blood, sweat and dirt made her gag, but she held on. The man released her hands and shoved her roughly to the ground. Murder was in his eyes as he advanced on Katherine.

Out of nowhere, Katherine was picked effortlessly up from the ground at the same time the rebel was grabbed from behind by Kimya. He held him aloft for long seconds and then unceremoniously tossed him to the ground.

The rebel's anger quickly turned to terror when he recognized Jackson as the one holding Katherine. "Stay there," Jackson commanded as he put her down.

Though she knew he wasn't angry at her, the expression on his face had her blanching. His eyes were unblinking, their golden depths obscured by a hot, searing fury. "Jackson, no," Katherine pleaded, her eyes wide in her drawn face. The hand she placed on his arm was shrugged off as if it were a worrisome forest insect. He stared at her until she backed up out of harm's way.

Fear rendered Adam incapable of standing and he scurried back on his hands and haunches, his own eyes bulging as he tried to speak. He could not move fast enough as Jackson stalked him with purposeful strides.

Katherine looked to Kimya. He watched the two men, his expression unperturbed. She'd wanted

the man to leave her alone but, dear God, she did-
n't want him dead.

Jackson dragged Adam to his feet. "You will die
for touching her." He backhanded Adam in a cool,
deliberate manner. The sharp crack of knuckles
against flesh and bone reverberated in the atmos-
phere. Adam stumbled from the force of the blow.
Jackson caught him before he fell, hitting him a
stinging blow across his face again. The force of
this blow was louder than the first.

"Damn you, fight back. What kind of man are
you?" Jackson snarled, shaking Adam when he
refused to defend himself.

"She wants me, she wants me!" Adam babbled
when Jackson raised his fist in the air. "What are
you saying?" The rage in Jackson's eyes intensified.

"She came to me. She did!" Adam insisted.
"Before you came, I denied her. She tried to
seduce me. She rubbed her body to mine." When
Adam realized he had Jackson's attention, he
pressed his advantage. "I pushed her away...I—"

"Why would Katherine come to you?" Jackson
demanded, disbelief written on his face. "She
fought you. The evidence is on your face!"

"She wishes to leave," Adam answered quickly,
tucking his injured hand tight to his side. She says
you are too long in keeping your promise to take her

to her family. She would try to use me. But when I refused to do as she wanted, she said that I would be sorry and attacked me. Though she is a female, I had to defend myself."

Jackson's grip tightened on Adam's collar at the image of his hands on Katherine. The American was not submissive by any means. But to do harm to her despite the reasons only served to fuel his anger.

"She tried to bewitch me as she has tried to bewitch you," Adam said. "She says you want her body every night and now you do not wish to see her leave. She is desperate to get away."

Because there was truth in Adam's words, Jackson swung his eyes toward Katherine, who unconsciously took a step back. "What is it, Jackson? What is he saying?" Inhaling deeply, she moved forward and stopped when she read doubt mixed with something else on his face. He turned away.

"Please, Jackson, listen. That man has been after me almost from day one. He watches me. He is constantly trying to get near me when you're not around."

"All of the men watch you." There was bitter cynicism in his voice. "But they would not dare touch you! They are all aware of the outcome."

Katherine was confused. What was he saying?

Was he aware that this man wanted her, had stalked her? Did he think that just because he commanded these men, not one of them would dare defy him? She could see by the expression on his face that this was exactly what he thought.

"I don't care about those other men, Jackson. It's you I want, no one else," she said, barely above a whisper. Her voice carried to him, caressing his ear.

Jackson did not respond but his hard expression softened. He looked at Adam.

Adam, though he didn't understand English, could read Jackson's expression and feared he was losing his advantage. He chuckled nastily. "She has bewitched you. I can see it as does everyone. Even N Zee said the American bragged to her how she had bewitched you. "If you want him, you'll have to find some way or someone to get me out of here. That's what she said to N Zee. Everyone is talking about how the weak American has brought the mighty warrior low." Adam shot Katherine a look of loathing and spat on the ground near Jackson's boot.

Horrified, Katherine watched as Jackson's fist connected with the rebel's nose. Blood spewed from it. Adam at last tried to fight back as Jackson's blows rained down on him, unmercifully pummeling him.

"Stop it, Jackson," Katherine screamed when Kimya failed to intervene. She ran to Jackson and grabbed his arm. It was like holding a lead pipe. He turned furious eyes to the woman who had stolen his reason.

"Why are you protecting him?"

"You're going to kill him, Jackson. I thought your fight was with the Kenyan government, not your own men. "

Kimya stepped in and took the arm Jackson jerked from Katherine's hold. "Ac na [stop]. He is not worth it," Kimya said levelly. "Do not kill him. Katherine will never understand nor will she forget."

When Jackson released him, Adam staggered to his feet and wiped sweat and blood from his face with the back of his hand, as best he could. He backed away from the people watching him, his eyes trained on Jackson, until he disappeared into the dense foliage.

In silence Katherine regarded Jackson. His profile to her, he stood like a statue, muscles working under his skin. Tentatively she approached him. He flinched at the hand she placed on his shoulder.

Panic lodged in Katherine's throat. She tried to turn Jackson to face her. When he refused to budge, she stepped in front of him. "Say something, please."

"He said you offered yourself to him," he replied

flatly. "Because you wish to leave you offered your body as payment and attacked him when he refused." Jackson went on to list Adam's accusations, omitting the part about her bewitching him.

Unbelievingly, Katherine stared, openmouthed. Finally she uttered sharply, "Surely you don't believe him?" Receiving nothing but silence to her question, she whispered accusingly, "How could you believe that of me?" Dispirited, she turned to walk away.

Chapter Twenty-Five

Jackson watched her take a step away. "Wait," he called. "Adam said you spoke to N Zee. Because you want to be away from here, from me, you went to her for help."

She turned and faced him. Jackson's eyes were intent on Katherine's face, watching every nuance as he spoke. "I know that he lied about your asking N Zee for help."

"But you believe me capable of trying to seduce that...that piece of scum so that he would lead me out of here?" Katherine's fury knew no bounds. She wanted to lash out at him for his doubt of her. "I would risk getting lost before I asked those two for anything," she replied acidly, her voice filled with loathing.

"Maybe." There was no mistaking Jackson's skepticism.

"Maybe?" Katherine tossed back at him. "How can you think I would have anything to do with that pair? A woman who attacks me without cause and a man who has been leering at me since I set foot in this place."

Without warning Jackson's hand clamped around Katherine's arm. The searing fury flared behind his eyes. Katherine flinched and he relaxed his tight hold, finally releasing her arm. "If he comes near you again, you are to tell me immediately."

"He won't get the chance after today, will he?" Katherine quipped, flicking her wrist. "I don't plan to see him or anyone else once I leave here." She eyed Kimya, who was standing nearby, wondering how much of their conversation he understood.

"Don't take offense, Kimya. You've never done anything to try and harm me."

Kimya didn't speak but Katherine was shocked to discover a smile in the depths of his brown eyes. She smiled at him in return.

"Because Adam wants you, maybe you will go to him for help," Jackson said.

"Excuse me?" Feeling confused, Katherine blinked. Unable to read his face, she turned back to Kimya, hoping his expression would shed some light on Jackson's remark. Kimya's face gave nothing away. Katherine's heart fell behind her ribs and unease began a slow descent through her body.

"Why would I need Adam's help for anything?" she asked, injecting as much disdain as possible into her tone.

Noises from the bush behind them distracted the trio. The rebels were returning but, Katherine realized with a jolt, more than half of the men were missing. The remaining rebels filed past the trio looking preoccupied. A few spoke quietly to Jackson and Kimya who responded with nods of their heads.

"Answer me, Jackson," Katherine demanded stridently when the last man had filed by. She swung to Kimya when Jackson failed to readily reply. "What does he mean by what he said? Please tell me, Kimya. I know you understand some of what I'm saying." Her eyes pleaded with him and unconsciously she caught hold of his arm, conveying her growing anxiety.

Kimya regarded her thoughtfully, his concern engaged. His eyes turned to Jackson, and he opened his mouth as if to respond. But in a light-ning fast motion Katherine was spun around and away from him.

"You will not be leaving here today." Jackson's tone was as cold as his eyes.

Telling herself not to panic, Katherine quelled

her growing fear. Something else as serious as the bombing must have happened to cause Jackson to temporarily delay their trip. "When, Jackson?" she managed. "Tomorrow? The day after? Just tell me when."

Silence greeted her request. "You promised me, Jackson." Katherine's voice shook but she had no room for pride. "Take me back today." Tears filled her eyes and spilled over, coursing down her cheeks unheeded. Jackson reached out a hand to brush them away. Recoiling from his touch, Katherine turned to Kimya.

"He won't take me back. He can't do this. I am an American citizen. Why does he want to keep me here? My uncle is an important man. There is no doubt in my mind that he's been looking for me since my disappearance. Take me to him, Kimya.

Kimya's eyes latched onto his friend's as if seeking an answer himself. Jackson's expression was inscrutable.

"I am not some piece in a chess game," Katherine cried brokenly. She had to leave while she had the will to do so. Already a small part of her rebelled at the thought of leaving Jackson.

Jackson recaptured Katherine's arm. She shrieked in protest, straining away from his hold. It was useless. He held her without much effort. The men some yards away watched them with keen interest.

"I despise you," Katherine uttered through stiff lips.

A muscle twitched in Jackson's cheek. "It does not matter," he answered evenly. "You will get over it."

"Never," Katherine hissed, narrowing her eyes on his handsome face.

"And you will not try to escape," Jackson said, as if Katherine had not spoken. "No one will help you."

How could she have lain so blissfully in this cold, emotionless man's arms mere hours ago? He was cut from the same fabric as the man he'd beaten to a pulp. As quickly as the thought came, Katherine tossed it aside. She would never be indifferent to Jackson's touch or shrink from it in distaste as she had Adam's.

Escape was what she needed. To escape from Jackson's hateful presence. She twisted her arm and Jackson allowed her to pull away. Moving swiftly, Katherine gave him a wide berth as she headed for the only place where she had a modicum of privacy, the shelter. Jackson pivoted around to watch her go, his expression brooding.

Kimya watched Jackson watch Katherine until a sentry rushed from the bush grabbing his arms. Jackson pulled his attention away from the closed door and turned to the agitated rebel.

Katherine paid little heed to the men milling about in front of the shelter. They kept their eyes averted as she passed, pretending interest in the various weapons at their sides. After entering the darkened interior she paid even less heed to the curses and shouts in Swahili intermingled with English and the sound of rushed footsteps.

The sound of Jackson's voice, unusually urgent and insistent, served to infuriate her more. How dare he think she was at his beck and call. Here only to serve his sexual needs. "Damn him!" He'd find her not so willing the next time.

"Katherine!" Jackson shot through the opening, his eyes wide and searching. Holding out his hand he commanded, "Come with me."

"I will not!" Katherine refused haughtily. Her chin came up. "You may be able to keep me here against my will but I will fight you every step of the way in everything else."

Jackson's eyes lighted on Katherine's small purse. He snatched it up and jammed it into his cargo pocket. He grabbed both her arms and hauled her out before she was aware of his doing it. "Let me go!" Katherine slung a look of disgust his way.

"Our camp has been found," Jackson said without ceremony. He released Katherine to smoothly slide bullets into the magazine of an assault rifle. "Biwott's men are close on our heels as we speak."

Katherine sucked in a breath, all of her right-eous anger forgotten. Her memories of the name and the man from the dinner party were clear. He was the same man who had warned them all about the rebel leader Jackson. He was on his way here. At least his men were. Her desire to get away from Jackson mysteriously vanished. Katherine willingly allowed him to lead her without further resistance.

The few remaining rebels were quietly and effi-ciently gathering their weapons and disappearing into the dense forest. Kimya met Jackson at the edge of the camp and tossed him a Rossi, which Jackson deftly belted at his back.

"How did this happen?" Jackson asked, peering down the barrel of the assault rifle. He didn't look at his friend but gave his full attention to his weapons, his movements quick and sure. Kimya's careless shrug was at odds with his expression of defeat. He spoke something in quiet Swahili which caused Jackson's lean form to stiffen in shock. For the first time since she'd known him, Katherine was able to read his expression. Disbelief and pain.

Regaining his composure, Jackson spoke to Kimya in clipped tones before Kimya disappeared into the underbrush. Jackson linked Katherine's arm with his and faced her. "Stay at my side. I will not allow any harm to come to you."

Katherine's heart turned over on meeting Jackson's eyes. Despite the impending and very real danger, a familiar tug of awareness danced over her. She loved this man. She could no longer deny that.

Jackson looked as if he might kiss her. She wanted him to, craved the touch of his lips. She leaned into him. It might be the last time. His breath fanned her cheek. "Jackson I—" Rifle fire exploded around them, breaking the spell.

"Lets go," Jackson commanded. Katherine moved at a trot abreast of him until they reached the clearing where Victor was. Katherine wondered how Jackson was going to get the wounded rebel to safety.

Careful to stay away from the open, they inched to the platform where Victor lay. Reflex brought Katherine's hand to her mouth, pressing hard to stifle her screams.

Half of the right side of his face was missing. Cleanly sliced away. Blood had spilled onto the platform, soaking into the wood. The wound Rose had worked so diligently over was untouched. Katherine prayed that his death had been instantaneous.

"Oh God, oh God," she wailed softly. Jackson could not die like this. Please, no! When tremors threatened to overtake her, she reached for her inner strength. Now was not the time to fall apart.

Jackson spoke quietly. "We must leave here, Katherine. Be prepared for worse before we reach safety." Heads low, they backed off the platform. His unspoken request had asked her to hold herself together.

"O.K." Squaring her shoulders, Katherine looked Jackson directly in the eyes, drawing on some of his strength.

"What will they do to you if you are caught?" Katherine and Jackson had been traveling through dense forest for close to five hours, barely speaking. Hunger and terrible thirst gnawed at Katherine but she refused to complain or make unreasonable requests. She would not burden Jackson with her wants. He was pushing them because time was of the essence.

Unless it was absolutely necessary, they avoided those areas where trails were frequently traveled or fallen trees provided large spaces overhead and on the ground. Jackson didn't want to chance being exposed if they happened upon the men looking for them.

They were some distance from the camp,

Katherine assumed, because they had been walking for such a long time. Each time Katherine had begun to believe they were traveling in circles or in the midst of nowhere, they had come upon a camp of sorts. One was always different from the other but all were abandoned.

"They will torture me, then kill me," he answered simply, as if he were giving ingredients for cake baking. They were on the edge of a clearing when Jackson paused and backed her up to a tree. She leaned against the trunk, resting for the first time since they had begun. As she studied his face, the thought of him being tortured wrenched Katherine's insides.

"They will torture you to try to make you talk?"

Jackson's full lips lifted in a grim smile while his eyes and ears continued to scan and listen. " I will be kept alive for a time, to gain information, yes. But useful information they know they will never get. They have tried before. And at this point what I have to say will be insignificant. Because they will have the person they believe is the cause of their problems, me." Not waiting for an response, Jackson continued. "They will torture me because it is what they are good at and they like it. Many times victims have told all they know, even to the point of fabricating what they think the police want to hear, in the belief that they will be freed. It does not help. The torture continues long after information, true or false, is given."

"Aren't you afraid?" His blasé attitude was escalating her fear and concern for him. He was used to this way of life. She was not. Unable to stop herself, her hand swept over his sculpted face, cupping his strong chin. Her eyes were full of worry and love for him.

A breath blew through Jackson's teeth and his eyes held Katherine's. His voice was gentle when he spoke. "I knew what the risks were when I began this, kipenzi changu [my love]."

"What do they mean, those words you speak?" Her eyes swept over his face.

Pressing his forefinger against her lips, Jackson shook his head, his body suddenly tense.

"What is it?" she asked, instinctively lowering her voice. He was like stone, listening intently.

The faint rustling of leaves was the only sound Katherine heard, no matter how she strained to hear what Jackson heard. Another false alarm, she assumed, until Jackson's arm slipped around her shoulder, pulling her from the tree trunk. The faint rustling stirred again, moving their way.

There it was again. Her hands gripped Jackson's biceps. Leaves with voices, headed in their direction. They were like sitting ducks.

"Jackson," she whispered insistently. She didn't

have a clue about where to go or how to get there, but the least they could do was make a run for it and not stand here and deliver themselves into the enemies' hands.

It didn't occur to Katherine until long afterwards that she was thinking in terms of the two of them and not just herself. Or that she now thought of the Kenyan police, an entity she'd prayed to rescue her only days ago, as being the enemy.

As the voices got closer, Jackson was spurred to action. He drew Katherine to his wide chest. "Stay with me, Katherine." The velvet-edged voice near her ear was husky with emotion.

With her face buried in his throat, Katherine wasn't sure how to decipher his entreaty. She only knew what was in her heart. "Always," she promised fervently. Her arm circled his waist tightly. She drew courage from his steady, strong heartbeat.

In a single movement his hands swept caressingly over her back, then bent her over into a crouch. He didn't have to warn her to quietness. She could hear the voices as well as he. Silently and noiselessly, she followed him through the underbrush, keeping low to the ground.

They had gone about twenty feet when Jackson paused. Katherine's heart pounded as loud as any African drum when she heard the voices once more. Jackson's shoulder was tense under her hand. Katherine couldn't see his face clearly when he swung around to her, but a warning rang in her head.

Chapter Twenty-Six

The voices were a different set. Pitched high, less vital. They came from in front of them instead of behind. And Katherine heard English, she was sure of it. She strained toward the voice speaking her language.

"The woman is with him, I am sure. He would not leave her; she is his ticket out."

Katherine understood every word of the accented voice. Which meant they were awfully close. And they were speaking of her and Jackson!

Holding her close to his side, Jackson kept a protective arm around her waist. Her leg muscles were cramping, screaming for release from the tight confinement.

As if sensing her discomfort, Jackson shifted his

rifle aside and allowed Katherine to lean heavily into him the instant the squawk of radio static pierced the air.

The voice on the other end of the radio could not be heard over the loud crackling noise. A male voice spoke into the radio but received no response. He spoke again, screaming in frustration. Finally giving up, he stormed to the man with him. "These damned things are useless! How can we be effective with outdated equipment?"

Both men stomped off, but not nearly far enough away to allow Jackson and Katherine an escape. Quiet reigned until a piercing whistle elicited a startled gasp from Katherine. She quickly clamped a trembling hand over her mouth. A second later she heard an answering whistle from the opposite direction. All too soon the sound of careless footsteps followed.

"What are we going to do, Jackson?" Katherine's voice was a hushed whisper in his ear. If the men had not found them yet they were bound to because they were at their front and their back. Jackson was about to make a move. She sensed it, dreaded it and hoped for it in the same breath.

Suddenly the brown and green leaves and limbs were ruthlessly brushed aside with the barrels of rifles. Two men, with surprised scowls on their faces, peered down at Katherine and Jackson.

They couldn't believe their luck. It was the one and only Jackson Shugaa! The man had been a thorn in the government's side for a long time. The man bringing him in would benefit greatly. Brown faces split with grins.

Their gloating was of short duration and was their undoing. As swift as the cheetah that roamed the game parks, Jackson was up, the butt of his rifle connecting with the chin and nose of the man directly in front of Katherine.

There was a sickening crunch of bones. Blood spewed from his nose and mouth as he crumpled to the ground. Before his companion could react, Jackson cut him down with a single bullet to the forehead. The man fell forward without a sound, landing by Katherine's foot.

Horrified and fascinated, Katherine's eyes flew to Jackson's. He exhibited not one iota of emotion at his neat and deadly handiwork. It had all happened before she could blink.

Jackson caught Katherine's hand in his and ran for the underbrush. The sound of excited voices seemed to spur them both on. Katherine tried to follow Jackson's lead and move soundlessly, but it was impossible. Her limbs were trembling with fatigue, and each time they paused to listen for sounds, she leaned heavily into him.

Finally, after what seemed like forever, they

stopped and remained where they were for an undeterminable length of time. The underbrush was so dense over their heads that Jackson had to nearly stand up to see above it. Dropping down beside Katherine, he put an arm around her. He could feel the tremors in her slim body as she leaned into him, but she did not complain. He held her closer and spoke into her ear. "I must go and find out where they are. You will remain here."

"Jackson, no," Katherine protested. She didn't want him to leave her.

"You will be safe here, Katherine. We cannot take the chance of stumbling upon them again. Do not fight me on this," Jackson ordered softly. She felt his warm breath on her cheek before his mouth covered hers hungrily. Too soon, he was up and gone without further words.

Katherine held her fingers to burning lips. Tears filled her eyes. "God, please don't let this be the last time I see him."

When Katherine heard the voices, she didn't know if she should remain where she was or seek a different spot. The men's voices made the decision for her.

"The American is not to be harmed in any way.

She will be taken to her uncle immediately. Jackson will not use her as a shield, for I will kill him like the scum he is."

"But the reward," another voice protested.

"He killed one of my men and seriously injured another. He is too quick, that one. His days are drawing to an end.

"The helicopters will be overhead at any moment. Surely he will be found."

As Katherine stood up in the brush, she didn't question whether she was doing the right thing. Her heart told her she was.

"Help me," she called out weakly. "Someone, please." Four pairs of startled eyes turned her way. Katherine looked down four rifle barrels and swayed on her feet

Voices started babbling all at once. A heavyset man, who was obviously their superior, signaled for quiet. He approached Katherine, his rifle held aloft. Katherine thought she'd better talk fast.

"My name is Katherine Wellington. I'm American and I was kidnapped by rebels. My uncle is Julius Wellington, a director on the board of the World Bank."

"We know who you are," the man answered. He came to stand by Katherine. "Where is Jackson? Where is he hiding?" He brushed by Katherine, poking the barrel of his rifle into the underbrush. "Come out, you coward. Hiding behind a woman is not like the Jackson Shugaa whose name means brave warrior! Ha." The man spat with contempt.

"He's not here." The relief in Katherine's voice was real. "He left me hours ago to find some of his rebels. He said I was slowing him down."

Spinning around, the man leaned toward Katherine, squinting. "Hours you say? Will he return?"

Her heart was thumping so loud she thought the man might hear it or read the lie in her eyes. She shook her head. "He left me here to fend for myself. He said some of you would probably stumble upon me. And he was right," Katherine added with a trembling smile when the veins in the man's neck doubled in size. For a few seconds, he seemed incapable of speech. He finally thundered at two of the men. "Search this immediate vicinity. If you find him, leave him to me. I will enjoy killing him."

They took off at the same instant Katherine heard propellers over head. With Jackson's acute hearing, she knew he'd heard them too. If he came back this way, he would try to rescue her. She had to get out of here without his being caught. "You must take me to my uncle immediately," she insisted. "I feel very sick."

Alarm crossed the man's face, but he protested.

"We will need to search some mo—"

Cursing harshly, he stared at Katherine's crumpled figure lying on the ground. He held the radio to his mouth and spoke rapidly in Swahili, then turned to the remaining policeman. Snapping a command at him, they picked Katherine up and walked towards the sound of the helicopter.

"You will not stay long to question her." The doctor's deep voice brooked no argument. Biwott's eyes narrowed in disapproval but Dr. Muiruri would not be swayed or intimidated.

"Ms. Wellington has had a traumatic couple of weeks. She is in a state of shock and her body is weakened from her ordeal. I will return in ten minutes, no more."

After Dr. Muiruri left the hospital room, Katherine scanned the faces of the individuals hovering over her. She'd awakened to voices arguing at the foot of her bed and was about to blissfully slip into slumber again when she recognized her uncle's anxious voice.

In and out of consciousness since yesterday, she'd spoken briefly to the persistent commissioner, but he hadn't been satisfied with her answers and had insisted on coming back today. Julius had refused to allow her to be questioned any more until Katherine convinced him that she was able to endure the ordeal. She wanted the entire matter over with. Biwott would not let her rest until then.

She learned that the man who had brought her to Nairobi was Jacob. Also at the commissioner's side was one of the men who had gone in search of Jackson. His face was bruised and battered, his lips swollen to twice their normal size, and his right arm was in a sling. He moved as if to sit in one of the vacant chairs but Biwott shot him a piercing glance. He tried to stand straight away from the wall, but leaned heavily on it instead, favoring his side.

Katherine wasn't a cruel person but she could only hope that if he'd found Jackson, his condition meant that Jackson had gotten away.

Julius was at his niece's side, her hand in his. Abra was furthest away, sitting with legs crossed and hands folded in her lap. She watched Katherine closely. She wanted to know what it was Julius wasn't telling her about Katherine's stay in the jungle.

"Did Jackson Shugaa tell you where his next target might be, Ms. Wellington?" Biwott asked in a smooth voice.

"Why would they tell me anything? I was kidnapped, remember?"

"Maybe you overheard something that may be of use," Biwott offered helpfully.

"I've told you more than once the rebels did not speak English around me," she replied testily.

The injured man pushed himself away from the wall with effort. "When he attacked me, Jackson demanded to know where she was. 'Where is Katherine?' he said. 'What have you done to her? If you have harmed her, I will kill you!' A man does not speak of a woman that way if he does not communicate with her," he insisted, throwing Katherine an angry glare.

So, he had encountered Jackson. Did that mean he was alive? Biwott's next words dashed her hopes.

"They are no more, you know," Biwott interjected gently, a smile curving his mouth, a cruel glint in his eyes.

Katherine gasped, one hand gripping Julius's, the other crumpling the crisp, white sheet. No, no, no. God no!

"They are dead, most of them. Their high ideals and pitiful weapons," he spat. "Thorns in Kenya's side with their lies and falsehoods. Dead, to bother us no more."

Slaughtered was more like it! Of that Katherine had no doubt as she watched Biwott, her dry eyes burning while her heart crumbled inside. Jackson dead. She could not bear it.

"You are telling us all, are you not, Ms. Wellington?" Biwott asked.

"Why would Katherine keep secrets after her ordeal?" Abra's voice vibrated in the small room with an underlying sneer. "Especially with that...that heathen still loose."

Katherine's heart sang. With every ounce of willpower she possessed, she kept the joy from her face, dropping her eyes quickly. But not before Biwott spotted the joyous relief written on her face.

"You are a very beautiful woman, Ms. Wellington." Biwott's eyes crawled over her in a rude manner. " Maybe you were with him long enough to share some of your thoughts and feelings." This last was filled with innuendo, but Katherine failed to rise to the bait.

"That's it. No more questions. My niece is the victim here, not the enemy." Julius pushed himself from his chair, his stance signaling the interview was at an end. "This Jackson Shugaa is your problem. I'm taking Katherine home to America in two days."

Katherine's fingers curled around her uncle's. She raised grateful eyes to his stern face. She was happy to see him again, but she didn't know if she could live with the knowledge of never seeing Jackson Shugaa again. Her thoughts were interrupted when Dr. Muiruri entered carrying a chart, the nurse behind him.

Biwott's lips tightened and all pretense at amicability was wiped from his face.

"You can be sure that if Jackson Shugaa sets foot in Nairobi and makes an attempt see you, Ms. Wellington, he will be shot dead like the dog he is. There will be no more toying with this animal."

Animal! Dislike for Biwott spewed within Katherine. Who really was the animal? Someone who would gloat in killing dozens of men and women? She wanted to smack his reptilian face.

"That is enough!" Julius snapped, recognizing Katherine's look of distress.

"I believe your niece cares for the heathen as your wife so aptly puts it. She is trying to protect him," Biwott said in a damning tone.

"I wouldn't be surprised," Abra stated with sarcasm. "Katherine doesn't—"

"I said that's enough, Abra!"

"From all of you," Dr. Muiruri added. "Please leave. Katherine needs her rest." Biwott shot the doctor a look which promised retribution, which the doctor studiously ignored.

Julius brushed his lips across her brow and ushered them all out of the room. The door closed quietly and Katherine shut weary eyes. Her bittersweet memories would be enough to sustain her for the days, weeks and years to come, of that she was sure.

Chapter Twenty-Seven

The soft brightness of the banquet room was reflected off diamonds, pearls and other gemstones glittering lavishly on the women and some men in the ballroom of the Hyatt hotel. A spotlight shone brightly on the man standing at the dias who was finishing his closing remarks about the man sitting to his left. Julius Wellington was valiantly struggling to maintain an interested expression. The banquet was being given as a tribute to him and three other successful businessmen in the Washington, D.C. area.

For the second time in as many minutes Katherine removed the hand of her date from her thigh. She turned to the man sitting next to her with a pleasant smile on her face, speaking for his ears only. "If you touch me one more time, in any shape, form or fashion, I will slap your face into the next decade." She smiled wider at Scott Strathmore, eyes glittering with determination, then rested her slender, manicured hands on top of the lace table-cloth next to the glass of water.

She was loathe to make a scene but Scott left her with no other alternative. If she moved from the table where she sat with Abra, her two cousins, cousin-in-law and close friends of her uncle, tongues would wag even more than they had in the past year since her return home. Family and friends of her uncle's circle flanked her, wedging her in tight against Scott's chair with little room to maneuver. That, however, did not give him an excuse to paw her.

Scott grinned innocently at her, showcasing white capped teeth. He lifted one of her stiff hands from the table and brought it close to his lips. His green eyes turned brighter when Katherine tried to slip her hand out of his. He blew a kiss across her knuckles before dropping her hand to the table, his remaining on top. Leaning in close, he spoke for her ears only.

"Damn it, Kathy. Do you realize you are the sexiest, most elusive and beautiful female I've ever met? I would like nothing better than to take you home with me away from all of these prying and jealous eyes so I can gobble you up." His eyes dropped to her cleavage visible above the neckline of her baby blue gown.

Katherine's spine stiffened at the despised, abbreviated use of her given name. She didn't know whether to laugh or throw up. She allowed the disdain she felt for the sexist remarks to show on her face. She almost wished that she'd accepted Alex's invitation to the banquet instead of Scott's. But she'd been in no mood to listen to his pleas or arguments. Their relationship was over. The fact that he wanted to "go back and start from the beginning" was the main reason she'd refused.

She was here because her uncle Julius wanted her; he'd insisted that she come. How could she refuse him after he'd stood staunchly by her side when gossiping tongues sought to tear her down? On the rare occasions she went out, she usually went alone, but for some vague reason she'd allowed Scott to talk her into allowing him to escort her here after she turned Alex down. Now she was living to regret that decision.

Without dignifying his dubious compliments with comments, she leaned away from him, picked up her wine glass and took a long drink. While she wasn't big on spirits, the semi-dry wine soothed her parched throat.

The voice of the speaker droned on and she

closed her eyes. When she opened them, she was staring into the reproachful eyes of Abra, who had watched the exchange between her and Scott. Her cousin Ja Lisa looked frustrated and sad at the same time. Caught staring, Ja Lisa dropped her eyes and turned to her husband, who was doing an excellent job of ignoring her.

Tilting her chin proudly, Katherine held Abra's disdainful stare. She wasn't under any illusions that Abra wanted her here. She, Katherine Wellington, who was a blight of shame on the family name, should be at home, away from prying eyes and wagging tongues.

Abra's scornful gaze dropped to the rise of Katherine's smooth bare breasts above the draped neckline of her gown. It said emphatically that Katherine was asking for trouble. She selectively overlooked the fact that she herself was wearing a clinging dress of chiffon fabric that rode well above her knees and revealed much more cleavage than did Katherine's garment.

Breaching etiquette, Katherine propped both her elbows on the table and thrust her shoulders forward. She didn't give a fat rat's ass what Abra thought of her. She'd stopped caring long ago.

"I don't understand why any of the eligible men in the city continue to want to date her," Abra replied nastily to her sorority sister, Patricia Becon. They were standing in front of the bar in the lobby of the Hyatt. Bored with the speakers inside the banquet hall, they had strolled outside for fresh air. They openly watched Katherine walk by, her satin purse hung from her shoulder on a long gold chain. Katherine walked to the large window facing the entrance of the hotel to stare out at the manicured grounds.

"You know how men are, sweetie," Patricia responded knowingly, nodding her perfectly coiffed head. She watched Katherine's straight back, the rounded bottom and long legs peeking through the side slits in the dress with an envy she would never reveal to her friend of two decades. The floor length silk gown with lace embroidery and beading hugged Katherine's youthful body enough to hint at the curves underneath. Her hair was slicked off her forehead and ended in a thick chignon. Small diamond studs adorned her lobes. The simplicity of the hairstyle and dress only added to her appeal. That figure, combined with her beauty and aloofness, increased the mystery surrounding her, even to those who thought they knew her best.

Everyone in their circle, female and male, had waited with bated breath for more than a year for

Katherine to give details of what she'd endured during her kidnapping. She had spoken to no one about her ordeal and had become a virtual recluse. So they had speculated, oh how they had speculated, and as it turned out, with good reason.

"They want to find out just what she learned in the jungle at the hands of that...that bandit." The two women stared at each other for the beat of a second before bursting into laughter.

"Did she tell you what happened out there?" Patricia asked, not for the first time, her voice dropping to a conspiratorial whisper.

"We know what happened, we've seen the results," Abra snapped, suddenly irritated.

"I know, I know." Patricia brushed Abra's agitation blithely aside. "But what we don't know is if she was forced to have sex with him or if she did it willingly. I'll bet she enjoyed it," Patricia said half to herself, her eyes lighting up with the probability. "She rarely goes out. You said yourself that she isn't serious about anyone. Poor Alex is still willing to jump through hoops for her, despite everything."

Abra hrumped disdainfully as both pairs of eyes turned to the slender back facing them. A semi-famous band hired for the evening's entertainment was having its intermission. Several of the male band members walking through the lobby spotted Katherine and paused to talk.

"Maybe Katherine's got a secret," Patricia replied, her eyes narrowed. "Good sex can happen when one least expects it. Especially if a man knows what he's doing. Something tells me that rebel knew just what button to push on our dear girl."

Snorting her contempt, Abra downed a swallow of her Merlot. Patricia's beginning and ending thoughts were about sex. The thought of food came in between. She ran a critical eye over her girlfriend in the too tight, too short silk dress that showed bulges in all the wrong places. Yet she held a plate laden with food.

Chills shook Abra's frame. "I shudder each time I think of what could have happened to my Ja Lisa. The idea of that man laying his filthy hands on her gives me nightmares."

It would be more than that husband of hers was doing at the moment. Hollis was laying his hands on someone all right. On Patricia's niece. Patricia prudently kept her thoughts to herself. What one didn't know sometimes didn't matter. A malicious twinkle entered her eyes as she popped a salmon canapé into her mouth.

The hotel lobby was teaming with activity,

patrons and guests coming and going in and out of the various rooms and halls in which their interests lay. Bellboys arrived with luggage while others carted luggage out to waiting vehicles. People buzzed around Katherine in small groups and large, laughing, discussing, having fun in general, but none approached her. After she'd gotten rid of the men from the band, she'd been content to continue staring out the window.

She would go home in a short while. That would mean going back to Scott whom she'd escaped as soon as she could. It was rude but at this juncture, she didn't care. He had breached all etiquette as far as she was concerned. Holding her too tight and too close on the dance floor, grinding his body against hers, placing unwanted kisses over her face. His behavior disgusted her. She was tired and wanting her bed. Prior to going to Kenya, she'd enjoyed the nightlife. Now she had other priorities which were more important and she didn't miss the "good times" at all.

The laughter and talking grew louder around her, piercing her reverie. Slightly curious, she looked over her shoulder to see what was causing all of the excitement. Some of the women from the banquet were clustered together talking, their attention glued to the bank of elevators at the end of the carpeted stairs leading to the second floor.

"Be still, my heart."

"Lord, Lord, Lord, I'm starting to sweat. I just hope there's more than one of him."

"Ssh. He's coming our way. Don't look."

"The hell if I won't look! I want him to see me, sister girl."

Uninterested, Katherine was about to turn back to the window when something about the precise gait and long legs of the man headed in their direction caught her attention. Her heart paused for long moments. Her jaw unhinged and the bag she was holding fell from cold fingers.

"Look at that, will ya," one of the women was saying, venom dripping from her tongue. "Shoulda known he'd head straight for her. They all do after finding out about her jungle adventure."

"If that one took me to the jungle I'd gladly go and not come back."

The women snickered and all nodded in agreement. Katherine didn't hear any of the snide babble or suggestive comments. She couldn't over the loud pounding of her heart in her ears. Her mind was telling her what she was seeing was impossible but her eyes were saying yes, it was possible.

"Jackson?" He came closer, wearing a chalk-striped rayon suit, dark shirt and matching striped tie. On his feet were Chelsea dress boots. A black mustache covered his upper lip and his eyes were as clear and golden as ever.

He'd lost weight, was leaner, and though she knew it wasn't possible, he seemed taller, his shoulders as impossibly wide as ever.

Katherine had never seen him in anything but battle uniform and combat boots. My God, he was beautiful! Her eyes drank him in. He came closer. A small raised scar on his jaw disappeared under his shirt collar. He smelled as good as he looked. Katherine's limbs trembled and she felt slightly dizzy.

She wanted to shout, stomp, scream. She wanted to kiss him, hit him! She had prayed for this day and thought her prayers futile. Tears filled her eyes. She cried so easily these days and despised herself for it.

"Jackson," she repeated, in a less shaky voice.

"Hello, Katherine." He stared across the small space at her, his golden eyes as impenetrable as ever. The full lips were tilted upwards in what appeared to be a smile.

Her insides turned to mush at the sound of the voice she'd longed to hear for hours, days, months. She wanted to fall into his arms. She despised herself for that weakness also.

"Katherine?"

Her uncle! He was coming her way. Too late Katherine remembered Abra and Patricia standing at the bar. Her eyes flew across the wide room filling up with people. The two heads were together, looking her way. Did Abra recognize Jackson? Julius was sailing across the marble floor, a big grin on his face. Panic numbed her for long seconds.

Suddenly she was galvanized into movement when Julius's eyes swung to Jackson, a curious frown between his brows. She pivoted to Jackson and whispered hurriedly, "You must leave here! You are in serious danger!" Without waiting to see if Jackson complied with her warning, her legs carried her to meet her uncle.

She slipped an arm through his, expertly guiding him away from the spot where Jackson was left standing. "Uncle, I'm sorry but I'm going to have to leave. Scott is being a total jackass and I have one of those tension headaches coming on." And indeed she did. Katherine massaged her scalp to relieve the tightness at her temple.

She chanced a glance over her shoulder. Jackson's angry eyes were riveted to her retreating back. The women were converging on him and Katherine wanted to run back and scratch out every pair of female eyes. Her satisfaction in seeing him brush them aside lasted for a brief period, until he took a step in her direction.

If she could only reach the stairs where there were throngs of people ascending and descending.

She tugged harder on Julius's arm.

"Katherine, honey," Julius laughingly protested, attempting to slow his niece down.

Finally they were at the stairs and climbing up. Midway Katherine looked down over the heads of people and was foolishly disappointed that she didn't see Jackson. Where had he gone that quickly?

Breathing easier after they reached the second floor, Katherine turned to Julius. "I'll find Scott. I'll talk to you in the morning..."

"Hey speedy-o," Julius called out, reverting to her childhood nickname, "hold on a minute."

Katherine paused, ready for flight. Jackson could come up those stairs at any second. Julius knew what he looked like and so did Abra. Reward posters had been posted all over Kenya before they left. The mustache only added distinction to an already arresting face. And who could forget those eyes? All hell would break loose if Abra recognized him.

"I thought—downstairs—you were talking—," Julius, stumbled, clearly confused.

Katherine's heart pounded, she couldn't breathe. She'd deny knowing him! she thought wildly. She'd go to her grave denying it if it was necessary! She curled stiff fingers inward and waited for the ax to fall.

"It doesn't matter," he finally said. He kissed her

forehead and stared into her eyes as if about to say something. Still looking a bit dazed, he went in search of his wife.

Chapter Twenty-Eight

By the time Katherine reached home, paid Mrs. Grant and walked the elderly woman to her car, her headache was full-blown. She threw two aspirin down her throat, slurped a glass of water and put on pajamas while waiting for them to take effect. When forty minutes passed and her temple still throbbed, she realized she was still too agitated for the pills to do any good. Jackson's visage filled her mind. Where was he now? What was he thinking? How had he gotten into the States, to the Hyatt, to her, as bold as you please? So many questions and no answers. "Oh, Jackson." The heartfelt sound of his name on her lips set her pulse to rapid beating.

Did her uncle know who he was? Something

about the expression he was wearing when they parted made her think he did. Please, Uncle, for my sake, have mercy. She squeezed her eyes shut. Julius now understood the reasons behind the fight the rebels waged against their government. He didn't agree with everything they believed in or the way they went about achieving their goals but he at least realized most of the men and women were recently law-abiding citizens until desperation drove them underground to exact a change by the only means at their disposal. The deplorable conditions in Kenya could no longer be concealed. The ethnic cleansing had become a part of the national evening news. The corruption of the current government was slowly being exposed. Matoi was extremely powerful, however, and did whatever was necessary to solidify his tenure in office.

And while Julius now knew that Jackson had nothing to do with her kidnapping, he held him responsible for taking so long in getting her back to him. Katherine did not reveal to him that Jackson had perhaps not intended to bring her back at all.

Each night of her life she prayed for his safety. She knew enough about the volatile situation in Kenya to know that she could not search for him. It would only place his life in greater jeopardy.

She scanned the large living room with all its trappings of comfort, from the sofa she was resting on to the antique, upholstered armchairs covered in elegant brocade. How she had longed to see this again. And now, it was just a place she came home to every day after work. One she kept reasonably clean but a place she could take or leave without regret.

The knock at the door brought her to her feet. She approached it with caution but not fear. It was late and she had few close friends. Only her uncle would be concerned enough to stop by.

Her heart fluttered in her chest when she peered through the peephole. She straightened the collar of her pajama top and ran her hand down the length of the silk material. Jackson Shugaa stood on the other side of the door. The street lamp illuminated his sharp features clearly. He stared back at the wooden door as though he could see through it.

Inhaling a deep breath while a thousand questions ran through her mind, Katherine twisted the knob with a shaky hand. Jackson stepped over her threshold, his eyes locked on hers.

She backed up further to allow herself room to breathe, then walked into the living room with Jackson on her heels. Katherine turned and faced him calmly enough as she tried to read what was in his eyes. They were gentler than she had ever witnessed. His mustache was thick and black. The scar on his chin was healed over, causing Katherine to wonder abstractedly how he'd gotten it.

Every muscle was tense, her nerves stretched thin. She had to say or do something to relieve the tension. "What are you doing here? In Washington?"

"I'm here to see you," he answered simply.

Katherine's heart leapt with gladness. But she would not be sidetracked. She had so many questions.

"How did you find me?" Her voice was steady, belying her inner turmoil.

"Let's sit," Jackson invited. He sat on the sofa, his long legs stretched out in front of him, crossed at the ankles in a pose reminiscent of the way he used to sit on the stump stools or the ground. Katherine licked her lips and complied, careful not to sit too close to him. Her hands were primly folded in her lap. She could still smell his scent of fresh air, woods and pine. She swallowed and licked her dry lips.

"Your uncle."

"What?" Katherine croaked, glad she was sitting. She wasn't sure she'd heard correctly. Jackson had to be talking of something else. "My uncle what?"

"I found you through your uncle."

"Impossible!" Katherine shook her head in

denial.

"I am here in the United States with the help of your uncle. Tonight he helped me find your home. It is true, Katherine." Jackson's smile revealed white teeth. He was stunning when that stoic, dignified persona was pierced.

It was totally improbable, impossible. But she knew Jackson was telling her the truth. At a loss for words, her hands fluttered up to her cheek to fall limply to her thigh. Jackson caught her hands in his and her heart went pitter-pat.

"I've been living in exile in England and trying to get to the United States for months, Katherine," he explained softly. Amnesty International and your uncle helped me get here. Your uncle was the man who made everything possible."

"How?" she asked shakily.

Lifting wide shoulders, an ironic smile on his lips, Jackson answered languidly, "Your uncle warned me to 'ask no questions and he would tell me no lies.' I am no fool, Katherine. I would not—how do you say it—look for a gift in a horse's mouth."

"Look a gift horse in the mouth," she automatically corrected, too agog to laugh at Jackson's attempt at American slang. "Why?" she asked, mostly to herself.

"Your uncle loves you very much."

At a loss for words, Katherine was the one staring now. This explained her uncle's bewildered expression when she rushed him from the hotel lobby. He'd recognized Jackson all right. He was the reason for him being in the country! Her throat was tight and her body trembled with emotion. Jackson rubbed his fingers over her knuckles. Katherine's lashes swept her cheeks. The touch of his hands brought back so many memories.

She wasn't aware she was crying until Jackson reached out with his fingers, caught her tears and gently wiped them away. "Do not cry, Katherine, kipenzi changa. I am here now."

Katherine's fingers gripped Jackson's. She recognized the endearment. Understood its meaning though Jackson wasn't aware she understood it. Did he really mean it? Or was it something he said in the throes of passion or to soothe a woman in distress?

"When your uncle learned I was trying to find a way to get here, he got in contact with me and we talked by phone. He was in England some time ago for a World Bank Conference and we met and talked some more. With the help of him and a few of his friends in the state department, I was able to enter your country with a record that is almost clear."

"He never breathed a word to me," Katherine

replied, unsure of how she felt.

"He told me he did not want to get your hopes up." Jackson dropped his eyes to her hands which he turned palm over in his large hands. "He said you had changed since returning home."

Uncle Julius had said a mite too much, she thought, a frown marching across her brow. "What else did he tell you?" Katherine asked, watching him carefully.

Spreading her hands wide, Jackson's lips curled upward. He placed a kiss on the back of her hands.

Katherine sucked in a breath. Her pulse was beginning to beat rapidly. "How did you get away?" It was a question uppermost in her mind.

"Thanks to you, it was easy to avoid Biwott's henchmen." His eyes flashed with renewed anger and fear, remembering that day in the forest. When he'd spied one of the policemen coming from the direction he'd left Katherine, he ambushed the man and made him talk. When he heard what she'd done, he felt anger, pain and a great sense of loss. Later, when he'd had time to reflect on the events of that day, he realized why she had acted as she had. Still it did not lessen his sense of loss or his fear for her safety.

"Those men were so desperate to have me in their clutches they could have done you great harm, Katherine. You will not put your life in jeopardy in such a way again, do you understand?"

Katherine wanted to laugh at the ludicrous statement until she read the seriousness in Jackson's eyes. "Do you plan to kidnap me and take me back to the jungle?" she asked laughingly.

"If that is what it takes."

Sobering quickly, Katherine stared at Jackson, speechless. She didn't ask him to expound on his statement. She had a feeling she wouldn't like or agree with his answer.

"What about Kimya? Is he alive?" she asked instead.

"Kimya is alive and in China. He will be returning home soon, a free man."

"My uncle's doing?" Katherine questioned, knowing the answer.

Jackson smiled enigmatically. "And that of some others in high places."

"And N Zee?" Katherine did not look directly at Jackson.

"N Zee is dead," he replied flatly. "She is the reason for the deaths of so many."

Her eyes flew to Jackson's. He read fear and aversion in their depths. "N Zee's death is her own doing," he explained. "After attacking you, she slipped into town and made contact with Biwott through one of his men. She made arrangements for his men to invade our camp. " At Katherine's gasp of disbelief a bleak look entered Jackson's eyes.

"The moment she made contact with him she set into motion events she was unable to stop. Because of her arrogance, she thought she could control Biwott. She expected a man of his poor character to hold true to his word to take only the American woman.

"She assumed that Kimya would take you back. That she was putting at stake the life of a man who cared very much for her, she gave no thought to. That the soldiers might do you harm, she did not care." His eyes hardened and his tone chilled Katherine, though it was her well being he spoke of.

"When she learned you were not going back as originally planned, she led Adam to you, knowing that he wanted you and would force himself on you. Afterwards he was to hold you there until Biwott's men arrived. She allowed selfishness and jealousy to control her. Biwott's men would never have stopped with taking you. They wanted the glory of wiping us out. When they did not get what they wanted the most, me, N Zee paid the price."

Katherine let go a breath filled with regret. N Zee was a human being who should merit some sort of feeling but Katherine felt little sympathy for the spiteful woman. She'd sought to hurt Jackson by hurting her. Katherine would never forgive her for that.

Rose! The diminutive, proficient Rose. Katherine didn't want to see her dead, even if the woman had withdrawn from her.

"Rose?" she questioned anxiously.

Pain entered Jackson's golden eyes. He closed them briefly. "Rose is dead." The subject was closed. Katherine had no desire to pursue it.

So much pain and destruction. Good people dead. Katherine shook her head sadly. In a detached manner she noticed Jackson reaching to the inside of his breast pocket for something. It was enclosed in soft white tissue paper, the kind used inside gift boxes. He balanced it carefully on a muscled thigh. As he unwrapped the small, flat object, he spoke.

"Throughout everything I endured I managed somehow to keep this with me. When I thought I would never see another day, I would hold this to my nose and think of you. The way you looked, the scent you carried, despite your dips in the cool lake."

The huskiness of Jackson's tone drew Katherine's eyes to the purse on his knee. Her small beaded purse that she'd completely forgotten. He'd carried it with him for over a year. It was still in reasonably good condition. The tube of lotion, was it still inside? It couldn't be!

As if in answer to her question, Jackson unsnapped the purse and withdrew the small tube of lotion to hold up to her eyes. She'd used the lotion during one of her most despondent moments.

"This is you, Katherine. The you I will always think of." He gave her the purse, which she clutched with nerveless hands, but not the tube of lotion. This, he held under his nose, sniffing delicately, his eyes holding hers.

Sucking in her breath, she met him halfway as he leaned towards her. Her heart fluttered in her chest and her lips parted for something she had thought was gone forever. The sound of a baby's cry broke their sensual spell. The cry came again, persistent, louder. Katherine moved swiftly, oblivious to the astonished expression on Jackson's face.

Chapter Twenty-Nine

*H*olding the whimpering baby close to her breasts, Katherine bounced him up and down in her arms, crooning soft words in his ear to quiet him. Jackson, his jacket off, his dark shirt stretching across the width of his shoulders, stood just inside the doorway. The lamp in the nursery was covered with a Winnie the Pooh shade and provided a soft light that did not quite reach Jackson's eyes. Katherine didn't know what he was thinking.

He came further into the room as she shifted the now quiet child across an arm. Billy made sucking noises with his lips and opened his eyes to stare unblinkingly up at the man staring down at him. Deep golden eyes held darker golden eyes.

Jackson touched the downy soft cheek, caressing it lovingly. Billy's chubby fingers reached for the finger that Jackson held before his eyes, clamping it tightly in his baby grip. Jackson pressed a kiss to the baby's knuckles. Billy gurgled and smiled up at him.

"What is his name?" Jackson asked, his attention not straying from Billy as he gave him an answering smile.

"William Kirk. I call him Billy, for short," Katherine answered evenly.

His finger still in Billy's, Jackson lifted his head. Something hot and tender flared in the depths of his eyes. Once she reached home Katherine had set about to find out as much as she could about Jackson and his family. Information had been sparse but she did learn that his father's name was William Shugaa and that the popular lawyer had died mysteriously while in police custody. Kirk was her father's first name.

"How old is my son?"

Katherine stiffened. She could not deny it if she wanted to. It was written all over Billy's small round face. She kissed the soft tuft of hair. Billy giggled when her lips touched his head. "He'll be five months in three days."

He eased his finger from the baby's hold and cradled his arms. Katherine put Billy into the protective fold. Now wide awake, the baby was no longer content to lie still. He squirmed, clamoring for an upright position. Jackson sat him up and Billy began to investigate his father's face with fat fingers. Jackson placed a soft kiss at his temple.

Katherine's heart tilted and love filled the space. No matter what happened between the two of them, she would always cherish these moments between father and son. Jackson's eyes lifted to hers. The emotions written in his drew her in. She raised a hand to the prominent cheekbone.

"He must have my name right away," he stated firmly.

Nodding, Katherine agreed. She had no problem with that. "It's not a lengthy process these days. We can add your last name to his at the beginning of the week, Monday or Tuesday."

Jackson's eyes narrowed and his lips compressed. "We will marry Monday or Tuesday," he stated firmly.

Katherine's temper flared. "We will do no such thing," she stated just as firmly, dropping her hand. He was back. The old autocratic Jackson. The same man she'd loved almost to distraction. If he thought he could waltz in here after more than a year, making demands on her, she had a reality check for him well in hand.

The problem was, he wasn't giving her a chance

to say yes or no. He was ordering her to do his bidding just as he had while she was his reluctant captive. Where was his declaration of love? She wasn't about to enter into a union with a man who thought he had all of the answers, no matter how much she loved him. If he didn't return her affections, he could just go to Halifax.

"My child will not grow up to be called a bastard." Jackson's arm closed protectively across the small back and Billy wiggled in protest. Loosening his hold, Jackson's harsh features relaxed as he watched his son watch him.

"This is America," Katherine snapped cooly. "Times and conditions have changed. People pay very little attention to that moral code." Even as she spoke, she cringed inside at the thought of someone calling her child names because of a lack of a father in his life.

But she could no more marry a man who decreed without love what she must do than she could marry a man who professed his love, whom she did not love in return. Alex had offered to give her and Billy his name on more than one occasion. Katherine had once thought she could marry without loving the man or the man loving her. After knowing Jackson, she knew she could not.

"Why will you not marry me, Katherine?" Jackson's anger was growing. His curt voice lashed out at her. Billy, sensing a shift in his father's emotions, stared up with at him with wide, tawny eyes which began to fill with tears, prompting Katherine to take him and sooth his anxiety.

When he was calm, she placed him in his bed, cranked up his Winnie the Pooh mobile which made soft, tinkling music. Jackson stood over the crib watching his son fall asleep until Katherine beckoned him to leave the room with her.

The instant they were in her living room she rounded on him with fury. He beat her to the punch. "Is it because you are interested in that fop who was hanging over you tonight?"

Katherine sucked in a breath. She'd had no idea Jackson had been in the vicinity watching Scott put his hands all over her. Had he observed her every move before, during and after the banquet? Well, she didn't like him spying on her!

"Is that the fiancé you told me about?" His face was a glowering mask of rage. "My first thought when I saw him touch you was to loosen his teeth. It took every ounce of control I had to keep away from the both of you. I did not want to embarrass your uncle and insult his generosity. After all, he was the reason I was in the States."

Embarrass her uncle! Of all the nerve. What about embarrassing her? Growing angrier by the minute, yet fascinated at the play of emotions on

Jackson's face, Katherine could only listen.   His
gold eyes were the color of mud and she swore she
saw steam coming from his proud nostrils.

"He will not have you," he stated forcefully. "You
set him straight or I will. I promise you neither of
you will like my way."

"Now you listen to me, Jackson Shugaa,"
Katherine bit out, seething with fury. "This is not the
jungle. I am not one of your rebels or a captive you
can order about any longer. You cannot, I repeat,
cannot waltz in here telling me what to do. And,"
she added for good measure, "you'd better be glad
you didn't cause a scene at the banquet tonight. My
aunt would have had you carted away in handcuffs
once she found out who you were."   She was
absolutely furious at him but a tiny part of her was
thrilled at his unmistakable jealously.

"He will not have you, Katherine. I mean it,"
Jackson replied, advancing on her. His expression
was thunderous and his voice was barely edged
with control. He dragged her none- too-gently to his
long, lean frame.   His warm breath fanned her
cheeks and Katherine's pulse ran rampant.

"No man will have you while I am alive. If I die
before making you mine and another captures your
heart, I promise to haunt you from my grave." His
mouth slammed down on hers, persistent, demanding. His tongue swept across her lips, sending shiv-

ers of longing down her spine while his arms crushed her to his hard body.

Whatever resistance Katherine had mustered fled with his knowing touch. It had been so long since his lips held sway over hers. So long since his arms held her as they did now. Leaning into him, Katherine drank in his hot, furious kisses. Her mouth opened and his tongue delved in. His demanding lips, sweet and moist, plundered and ravaged. Katherine was willing putty in his hands and still Jackson carried on as if he couldn't get enough.

Before their lungs burst from lack of air, Jackson drew away. He pressed his forehead against Katherine's, his breathing rough and labored. Incapable of speech, Katherine trembled in his arms as hers hugged his waist. He touched his lips to her forehead and both cheeks, working his way across her nose to her jawline. Gathering her hands in his, he pressed a kiss into the center of each palm. His thumbs caressed the pulse beating erratically in each wrist while his eyes held her captive.

His head lowered and his mouth captured hers in another drugging kiss, this one less frantic but no less demanding. He raised his head, the fire in his eyes a tawny gold. "Will you marry me, Katherine?" His voice was husky with longing. "Please."

Katherine's heart sang. He had not said he loved her yet, but there was a sound of caring in his request and he was asking, not demanding. "Jackson—" Senses befuddled, Katherine wasn't sure what she was about to say.

"Nakupenda, simba shugaa ," Jackson intoned softly, nibbling at her earlobe.

"What did you just say?" Katherine asked, breathless, averting her head to allow Jackson easy access to her neck.

"I said I love you, brave warrior."

When Katherine's heart started to beat again, she stared at Jackson, not sure she had heard him correctly. Swallowing the lump in her throat, she asked, "Can you repeat that, a bit louder this time?"

"Nakupenda. I love you, Katherine. With every fiber of my being." He smiled a seductive smile. "If you don't know that after all I've done to get here to you, I do not yet know what else I can do. You must let me know." He shrugged nonchalantly. "If you do not love me yet, I will teach you how," he stated confidently. "I promise to be patient."

A warm glow enveloped Katherine and her joy shone in her eyes. She cupped Jackson's face in her hands, her expression conveying all of the love she had in her heart for this man. "Nakupinda. Nakupinda. I love you, I love you," she cried. " Oh Jackson, I love you so much. Tears stung her eyes.

She was always tearing up around this man but this time she didn't mind.

As she pressed kisses to Jackson's startled face, laughter bubbled to the surface. It was cut short when Jackson crushed her to him. The light of desire visible in his eyes turned Katherine's already weak knees to butter. He scooped her up in his arms. "It has been so long, my love. I want you so badly. I would go through hell and back again to have you in my arms like this. I need you desperately."

The longing, desire and need were clear in his magical voice. It seeped into her, increasing her own. "In there." She nodded in the direction of her bedroom. The single burning candle caused Jackson to pause after setting Katherine on her feet.

"It's a habit I've developed," she stated simply. One she could not seem to break, nor did she try. It was the one way she could have a restful night.

Easing the pajama top off her creamy brown shoulders, Jackson pressed moist kisses on her collarbone, drifting to the rise of her breasts. Katherine began undoing the buttons on his shirt as his mouth closed over an engorged nibble. She moaned, snatching the shirt from the waist of his pants.

Need spiraled out of control through her. He slid

a hand into the waist of her pajama bottoms, working his way over the rounded curve of her hip, measuring, sculpting, before slipping between the apex of her thighs. Jackson found her warm, tight and moist. He groaned deep within his throat and pushed the bottoms fully off her hips so that she could step out of them.

Katherine made quick work of his pants and briefs and gasped when he sprang free, long, thick and hard. Guiding her to the king-sized bed, Jackson laid her down on it and stretched out beside her. "So many nights I have wanted you beside me, inside me," Katherine said huskily, stroking the silky length of him.

Smoothing a hand across Katherine's stomach, Jackson rained kisses from her thighs up past her navel, over her breasts, capturing her mouth. "I am here, my Katherine," he replied, raising his head to look into her eyes. "Now you can do with me what you will."

Needing neither encouragement nor permission, Katherine proceeded to do just that as they ravaged each other's body well into the night. Still they could not get enough of each other. When Katherine would drift off to sleep, Jackson would awaken her with his mouth and tongue. When Jackson grew drowsy, Katherine brought him to wakefulness with the stroke of her hands and smooth glide of her tongue.   At last both were exhausted and had to be content to lie in each other's arms.

Katherine was resting limply on Jackson's chest when he spoke near her ear. "If we do not marry next week, it will be soon." It was less of a demand and more of a question.

Because Katherine was secure in the knowledge of his love for her, she did not take umbrage. There was some hesitation in her response however. "I'm not sure I can marry you, Jackson."

The hand at her waist stilled. "What is this nonsense you are speaking, Katherine?"

Her hand fluttered helplessly on his chest. She lifted her head, attempting to convey her dilemma to him. "I love you so very much, Jackson, but I cannot come to Kenya with you. I have to put our son's safety first."

A smile curved Jackson's full mouth. His fingers snaked into Katherine's thick hair which fell across her shoulders. "I will return to Kenya in three months for the presidential election. I will be there with other members of the international community, some of your Washington politicians and your uncle to monitor the two party voting—the first time this will be done in my country."

Jackson's hopeful expression was tempered with caution. "This is one small step in the right direction. However, Kenya has many uphill battles, especially if Matoi retains his office. Even if he does, Kenyan citizens will not give up fighting, nor will I. But I will not remain in Kenya. I have been working with Amnesty International these past months and I will continue, through your government and other legal means, to help my country in any way I can. I will remain in America to do this." His eyes held hers, full of meaning. "With you by my side."

Stretching up, Katherine kissed Jackson with all of the love and joy she carried inside. Her heart swelled. He was making a huge sacrifice for her. It was something she would have never asked him to do. "You will not regret your decision later?" Her expression was full of earnestness. She would give him up rather than see him unhappy.

"The only thing I would regret is not having you by my side," Jackson replied with quiet assurance. "I can go home to visit my mother and family; however, I will remain here. I cannot live without you, Katherine."

Katherine drew his hand in hers and kissed the calloused palm. "I want to meet your mother."

"She is waiting only for me to tell her the day we will marry and she will be here."

"We will marry right away." She smiled radiantly.

Jackson drew her to him for a gentle kiss. He was the first to pull away and tunneled his fingers into her hair, drawing her head back so that he could stare into her eyes. "When I found you gone with Biwott's men that day in the thick brush, I was like a crazed man, even knowing it was best for you." His fingers were gentle but his expression was fierce.

"I only knew I had to get those men out of there somehow, before you returned. Do you think I could have lived if they had killed you?" she asked quietly. "Then when I returned to Washington and found out I was carrying your child, it became my one and only reason to keep going."

Seemingly at a loss for words, Jackson peered down into her face. Finally he said, "I do not want to see you unhappy at any time, Katherine. I promise to do everything in my power to care for you and our child, always."

Hoping to put his mind at ease, Katherine replied, "You don't have to worry about us while you're working to help your government. I have a very good job. I also have money left to me by my parents that I have not touched."

Jackson was shaking his head. He was a very proud man and Katherine assumed she had offended him with her statement. "I will work also, Katherine." His smile told her he understood her offer. "I was working on my doctorate in physics when my father was killed. I have interviews scheduled at three of your universities in the area, two at chemical companies, several at hospitals and one with a toy manufacturer."

Frowning, they both laughed at the incongruity of the last job interview. "Those are scheduled for my second week here," Jackson continued. "The following week—"

Katherine held up her hand laughing. " Uncle Julius did all of this?"

Nodding, Jackson answered, "After discussing them with me a short while ago, he set them up. All except the toy manufacturer. That one he handled entirely on his own. He's taking no chances, that uncle of yours. He loves you a lot, Katherine."

"And I love you a lot, Jackson Shugaa. So very much." She touched her lips to his in a tender kiss.

"You are my heart," Jackson said softly. " No one can touch me the way you do, beautiful, brave Katherine."

As his mouth covered hers, Katherine realized her world had come full circle. She'd discovered love a continent away, and that love was with her now in the form of this brave, tender warrior. Her life was complete.

INDIGO

Winter, Spring & Summer
2001

❦ January

Ambrosia	T. T. Henderson	$8.95

❦ February

The Reluctant Captive	Joyce Jackson	$8.95
Rendezvous with Fate	Jeanne Sumerix	$8.95
Indigo After Dark Vol. I	Angelique/Nia Dixon	$10.95
In Between the Night	Angelique	
Midnight Erotic Fantasies	Nia Dixon	

❦ March

Eve's Prescription	Edwina Martin-Arnold	$8.95
Intimate Intentions	Angie Daniels	$8.95

❦ April

Sweet Tomorrows	Kimberly White	$8.95
Past Promises	Jahmel West	$8.95
Indigo After Dark Vol. II	Dolores Bundy/Cole Riley	$10.95
The Forbidden Art of Desire	Cole Riley	
The Erotic Short Stories	Dolores Bundy	

May

Your Precious Love	*Sinclair LeBeau*	*$8.95*
After the Vows	*Leslie Esdaile*	*$10.95*
(Summer Anthology)	*T. T. Henderson*	
	Jacquelin Thomas	

 June

Subtle Secrets	*Wanda Y. Thomas*	*$8.95*
Indigo After Dark Vol. III	*Montana Blue/Coco Morena*	*$10.95*
Impulse	*Montana Blue*	
The Erotic Short Stories	*Coco Morena*	

INDIGO BACKLIST

A Dangerous Love	J.M. Jefferies	$8.95
Again My Love	Kayla Perrin	$10.95
A Lighter Shade of Brown	Vicki Andrews	$8.95
All I Ask	Barbara Keaton	$8.95
A Love to Cherish (Hardcover)	Beverly Clark	$15.95
A Love to Cherish (Paperback)	Beverly Clark	$8.95
And Then Came You	Dorothy Love	$8.95
Best of Friends	Natalie Dunbar	$8.95
Bound by Love	Beverly Clark	$8.95
Breeze	Robin Hampton	$10.95
Cajun Heat	Charlene Berry	$8.95
Carless Whispers	Rochelle Alers	$8.95
Caught in a Trap	Andree Michele	$8.95
Chances	Pamela Leigh Star	$8.95
Cypress Wisperings	Phyllis Hamilton	$8.95
Dark Embrace	Crystal Wilson Harris	$8.95
Dark Storm Rising	Chinelu Moore	$10.95
Everlastin' Love	Gay G. Gunn	*$10.95*
Forever Love	Wanda Y. Thomas	$8.95
Gentle Yearning	Rochelle Alers	$10.95
Glory of Love	Sinclair LeBeau	$10.95
Indescretions	Donna Hill	$8.95
Interlude	Donna Hill	$8.95
Kiss or Keep	Debra Phillips	$8.95
Love Always	Mildred E. Kelly	$10.95
Love Unveiled	Gloria Green	$10.95
Love's Decption	Charlene Berry	$10.95
Mae's Promise	Melody Walcott	$8.95
Midnight Clear	Leslie Esdaile	
(Anthology)	Gwynne Forster	
	Carmen Green	
	Monica Jackson	$10.95

Midnight Magic	*Gwynne Forster*	*$8.95*
Midnight Peril	Vicki Andrews	$10.95
Naked Soul (Hardcover)	Gwynee Forster	$15.95
Naked Soul (Paperback)	Gwynne Forster	$8.95
No Regrets (Hardcover)	Mildred E. Riley	$15.95
No Regrets (Paperback)	Mildred E. Riley	$8.95
Nowhere to Run	*Gay G. Gunn*	*$10.95*
Passion	T.T. Henderson	$10.95
Path of Fire	T.T. Henderson	$8.95
Picture Perfect	Reon Carter	$8.95
Pride & Joi (Hardcover)	Gay G. Gunn	$15.95
Pride & Joi (Paperback)	Gay G. Gunn	$8.95
Quiet Storm	Donna Hill	$10.95
Reckless Surrender	Rochelle Alers	*$8.95*
Rooms of the Heart	Donna Hill	$8.95
Shades of Desire	Monica White	$8.95
Sin	Crystal Rhodes	$8.95
So Amazing	Sinclair LeBeau	$8.95
Somebody's Someone	Beverly Clark	$8.95
Soul to Soul	Donna Hill	$8.95
The Price of Love	Sinclair LeBeau	$8.95
The Missing Link	Charlyne Dickerson	$8.95
Truly Inseparable (Hardcover)	Wanda Y. Thomas	$15.95
Truly Inseparable (Paperback)	Wanda Y. Thomas	$8.95
Unconditional Love	Alicia Wiggins	$8.95
Whispers in the Night	Dorothy Love	$8.95
Whispers in the Sand	LaFlorya Gauthier	$10.95
Yesterday is Gone	Beverly Clark	*$10.95*

All books are sold in paperback form, unless otherwise noted.

You may order on-line at www.genesis-press.com, by phone at 1-888-463-4461, or mail the order-form in the back of this book.

Shipping Charge:

$3.00 for 1 or 2 books
$4.00 for 3 or 4 books, etc.

Mississippi residents add 7% sales tax.

ORDER FORM

Mail to: Genesis Press, Inc.
315 3rd Avenue North
Columbus, MS 39701

Name _____

Address _____

City/State _____ Zip _____

Telephone _____

Ship to (if different from above)

Name _____

Address _____

City/State _____ Zip _____

Telephone _____

Qty.	Author	Title	Price	Total

Use this order form, or call 1-888-INDIGO-1

Total for books _____

Shipping and handling:
$3 first book, $1 each
additional book _____

Total S & H _____

Total amount enclosed _____

MS residents add 7% sales tax

Love Spectrum Romance

Romance across the culture lines.

Forbidden Quest	Dar Tomlinson	$10.95
Designer Passion	Dar Tomlinson	$8.95
Fate	Pamela Leigh Star	$8.95
Against the Wind	Gwynne Forster	$8.95
From the Ashes	Kathleen Suzanne	
	and Jeanne Sumerix	$8.95
Heartbeat	Stephanie Bedwell-Grime	$8.95
My Buffalo Soldier	Barbara B., K. Reeves	$8.95
Meant to Be	Jeanne Sumerix	$8.95
A Risk of Rain	Dar Tomlinson	$8.95

Tango 2 Romance

Love Stories with a Latino Touch

Hearts Remember	M. Louise Quesada	$15.95
Rocky Mountain Romance	Kathleen Suzanne	$8.95
Love's Destiny	M. Louise Quesada	$8.95
Playing for Keeps	Stephanie Salinas	$8.95
Finding Isabella	A. J. Garrotto	$8.95
Ties That Bind	Kathleen Suzanna	$8.95
Eden's Garden	Elizabeth Rose	$8.95

RED SLIPPER

Romance with an Asian Flair

Words of the Pitcher	Kei Swanson	$8.95
Daughter of the Wind	Joan Xain	$8.95

New from
Genesis Press

Coming Febraury 2001

Visit www.genesis-press.com for an excerpt